UFOs and GOD

A Collection of Short Stories

Also by Michael R. Lane

<u>Fiction</u>
Emancipation
The Family Stone

<u>Mysteries</u>
The Gem Connection
Blue Sun
The Butcher
Six Weeks

<u>Poetry</u>
A Drop of Midnight
Sandbox
Mortal Thoughts
Love & Sensuality
A Leap Year of Haiku

UFOs and GOD
A Collection of Short Stories

Michael R. Lane

BARE BONES PRESS
P.O. Box 9653, Seattle, WA 98109

ISBN: 979-8-9889722-0-4

Published by Bare Bones Press, Seattle, Washington

The characters and events in this book are fictitious. Any similarity to real persons, living or dead, is coincidental and not intended by the author.

Design: Bare Bones Press
Production: Bare Bones Press
Cover Art: Monika Younger

Bare Bones Press
P.O. Box 9653
Seattle, WA 98109

www.michaelrlane.com
www.barebonespress.com

Second Edition: September 2023

*To the overworked, underpaid and
underappreciated educators the world over.
A heartfelt, soul-felt thank you!*

Acknowledgements

Many thanks to the following publications in which versions of the following stories first appeared:

"The Zany World of Al, Nitro, Dynamite & Their Dog Blaze" originally published in The Roswell Literary Review, Spring 1999, Volume 3, Number 2.

"The Poet's Touch" originally published in African Voices, Volume 12, Issue 24, Spring/Summer 2008.

 "UFOs and God" originally published in Crack the Spine, December 2013, Issue 94.

"Tripwire" originally published in Potluck Mag, September 2, 2014.

CONTENTS

The Well

Gahiji and Sentwali peered down into the black water. Their thin forearms rested on the protective cool stone wall encircling the well. Gahiji stood flatfooted. His little brother stood on a wooden water bucket to gain the same view.

"What's down there?" Sentwali asked.

"Water, stupid," Gahiji said.

"I mean below the water," Sentwali said.

"How should I know?"

"Don't you want to be a geologist?" Sentwali asked.

"Yes," Gahiji said.

"A geologist would know."

"Without a core sample and lab I could only guess," Gahiji said.

"Take a guess," Sentwali said.

"This conversation is over," Gahiji said.

A welcomed cool dampness drifted up from the well. Gahiji dropped a pebble. He and Sentwali counted by thousands until they heard a liquid plunk.

"That well is deep," Sentwali said.

"Not much water in it because of the drought," Gahiji said.

"It's hot," Sentwali said.

"Yes, hotter than yesterday," Gahiji said.

"And the day before," Sentwali said. "I wish it would rain."

"So do I."

"How long has it been?" Sentwali asked.

"Three months past the rainy season," Gahiji said. "I heard dad tell mom the village crops didn't make it."

"Mom says if you make a wish before you drop a pebble in a well it'll come true," Sentwali said.

"That's stupid," Gahiji said.

"Mom's not stupid, you are!" Sentwali's words echoed in the well.

"I didn't mean it like that," Gahiji said.

"You'd better not."

Gahiji held out a pebble over the water for a few seconds before letting it fall.

"Did you make a wish?" Sentwali asked.

"Yes, did you?" Gahiji asked.

"Yes. What did you wish for Gahiji?"

"I wished for this drought to be over," Gahiji said. "What did you wish for little brother?"

"A football," Sentwali said with a hopeful grin.

Whiff

The Embassy corporate car pulled up in front of its first sales stop on Pride Street. The corporate vehicle was pristine. The Embassy Elite Fleet team had done an immaculate job of cleaning it inside and out before turning it over to their top sales person. Inside the modern hybrid branded with the Embassy logo and contact information, Dominic Dinfield gathered himself to begin his rounds. Dominic normally made his rounds in the morning and caught up on paperwork in the afternoon. Intermittently, he would do an afternoon visit mostly as a follow-up to customers he had already signed or were on the fence. His numbers were amongst the best in the region so no one griped about his schedule.

Dominic was ten minutes late from his normal eight a.m. start. He wrestled with organizing his sales materials and customer information that had been mysteriously scrambled into disarray. The muddle of his briefcase was a fitting metaphor for the way his life had been for the last three months. For the last couple of days his son had been ransacking the house in search of his hidden birthday gifts. This time Dominic suspected his youngest had rifled through his leather briefcase on such a quest and decided not to mention it to his father. Little did his son know all of his presents were neatly and brightly wrapped and waiting for him at his mom's place. Three months prior a joint divorce decree had been finalized for Dominic and his wife. It had marked a new dimension in his life; one that had emerged from structured discontent.

Without realizing it Dominic had come to place Teresa, eleven, and Mason, eight at the center of his universe. His children provided him with the impudence to ride the dive-bombing effects of lost love and shameful divorce and move forward into the light of redemptive hope. Just when he thought he was getting a handle on things the school year started. Dominic had only begun to work out the kinks of readying his children for school and himself for work. He had, of late, found himself feeling as though he was behind. Most times, he was correct.

It was also the first time Dominic had to handle all family responsibilities on his own. During the best of times, he would drop their children off at school and Rosario, who everyone called Rosa except Dominic, would pick them up after work. Rosario was also the one who herded their children in the morning while he prepared breakfast and readied their lunches. He and Rosario were rock solid as far as their parenting teamwork went. It was as husband and wife where they eventually faltered.

Rosario was a dynamo when it came to her professional career. She had an insatiable passion for business success and upward mobility. Her voracious appetite along with her stellar brilliance had landed her in no time a top executive position at one of the largest corporations in the world. Rosario was destined for a presidency that would be her gateway to a CEO position. Dominic had much more modest aspirations. He was content making a living wage at jobs with decent benefits as long as it meant he would have quality time with his family. Rosario put in long hours at the office. He did the minimum forty with few exceptions. Rosario always brought work home. He rarely did. As his wife sprinted up the corporate ladder, his advancement was at best modest until it ultimately became stagnant. To Rosario her work was divine. She cherished and relished her professional achievements. While Dominic was always proud of her accomplishments, he savored most when they functioned as a family.

The idea of Dominic becoming a househusband had been discussed between him and Rosario. Try as he might, Dominic could not bring himself to accept that singular role. He did not mind bringing home a fraction of the income his wife generated, but he felt it necessary he financially contributed as a matter of principal. His male ego required it. He was the type of man his father had raised him to be. It was how Dominic was bringing up Mason. Archaic or not, that was the way of Dinfield men.

Dominic never doubted Rosario remained faithful throughout their marriage, as had he. It was not in their natures to cheat, although their reasoning for fidelity he believed differed. For him it was a promise of the heart. Dominic had not only married the woman he loved but had intended to spend the rest of his life with her. For Rosario love was only part of the equation. Marriage for her was a binding agreement to spend their lives together and contracts were something Rosario held sacred. This was, of course, supposition on Dominic's part. He had no desire to discover if his speculation was true. Rosario was his wife and for Dominic that was all that mattered.

Some viewed his ex as a cold fish. Dominic knew better. It was not only because after fourteen years of marriage their passion never dwindled in the bedroom; nor was it because Rosario was thoughtful and considerate when it came to matters she deemed important like family birthdays, holidays or anniversaries. Rosario was the tale of two women. On the one hand, she was a hard charging focused professional. On the other, she was caring and thoughtful but only rudimentarily affectionate as a mother and spouse.

As a result of Rosario's blazing success, they moved into a larger house in an upscale part of town. It seemed to alter their family dynamic. As Rosario skyrocketed toward her goals, their family found themselves further and further back in her rearview mirror. Rosario insisted they employ a nanny to help with the children. Dominic objected. Rosario won out. His wife insisted they hire staff to attend to household chores. Dominic argued they should handle those duties themselves. Rosario was once again the victor. Rosario insisted they hire a gardening service to tend to their landscaping needs despite Dominic's adamant protest that he enjoyed doing the work. Dominic conceded on that point as well.

The large house they moved into became more of a residence than a home. A full time chef relieved Dominic of his cooking contributions. Dominic tried to reclaim a modicum of his role as chef by making his once family favorite strawberry waffles for breakfast. Rosario had already left for the office on that morning. Missing breakfast had become such a common occurrence for their mother that their children took no notice of her absence.

With a proud smile, Dominic placed his golden brown waffles teeming with fresh strawberries in front of his children.

"What's this?" Teresa said.

"Strawberry waffles, your favorite," Dominic said.

"Not anymore," Mason said.

"Since when?" Dominic asked.

"Since Jesse started making us breakfast," Teresa said. "Where is Jesse?"

"I gave him the morning off. So what is your favorite now?"

"I like omelets, crepes, and the special hot cereals Jesse makes like honey almond polenta," Teresa said.

"Mine are French toast, scrambled eggs and frittatas like the mushroom cheese frittata Jesse made for me yesterday."

"I was only expecting one dish," Dominic said.

"Sorry, Dad," Mason said.

"And don't forget about his homemade pastries," Teresa said.

"How can I," Mason said. "My mouth's watering just thinking about them."

"OK, I get the picture," Dominic said. "Jesse's a good cook."

"More like a great cook," Teresa said. "You should know, Dad. You eat breakfast and dinner with us every day."

"There's no denying Jesse is an excellent cook. Not even Jesse the great can make waffles like these. Give 'em a try. Discover what you've been missing," Dominic said, his smile fading along with his hopes.

Teresa and Mason poked at his best effort with frowns.

"Are we being punished?" Mason asked.

"Why would you think that?" Dominic asked.

"Just wondering," Mason said, shrugging his shoulders, picking at his waffle as if it were broccoli, which he hated. Teresa felt similar about zucchini and treated her waffle the same.

Dominic had made himself a waffle. He cut out a bite size piece and ate it. He grinned with genuine pleasure as he chewed. His reaction had no effect on the children.

"Can we at least have some syrup?" Mason asked.

"And butter?" Teresa added.

"You've never needed syrup and butter before with my strawberry waffles," Dominic said.

The picking continued.

Dominic had expected he would be hurt by a waffle rejection. Instead, to his surprise, he felt amused by the development. He leaned in close to his children. His smile as warm as his waffles. His voice confident, calm and reassuring.

"I'll make you a deal," he said, looking back and forth between their questioning eyes.

"Take one bite. If you don't like it, we'll throw them away. *And*, I promise never to darken your breakfast with my strawberry waffles ever again."

"Can we get that in writing," Teresa said.

They laughed.

"My word is my bond," Dominic said.

"No exit or arbitration clauses, or loopholes, and no statute of limitations on the aforementioned promise regarding the immediate termination of strawberry waffles?" Teresa asked.

"I give you my solemn word as your father."

Teresa and Mason looked at each other. Dominic marveled at the way his children could communicate with just a glance. He loved the fact they were that close.

"Deal," Teresa said, extending her hand to seal the agreement. Dominic shook his daughter's hand while thinking of how much she was like her mother when it came to negotiating.

Teresa took a nibble. Dominic could tell it was still zucchini in her mind. Her face lit up. Teresa cut herself a bite size piece and ate it.

"This is really good, Dad!"

Teresa proceeded to dissect her waffle into bite size pieces.

"Are you sure you don't need some syrup and butter?" Dominic asked.

Teresa shook her head not wanting to talk with her mouth full.

Mason had observed them closely. He had inherited his father's gift of healthy skepticism. Due to urging from his sister, Mason tried a small bite. He smiled.

"Now I remember why I liked them so much," Mason said. Like Teresa, Mason dissected his waffle and ate.

The children inhaled their waffles and asked for more. Dominic had been prepared for such a request. He stopped them at three. Teresa and Mason tried changing their dad's mind with no success. They were disappointed. Until Dominic promised to make strawberry waffles for breakfast once a week contingent upon Teresa nullifying their oral contract. Teresa agreed air ripping up their formal agreement. Father and daughter sealed the deal with a hug.

While Dominic was pleased with his small victory, he accepted the fact things would not return to how they once were. His children had tasted the fine cuisine of a professional chef and there was no going back to amateur offerings. Along with his strawberry waffle day, Dominic maintained the privilege of taking his children to school. The nanny had taken over Rosario's duty of picking them up afterwards.

Their mother had always treated Teresa and Mason with aloofness. In part, it may have been because Rosario was never keen on having children. Rosario felt more obligated to become a mother to fulfill her debt as wife and to deafen the nagging voices of their families on the matter. Once Teresa and Mason were born, Rosario seemed to accept them as solutions to a problem, as opposed to a glorious addition to their lives. In private, Rosario had tearfully confessed that shameful sin to her husband. A brutal secret they still shared.

In no way had his wife shown any bitterness, resentment, or spite toward Teresa and Mason. Rosario could even have been said to love them. When it came to nurturing, his ex didn't have that natural instinct. Rosario had a tendency to treat her children more like pupils at a boarding school rather than the woman who gave them life. Her instincts ran more toward fostering her career rather than motherhood.

For the children this was not an issue. They had been weaned off their mother since birth. Many of their mother's qualities had filtered into them. Their mom was different from those of their peers. Their mother was not doting or affectionate. She did not bask them with unworthy praise or drown them in positivity. Those qualities they received in droves from their father, grandparents and other relatives. Their mother was direct and honest in her dealings with them without being mean or corrosive. She was a practical, forward thinking individual in all matters, it seemed to them. This was her way. They accepted and loved their mother for who she was.

Teresa and Mason took the divorce in stride as if it was the inevitable outcome of a formula film. It wasn't because they didn't love their mother nor did they believe for a second that their mother didn't love them. They simply knew her better than her husband did. For that reason, they worried about their father. His strength was in question. They saw their mother as the strong reserved type whereas their dad kept his emotions in his shirt pocket ready to be extracted at a moment's notice. Their mom would be okay. He was the vulnerable one. His love ran so deep for their mother they were concerned as to how he would get along without her.

Dominic and Rosario agreed to joint custody with Dominic being the primary care provider of their offspring from their fourteen-year nuptial.

Her career came first. Rosario had come to accept that realization. Rosario would pay child support. Dominic had not requested alimony although his attorney believed he could have won citing the fact Rosario made considerably more money as a corporate executive than he made as a cable TV sales representative. Rosario turned over the deed of the residence that she had purchased outright to Dominic. His ex had moved into a condo downtown that seemed to suit her fine. She verbally agreed to help in every way. Rosario always kept her word. His ex cautioned Dominic not to allow his stubborn pride to get in the way of asking for help.

An example was Rosario felt Dominic should have kept the nanny. She would have gladly continued to pay for her service. Rosario believed why make parenting more difficult than it already was especially now that Dominic was for the most part a single dad. Rosario grudgingly remained mute on Dominic's firing of the nanny, but she insisted that the rest of the household staff, gardening service and chef remain at her expense. When Dominic resisted Rosario played one of her trump cards. Rosario told Dominic if he did not accept her terms she would fight him for custody of the children. Dominic knew Rosario would win hands down. His ex was never an unfit mother. Even a court with cataracts for justice could see that fact.

Dominic promised Rosario he would not allow his pride to stand in the way of the welfare of their children. Dominic knew he would have no trouble honoring that promise. It would be unfair to uproot Teresa and Mason from a community and lifestyle they had come to appreciate. Dominic adapted. He wanted to regain some of the wholesome working class character his family had before the wealth. He was taking cooking classes. He had wanted to win back the culinary praise of his children and believed the classes would help. His plan was to make more than the once a week strawberry waffles. When the time came, he would reclaim one of his roles as breakfast chef. From there, who knew what other family virtues could be restored.

*   *   *

Dominic finished reorganizing his sales and sign up materials. He carried only what he needed with him in the tan leather portfolio that matched his briefcase for his first contact. The remainder he left behind in his briefcase placed out of sight inside the locked company car.

In many ways Dominic Dinfield was a run-of-the-mill forty-something year old man. Dom, as most people called him, had an average gait and was of average height, weight and build. His skin was brown as were his eyes. His natural tight curls of Black African lineage were barbered short and razor lined all around. From the same race, he inherited his eyes and fullness of mouth. His prominent nose and cut of his square chin came from Welsh stock, and his high cheeks and proportioned ears waded in from his Wapanahki gene pool.

Dom was also a man of standard intellect and aptitude. He enjoyed playing and watching sports but was not passionate about them. The same could be said of music, video games, television, cars, art, poker, travel and a wide variety of other subjects that served more as entertainment for him rather than obsession. While he appreciated learning new things, Dom generally lost patience if the challenge became too steep. He liked hanging out with his buddies, but preferred the company of his family. In short, there was nothing remarkable about the man people called Dom until you talked to him.

What Dom had that could be defined as above common were his personality and smile. Dom had a certain charisma, a certain charm, a quintessential character that flamed beneath the surface and sprayed forth like water from lawn sprinklers once turned on. People liked Dom. Dom liked people. Dom was exceptional at sizing up a person within minutes of meeting them. An endowment he had honed under the careful tutelage of his equally gifted grandfather. Rosario referred to her husband as insightful in ways of the human condition. Rosario had come to trust his advice on how best to handle difficult employees and coworkers. Within moments of meeting some of her challenges, Dom demonstrated to Rosario subtle methods by which to muster what she wanted or needed from each person in question. He would follow up his demonstrations in private conference with Rosario with a general break down of their personalities and how best to appeal to their sense of self while maintaining hers and their respect in the process.

From Rosario's perspective, Dom was clinical in his analysis of people. Rosario tried mimicking her husband's gift when needed in order to achieve certain job goals but her sham worked only to a point. Most people saw through what Rosario was trying to accomplish and would acquiescence anyway. Dom was so adept at reading people that Rosario had encouraged him to earn a degree in psychology. Her husband warmly dismissed his wife's occasional prodding. Dom was convinced he could learn nothing in the classroom that he hadn't learned from his grandfather or life.

His charm, wit, and winning smile endeared Dom to people and he was reverential of their welcoming embrace. Compassion he adopted from his mother kept him from abusing his gift. His personality won over the lovely Rosario from much more worthy suitors. Those same endowments along with self-induced discipline made Dom a great sales person.

Dom approached the impressive two-story traditional country cottage styled dwelling with confidence born of repetitive success. He wore dry cleaned dark slacks and white shirt, black socks with spit shined comfortable black leather shoes. Dom called it his field uniform. On crisp days like this one, he added a fashionable jacket, dark brown corduroy in this case, topped off with the company baseball cap. He had been pleasantly surprised to discover a handful of people in the thriving Foehn community had, in his mind, neglected to subscribe to cable or satellite TV or the internet. Opportunity beckoned and Dom intended to heed its call.

He had been a sales person for Embassy for half a decade. Dom found he thoroughly enjoyed the job. One reason was because he liked meeting new people. Second, he truly believed in the products he was selling. Dom rehearsed the standard sales pitch in his head as he strode from flat even gray concrete sidewalk to smooth flagstone walkway.

May I speak to Mr. Smith or Miss Jones?

If the person you need to speak with answers the door, begin forming a bond.

Hello, Miss Jones or Hi Mr. Smith, my name is Dominic Dinfield but you can call me, Dom. I'm with Embassy, as if you couldn't already tell from my hat.

Smile as you draw attention to the Embassy logo on your hat. If the potential customer or PC returns your smile, continue your pitch with a smile. If the PC does not respond in kind, precede in a more serious, professional tone.

We are the premiere telephone, internet and cable company in the region. I was wondering do you have cable or satellite TV?

Never let on that you already know the PC does not subscribe to cable or satellite TV. Feign surprise when they answer "No" and continue.

May I ask why?

Etcetera, etcetera, etcetera, Dom knew the customary sales pitch backwards and forwards. He had also learned when to vacate the script and go with his well-honed instincts. While the generic sales script worked well about fifty-five percent of the time, his gut was closer to one hundred.

Without warning, thoughts of his divorce bludgeoned his mind like hostile stones hurled by badgering bullies. Thinking of his divorce made Dom's heartache and his blood pressure rise. Rosario had dropped the hyphen Dinfield from her last name, returning to her maiden name of Rosario Garcia Arroyo. Dom missed Rosario and probably always would. Just as he still loved his ex and probably always would. As evidenced by the fact he still wore his platinum wedding band.

Dom resisted the urge to torture himself forecasting when Rosario would be adding another hyphenated name to her own. Deep in his heart, he wanted Rosario to be happy. The selfish side of him wanted him to be included in that scene. Their children would keep their hyphenated last name of Arroyo-Dinfield. Dom didn't mind. It only seemed fair to Teresa and Mason to be allowed to hold onto their legacy.

While on the freeway, Dom had eyed his speedometer after spotting a state trooper parked on the side of the road checking for speeders. Eyeing his speedometer was something Dom customarily did when in the presence of police patrols since he had a tendency to exceed almost every speed limit; hospitals and school zones being the only steadfast exceptions. As he slowed by tapping his brake, a peculiar thought grazed him. If you replaced the MPH on the speedometer with YEARS then the car would become like a time capsule. The faster you drove the older you were and the faster life passed you by, a sort of forward to the future experience.

Dom had shaken loose the random thought. Speculating about speedometers and life like reflections of Rosario were wasted distractions. Distractions he couldn't afford if he was going to be at his best.

He took a deep cleansing breath before ringing the doorbell. The natural potpourri scent of autumn was in the air. He stepped back from the door about three feet in order to give the PC comfortable space. Dom put his shoulders back, stood straight and relaxed. He was prepared to look his PC directly in the eye and greet him as if he were a dear friend.

Dom heard uneven footsteps approach near the dying echo of the gentle electronic chimes. At every other step, there came a dull thud from the other side of the door as if made by a person wearing a leg brace or cast or possessing a clubfoot. As the footfalls became louder Dom made a mental note not to in any way draw attention to the PC's deformity should that turn out to be the case.

The irregular footsteps came to a sudden halt. Dom could sense the PC eyeing him through the peephole. He heard the hard metal snap of the deadbolt being disengaged. As the doorknob turned, *It's show time,* Dom thought with a warm inner glow. The door casually swung open. Dom leaped into his sales pitch before the PC came into full view.

"May I speak…?"

Dom broke off his pitch with an involuntary gasp in the middle of his opening line. He was stunned into silence by the face of the man before him. He recognized it immediately as a result of skin grafting. It consumed the man's entire face, making him appear inhuman. The deformed dream stalker character Freddy Krueger in the "Nightmare on Elm Street" film series leaped to mind. Dom assumed his naturally looking brunet hair was a top-drawer hairpiece since he couldn't imagine whatever happened to his face had stopped there. The hair gave only a small measure of pleasantness to his otherwise grisly countenance.

"Can I help you?" the man said as if nothing occurred.

"May I speak to Mr. Jacob Marsden?" Dom mechanically proffered after clearing his throat.

"I'm Jacob Marsden," the face said.

Remaining centered on a goal was a discipline he had learned from observing Rosario. Dom had developed a Zen-like focus when it came to signing new clients, following her example and utilizing his highly developed instincts. He would need every parcel of that resolve to survive this sales session.

"Mr. Marsden, I was wondering," Dom audibly swallowed, "do you have cable TV?"

"Nope," Mr. Marsden answered.

Dom pressed on forcing himself to look Mr. Marsden in his stark blue eyes made so by his embroidered skin. Dom felt his epalpebrate eyes stare right through him into the meat of his person. The only part of his face that appeared human. "May I ask why?" Dom asked.

"Don't need it," the face said.

Dom swallowed again only this time without the gulp. "Do you watch television, sir?"

"Sometimes, not much on I want to see."

Mr. Marsden had a soothingly pleasant baritone voice. Dom added Mr. Marsden's voice to one of the areas he could concentrate on to distract him from his repulsive face. "Do you like sports?" he asked.

Mr. Marsden answered with a shrug. The casual action made Dom glance toward his chest. Dom could see skin grafting consuming his neck from his open collar, disappearing underneath his plain white T-shirt that crested from beneath his long sleeve, cash green dress shirt. He imagined the rest of him clothed in black slacks and black leather shoes had suffered the same blighted fate. Mentally Dom slapped himself back into focus.

"What about comedies?" Dom asked.

"Most of what I've seen that's supposed to be funny these days is more stupid than anything," Mr. Marsden said.

"You get no argument here, sir." Dom didn't agree with Mr. Marsden about today's comedies but in order to forge a bond he felt it best to comply.

"I take it you've never seen a severe burn victim before." Mr. Marsden flashed a gentle smile as if asking Dom for the time. Mr. Marsden had straight white teeth with pale pink gums. Dom couldn't determine if they were real.

"No sir, I haven't." Dom felt ashamed. He had always prided himself on his ability to take people as they came. Standing before this unfortunate soul, met with the stern challenge of looking past the surface in order to discover what lay beneath, he felt like a failure.

"Good," Mr. Marsden said with spirit. "I hope I'm the last person you'll ever see that looks like me. Call me Jacob. Calling me sir is not going to help you sell anything here." Jacob smiled.

Dom was speechless. He nodded his response. Dom found himself returning a smile from a place of both sympathy and respect. He could not help but commiserate with the man's ill-fated condition. On the other hand, Dom respected the courage Jacob possessed in dealing with it head on.

"So what is it that you think you're going to sell me?" Jacob asked.

"A trip to the modern age," Dom said, feeling more at ease, abandoning his script and going with his gut. "And call me Dom. Everyone does."

"Really," Jacob said with a mischievous grin. "And you prefer that do you?"

Dom hadn't thought about his abridged name in years. The truth was he preferred Dominic. Since most people routinely shortened his name to Dom, he had learned to accept it. He shared that insight with Jacob.

"But do you prefer it?" Jacob asked.

"To be honest I prefer Dominic," Dom said after a moment's deliberation. "It's my birth name and I'm proud of it."

"Dominic it is," Jacob said.

"Jacob, it's a real pleasure to meet you." Dominic extended his right hand before he realized what he was doing. Jacob seemed touched by the gesture. Jacob had both hands shoved deep into his pants pockets as if searching for a tiny diamond at the bottom of each. He extracted his right hand. It was as badly damaged as his face. Dominic noticed Jacob's gleaming gold wedding band that seemed an abomination against his grafted skin. Jacob firmly shook the hand offered him. Dominic expected Jacob's hand to feel as it looked, dry and leathery. Instead, his skin was as smooth and soft as silk. Dominic neither flinched from the sight of Jacob's hand nor averted his eyes from his encompassing stare. The two held hands longer than is sociably acceptable for two men shaking hands. Quiet ensued until their hands reached their sides.

"You brought a time capsule with you," Jacob said. Dominic's speedometer metaphor came to mind.

"Pardon," Dominic said.

"How else are we going to take a trip to the modern age?" Jacob winked at him.

Dominic gave Jacob a burst of genuine laughter. "My company's car is nowhere near as fast, or as high tech, as that Ferrari in Back to the Future, but I have something to offer that can catapult you into the modern age without you ever having to leave the comfort of your home."

"You're not selling drugs are you?" Jacob said. "Because I've been on a few of those trips and they're overrated."

"What I have is legal and chemical free," Dominic said with a smile. "I can't promise you won't become addicted once you sign up."

"I'll give you this," Jacob said. "You're a hell of a lot better than that dish person who tried to sign me up. Although you're not as good looking as she was."

"We can't have it all," Dominic said. "You'll find our products are superior to our competitors as well."

"You don't miss an opportunity, do you?"

"Jacob, may I be frank?"

"I thought your name was Dominic, but if you want me to call you Frank, well alright then."

They laughed. Dominic liked Jacob. He had started to see him as friend material rather than a PC. That was bad karma for closing a deal and Dominic knew it. For the moment, he didn't care.

"I honestly believe you don't need anything I have to offer. By the same token, I *do* believe that you'll enjoy having limitless entertainment and information right at your fingertips."

"You do huh?"

"Yes sir—I mean—Jacob, I do."

Jacob eyed Dominic for the eternity of a few seconds. After nodding as if answering a question in his own head he said, "Come inside and let's see what sort of deal you can offer me, Frank."

Dominic thanked Jacob, stepped inside his snug foyer, stood off to the side and waited. Jacob closed the door and led the way down the dim entry hall. The right leg of his host swung forward in an arc from the hip as if the entire limb were confined in a leg brace with every right step concluding as a dull thud on the hardwood floor. His pace was labored and deliberate but steady. Dominic took baby steps in order not to crowd him. In following his PC, Dominic took notice of his person; about six-three, medium build, wide shoulders, and exceptionally long arms were the qualities that registered.

The muted hall opened into a bright and cavernous family room with wall-to-wall plush beige carpet, vaulted ceilings, herringbone brick fireplace and tasteful furnishings. Jacob pulled up in front of the far end of his desert sand colored microfiber sofa. With a graceful gesture as a waiter might when seating diners at a fine restaurant, he offered Dominic the matching love seat perpendicular to where he stood. Dominic thanked Jacob and sat, placing his portfolio on the square, glass, merlot wood finished end table. The seat seemed to hug him in the way a child would feel in the lap of a doting grandparent. He graciously declined Jacob's generous offer of refreshment. While he could have used a glass of water, or even a stiff drink, he didn't want to put out his host. Jacob plopped down in his seat with his right leg sticking out as rigid as a tree trunk. Off to the side of the end table was a cousin oval coffee table. The two men settled in to begin their talk.

"You certainly have a lovely home," Dominic said.

"I'm a bit of a neat freak," Jacob said. "It's takes a lot to keep this place up. With a family, I have to redouble my efforts. It's worth it don't you think?"

"You do a great job."

"Thank you."

"Do you take care of the outside as well?" Dominic asked.

Jacob shook his head. "Yard service; I have a little garden I keep out back. That's all I can handle. This is the same house we lost in the fire," Jacob said, looking around as if surveying his living quarters.

"It's great you found a house with a similar floor plan."

"It's a duplicate," Jacob said. "I had it built. All of the furnishings are replicas as well. What I couldn't buy I had made."

Dominic found that peculiar. Most people treasured certain things about a house they called home for years but typically not everything. The same could be said of furnishings. To go through such pains to replicate what was lost, especially in such a traumatic way, Dominic found both odd and maudlin. Jacob addressed those issues as if reading his mind.

"My family cherished everything about that house including the furnishings, how could I deny them those creature comforts?"

"I see," Dominic said and he did. Jacob was clearly the type of man who would go to any lengths to ensure the happiness of his family. They shared that quality, in his opinion.

Jacob's face suddenly went blank. His pupils dilated. There was an involuntary twitch of his head. He became stone still as if an android that had been switched off. Dominic called his name. There was no response. As Dominic rose from his chair to investigate, Jacob twitched again and sprung back to life.

"Are you alright?" Dominic queried as he eased back down in his seat.

"As good as I can be. Why do you ask?"

"For a moment there you seemed distant."

"Oh," Jacob said with amused recognition. "I must have had one of my spells, as my wife calls them. I occasionally space out. The doctors say it's because the fire cooked some of my brain inside my skull. I black out when my synapses need a moment to reroute. So far it's only happened on occasions when I speak. The doctors say it could spread to other functions or not at all. Only time will tell. Between that and my bum leg, I can't drive or operate heavy machinery. Not that I could operate heavy machinery before."

Dominic gave Jacob a slight smile, knowing a reaction of that sort was expected of him. He suspected Jacob wasn't telling him the whole story. They had just met. Whatever reasons Jacob had for withholding information was not for him to speculate. It was also superfluous for him to make the sale.

"I'm listening," Jacob said.

Dominic was prepared to go into his pitch but discovered himself speechless. He stared at Jacob and was unable to stop. He found his appearance both revolting and intriguing, like a freak show at a carnival.

"Do I repulse you?" Jacob asked in a piercing hiss that sent a chill through Dominic.

The gentleman in Dominic wanted to say "No." The truth was Jacob's appearance did not as much repulse Dominic anymore as made him uneasy. Dominic's people instincts were telling him something altogether different. That aspect of him believed Jacob wanted to hear the truth.

"To be perfectly honest you're going to take some getting used to," Dominic said.

Jacob nodded knowingly. "An honest man," he said. His tone returned to his soothing baritone.

"I try to be, and I'm sorry."

"About your reaction or your honesty," Jacob said.

"About my reaction and continued unease," Dominic said. "I pride myself on being better than that. Again, I'm sorry."

"No need to apologize. By 'better than that,' I take it you believed yourself beyond judging people based on their appearance."

"Yes," Dominic said with a touch of disgrace.

"You've already admitted you've never seen anyone in my condition before?"

Without knowing why, Dominic gave the matter a moment of consideration before answering. "No, I haven't."

"Unless you were a trained medical professional or blind I would have expected nothing less." Jacob's kind words made Dominic no less ashamed of his behavior.

"Would you like to know how it happened?" Jacob said. "Most people do."

To Dominic's surprise, the question had not crossed his mind.

"If you wouldn't mind sharing," Dominic said. "I don't want to cause you any distress."

"I've told the story so many times once more won't hurt."

Dominic nodded.

"I came home from work—late as usual—after working a thirteen hour day. As I was pulling up to my house, I noticed what looked like the den on fire. I immediately parked and ran inside. There was smoke everywhere. Louise was passed out on the sofa. I tried arousing my wife to get her out and ask about the kids but nothing worked. I carried my wife outside, and laid her on the front yard a safe distance from the house before running back inside. The fire had already spread to the kitchen and dining room by then and was making its way toward the family room. I rushed upstairs to the kids' rooms. They were nowhere to be found. I later learned they were spending the night at my sister-in-law's on the other side of town. By the time I realized my children weren't in the house, the fire had blazed through our home like flame through a kerosene factory.

"I found myself trapped on the second floor with nothing but walls of flames everywhere. I panicked. I ran in the direction I thought was the stairs. I'd gotten turned around and found myself running headlong into a burning wall instead. The fire set my clothes ablaze. I became disoriented and hysterical. Who wouldn't under those circumstances?"

Dominic nodded.

"I fought and clawed my way, at first on my feet, then my hands and knees, then my belly, trying to escape. To drop and roll never crossed my mind. Then the strangest thing happened. It got to where it was painless. I mean I couldn't feel anything, not my body, not the fire consuming me, nothing. My life was going up in flames and I had become numb to the whole experience. I felt myself surrendering to its power. I don't remember much after that. I passed out. When I came to I was in the hospital."

Jacob slapped his right leg with his hand. It made a dull, fleshy sound as though he had slapped a side of beef.

"I learned in the hospital that the fire had fused the bones and cartilage in my right knee. I'm lucky they didn't have to amputate. The ankle is about fifty percent but my leg is shot. Skin grafting is why I look like this if you haven't already figured that out. If you think I'm hideous now, you should have seen before they were able to do any skin grafting. What you see covers my entire body. The end results of severe second and third degree burns. They say it's a miracle I survived and I'm lucky to be able to function at a normal level. Pain is constant. There's nothing can be done about that. I've learned to live with it rather than temporarily deaden it with medication. Fortunately, for me, I have a wife and children who still love me in spite of my condition. They give me strength. They give me a reason to carry on."

Dominic became embarrassed for another reason. He was ashamed that he had placed his feeble personal concerns ahead of the tragedy Jacob had and continued to endure each and every day following his horrible ordeal. They sat a moment in silence. The type of silence found in houses of worship when people are involved in hushed prayer.

"Faulty wiring in the den," Jacob said.

"Pardon," Dominic said.

"The Fire Marshall determined the fire was started due to faulty wiring in the den. We sued the contractor and won hands down."

"That's good to hear," Dominic said.

Jacob nodded. Dominic noticed an abundance of photographs littering the walls, mantel and end tables. Many of which could have found their way into a magazine as a family success story. Jacob was handsome. The kind of good-looking man Dominic imagined Rosario would take as her second husband. His son had inherited his father's good looks, his daughter the regal beauty of her mother. Dominic noticed all of the photographs had been taken before the fire. Why that revelation didn't surprise him, it left him with mixed feelings that ranged from pity to envy. On the one hand, he pitied Jacob for his physical condition. On the other, he envied the contentment Jacob had fostered from such trying circumstances and the unconditional love and devotion he received from his family in spite of it all.

"You're a very fortunate man," Dominic said with sincerity. "Those are your wife and children in the pictures?"

"Those were obviously taken before fire turned me into a ghoul," Jacob said with a chuckle. "I wasn't a bad looking guy in those days."

Dominic didn't know what to say to Jacob's self-defacing comment so he said nothing.

"Richard's my son. He's the oldest. He was six in that picture. His younger sister, Rachel, is four. The adults are my lovely wife, Louise, and me during better days." Jacob spoke with a great deal of pride and affection.

"You have a beautiful family," Dominic said while thinking of his own.

"That can still be said of them; of me, not so much."

Dominic knew it would be pointless to disagree with Jacob. For one, he couldn't differ with his statement. Two, taking shots at himself seemed to be Jacob's coping mechanism for dealing with his misfortune. Dominic realized he was really little more than a listening post at that juncture. He glanced around at the photographs. He noticed there appeared to be none of his children or wife taken after the one of his son at six that Jacob had pointed out. All of the photographs seemed to go from that point backwards. Dominic found that unusual. Even if Jacob were understandably camera shy, that wouldn't explain why his photogenic wife and children would feel the same, unless for some reason they did it out of respect for him.

"If you think you're going to become accustomed to the way I look, forget it," Jacob said to Dominic, drawing his attention away from the photographs and back to his person. "I've lived with it for years and I'm still shocked at times when I see myself in the mirror."

"Believe me when I tell you," Dominic said, "who you are shines through any physical challenges you may have."

"You're very kind to say so."

"I speak the truth."

Dominic had done just that. As he was becoming acquainted with Jacob Marsden, his personality, charm and wit made his physical shortcomings a mere distraction by comparison. The unexpected result of his well-meant comments served to dampen conversation. Whether Jacob was embarrassed or humbled by what he'd said, or merely a non-believer, Dominic couldn't determine. Before Dominic became too philosophical— or sappy—he refocused on why he was there. Jacob breached the mood.

"I used to be in sales—advertising to be more precise."

"Really," Dominic leaned forward with genuine interest, "television, radio, print, the internet."

"All of the above and then some; have you ever heard of Apex?"

"Who hasn't? They're one of the biggest ad agencies in the country."

"Try the world."

Dominic whistled.

"You can say that again," Jacob said with pride. "I helped them achieve that goal. Thanks to their executive stock options my holdings with Apex alone helps keep my financial portfolio rather healthy."

Dominic had presumed Louise was the breadwinner. Her, like Rosario, he assumed was the reason they were living large. Not that Jacob's admission discounted that possibility. Louise could still have much to do with their comfortable lifestyle. Having a lucrative financial portfolio clearly didn't hurt. Dominic wished he had been more money conscious. Maybe it would have made a difference in his marriage. Maybe he and Rosario could have worked things out. For reasons he chose not to examine, it also made Dominic wonder if Louise remained with Jacob because of his money.

"What did you do for them?" Dominic asked.

"I was president of marketing and promotion for the northeast region," Jacob said.

There was not only the light of steely blue brilliance in Jacob's eyes but also wattage of confidence and guile. Dominic had no problem accepting Jacob's story of being a top level executive. He saw in him all of the characteristics of every successful executive he had ever met, including Rosario. Dominic resisted the urge to mention Rosario. She was no longer his wife. There was no need to tout her achievements.

"Sounds challenging," Dominic said, easing back into the lap of his grandparent.

"It was," Jacob said. "You could do it. You've got what it takes to make it in the advertising business. I can tell. I've got a nose for ad people."

Jacob wasn't the first to have told him that. Dominic believed he would be successful if he had a passion for such things. "No thanks," Dominic said with a modest smile. "I've enough paperwork as it is."

Jacob laughed. Dominic wanted to ask Jacob if his condition caused him to quit or was he forced out. He held back because he felt the question inappropriate. Jacob spoke again as if he had read Dominic's mind.

"I had to give it up, though. After the fire, most of what we did seemed pointless. The company tried to talk me into staying, in a different capacity of course, one that would not be in the public eye, out of sight, out of mind. I declined."

Dominic nodded his understanding. They sat in silent contemplation. Dominic stared at the photograph of Jacob and his family, propped up on the end table at the opposite end of the sofa where Jacob sat. Jacob stared off in the distance reflecting, on a life that once existed in the gray ashes of his memories.

"My wife and children have been amazing," Jacob said. "They've shown me tremendous love and support throughout this terrible ordeal. Have I mentioned that?"

"Maybe once," Dominic said in jest. Jacob smiled then continued.

"Children will love their parents oftentimes no matter what. A wife has an option in the matter. Can you imagine a woman staying with you after you've gone from that to this?"

Dominic's candid thought was *No.* "I have no idea," was what he said. "I would like to think so."

Dominic thought of Rosario and their children. He imagined it would be as Jacob said with Teresa and Mason. They would love their father no matter what. Rosario he wasn't as certain. Dominic subconsciously rubbed his wedding band as he had been in the habit of doing over the span of his marriage. For the first time, it felt cold and dead to his touch.

"Louise is an amazing woman," Jacob said. "I'm truly blessed to have someone like her in my life."

Jacob dabbed at his eyes with a white cotton handkerchief he had whipped out of his left back pocket. For the first time, Dominic noticed that he had no eyelashes. As callous as it seemed, Dominic knew he would have to steer the conversation in the direction of why he was there in the first place. Waiting for the proper moment was crucial for such a delicate situation.

"You're a very fortunate man to have people in your life who care for you no matter what," Dominic said.

"I'll tell them you said so."

Jacob appeared distracted. As if, something only he could see was drawing his attention away. During that time, Jacob did not meet his gaze. Dominic patiently waited, looking away from his PC.

"I'd like to meet your family," Dominic said, rattling the tranquil quiet that had embraced them, "when the time is right of course."

Jacob jerked his head to the right as if spying an intruder in his home. Dominic followed his line of sight. He saw an empty, unspoiled dining room. Jacob sniffed the air. "Do you smell that?" he said, his voice on edge.

Dominic sniffed the air several times before responding. "I don't smell anything."

Jacob sniffed at the air like a frantic bloodhound hot on the trail of its fleeing prey. His body tensed; his movements frantic. "Smell that," Jacob said with mounting anxiety.

"I'm sorry, but I don't smell anything," Dominic said.

Jacob moved as quickly as his condition would allow from the living room through the dining room and out-of-view. Dominic sat still, baffled by what had just happened.

Try as he might, Dominic could not shake the troubling feeling that something was amiss. It was the house for starters. Everything about it was too ideal, too perfect. Nothing seemed out of place. Dominic knew from personal and observational experience that was rarely if ever the case, especially when you had children. Even with housekeepers, Dominic would still find abandoned items, unwashed dishes, and an untidiness that would surface in the midst of cleanliness. Sometimes his children were at fault, other times it was his own doing. That's the disarray of living with others. It was a natural mixture. Especially with family, there is a constant shuffling of conditions and energy to make life work.

Dominic didn't have the feeling that was going on here. He didn't sense that energy, that give and take. Dominic had only experienced otherwise when he lived alone. Looking around gave Dominic that itch he couldn't scratch. An annoying sensation, a nagging signal that things were not as

Jacob would have him believe.

Dominic resolved to stay. He had already made one derogatory impulsive judgment on the man based on his appearance. He wasn't going to allow the same mistake to happen again.

He looked around from his comfortable seat. The place was immaculate. He gave credit to Jacob since it seemed clear to him that he had accepted his domesticated role as a stay at home husband and father. It was safe to assume his wife was at work and his children were in school. The wife and children had not appeared in his preliminary contact record. Just as there was no mention of Jacob's condition. Those omissions happened often. Name, gender, age, birthday, address, contact info was most times all you had to work with. Dominic made a mental note to update Jacob Marsden's information when he returned to his office.

Jacob appeared after a few minutes.

"I'm sorry about that," he said. "I tend to get a little paranoid when I think I smell something burning. Our fireplace is electric rather than wood for that reason."

Dominic nodded.

"You don't smoke do you?" Jacob asked.

"No," Dominic said.

"Good," Jacob snapped, "filthy habit. Even the slightest whiff of smoke will set my imagination into five-alarm overdrive. It's like I'm trapped in those carnivorous flames all over again."

"That's perfectly understandable," Dominic said with genuine compassion.

Then as if another person stepped inside his skin, Jacob returned to his congenial self. "So you forgive me?"

The question surprised Dominic. It was spoken as a father asking a child for forgiveness from some unpardonable parental sin. There was gravity in his eyes that strongly suggested he needed immediate absolution.

"There's nothing to forgive," Dominic said with a slight grin.

"Are you sure I can't get you anything?" Jacob asked.

"A glass of water would be nice." Dominic no longer felt the compunction to empathize with Jacob because of his appearance. He was clearly capable.

"Coming right up," Jacob said and was on his way.

Dominic casually glanced around, taking unintended notice of the photographs, treasured relics or clan affection. Many of the pictures containing Jacob were vintage him in a happier, healthier time when his children were young and his marriage was green. Upon closer examination, Dominic could see there was something vacant. Some of the photographs appeared rigid. Almost too perfect, like staged family portraits orchestrated by widget photo studios framed in stilted poses fronting bland generic backgrounds. The ones that surfaced as most natural had Louise and their children emerging as bored or annoyed by the irritating process. The eyes of his family did not support their fake smiles in those photos. Only Jacob consistently exhibited great joy and pride in each portrait.

They contrasted in Dominic's mind with his own family photographs that appeared innate. A genuine affectionate glow emanated from each print that was undeniably heartfelt in his household. While not as bountifully displayed in their home, what appeared were sincere photos of a proud and happy family who were almost giddy at being photographed. All of their formal portrait sessions had to be ceased by him or Rosario because the children wanted more. While many of the portraits he saw around him could have made it into the pages of a family magazine, as he had thought before, Dominic had no sense of sincerity from the participants, only an obligatory requirement they were fulfilling.

Dominic became concerned Jacob may have had one of his spells or worse after being absent for what seemed like an excessively long time, a minimum of five minutes. He was about to check on him when Jacob returned with a smile, a tall glass of water, and a hand carved wooden coaster. He handed Dominic the glass and set the coaster on the end table nearest him.

"Thank you," Dominic said.

"Don't mention it," Jacob said.

Dominic took a long drink as his kind host made himself comfortable. The water tasted cool and clean, with no flavor or aftertaste. *Just the way water should taste*, Dominic thought.

"That's bottled," Jacob said with smugness. "It's all we drink in this house."

Dominic knew he had to wrap things up. Their time together was heading into mid-morning. He should have been closing a sale with his second PC by now. As much as he was enjoying Jacob's company, he had another five visits planned before his workday was through. He would have to hustle if he had any hope of making all five. Fortunately, they were in the same neighborhood, three of which were within walking distance.

Jacob regaled Dominic with tales of his children, his wife and his past advertising life. The delight he had for his family had no bounds. His business and advertising acuity was erudite to say the least. In between his anecdotes of kin and commerce, Dominic found ways to educate Jacob about his corporate products. Not an easy task since Dominic found his voice mesmerizing and his stories fascinating at best and delightfully entertaining at least.

Jacob chose the premium telephone and internet service with a moderate cable TV package. Jacob signed off on the final paperwork with a sidebar that he wanted to consult with his wife and children to discover if there was anything specific they wanted to add. Dominic had no problem with waiting. He told Jacob he would hold off processing his paperwork until he heard from him on what they decided.

In parting, the two men wished each other luck with well-intentioned promises of future family gatherings. They shook hands, firm, brief, affable, a genial gesture that surpassed the normal professional grip that generally transpired between customer and provider. For a moment, Dominic believed he saw a flint of sadness in Jacob's eyes as if parting were somehow an act of abandonment. Dominic strolled down the flagstone walkway toward his hybrid company vehicle to drop off Jacob's paperwork and pick up his next PC's, replaying one of Jacob's more entertaining stories in his mind. He could feel Jacob's eyes upon him with each casual step until the faint metal snap of the deadbolt nipped his ears like a distant gunshot.

*   *   *

Mrs. Gwendolyn Crawford had answered the door with caution. It took Dom but a minute to tap into her social demon and release her gossip girl. Dominic wasted no time capitalizing on his PC connection. He dove into his sales pitch and roped Mrs. Crawford in less than an hour of their meeting. Mrs. Crawford had chosen the premium cable, telephone and internet bundle. They were sifting through the paperwork in her cozy family room, tender sunlight streaming in from a vivid blue sky. Dom enjoyed a great cup of fresh brewed coffee and a delicious slice of homemade cinnamon coffee cake that Mrs. Crawford had kindly thrust upon him as they navigated the details of their agreement. Unlike Jacob's place, hers was tidy with the added sense of family aura and occupancy.

Mrs. Crawford was a jovial middle-aged woman with doe brown eyes, an engaging smile, and lilting voice that was perfect for gossiping. Poured into a five-three frame that his dad would describe as pleasantly plump, Mrs. Crawford put Dominic in mind of a woman who would never outgrow being regarded as cute or adorable. Her husband owned an auto repair shop that was doing extremely well, despite the incessant recession, according to Gwen as she insisted on being called after Dom offered up the abbreviated version of himself. Gwen had been the personal assistant for a top-level manager at a large corporation. According to Gwen, they had decided to fatten their bottom line by closing her branch office, a pungent fact that still left a bitter taste in her mouth, and stoked a raging fire in her belly.

The Crawford's had four children, two who were adults out on their own, one who was a sophomore in college, and the other a junior in high school. Gwen had been out of work for almost a year and found the forced hiatus boring. Her husband had offered her work with him, but she declined. They had tried working together before and it was a disaster, according to Gwen. They couldn't separate their personal life from their professional. She was in the process of changing careers but she hadn't decided on what. All of that data and more Mrs. Gwendolyn Crawford had gleefully volunteered.

As Dom summarized her services along with the conditions of their agreement, her black miniature poodle squirmed in her milky arms as if irritated by their conversation. Gwen set Princess down without taking her attention from Dom. Princess ran off as if starved for freedom, disappearing from view amongst the colonized living quarters.

Gwen signed the contracts where Dom instructed her, switching subjects like a driver suddenly changing course.

"I saw you coming out of Jacob's house," Gwen said with a tone that would be regarded as accusatory by others.

"I paid Mr. Marsden a visit," Dom said, not having taken offense.

"How's he doing?"

"Pretty good from what I could tell," Dom said, putting his guard up. He felt a wave of gratuitous information flowing his way. Dom prepared himself to separate the chaff from the wheat.

"Poor dear," Gwen said with compassion.

Jacob cut into Dominic's thoughts. The man he left, he left without pity. If anything, he had developed a sense of admiration for Jacob Marsden. A pining to lead the idyllic family life he had.

"It's unfortunate what happened, but he seems to be handling it well,"

Dom said.

"*You think?*" Gwen blurted out.

"Yes, I do," Dom said firm in his defense. "With the support of a loving family, I guess anything's possible."

"Support? Loving family?" Gwen said. "I don't follow."

"His wife and children are standing by him in spite of his appearance," Dom said.

"That's what he told you," Gwen said, shock igniting her face.

"Well, yes, he did."

Gwen shook her head as if acknowledging a disaster that was too terrible for words. "Jacob lives alone."

"Pardon," Dom said.

"His wife left him and took the kids."

"Are you sure?" Dom said.

"As sure as I am that I gave birth to four children," Gwen said. "The poor dear; apparently his youngest was going through a firebug phase."

Dom reflected on what Jacob had told him about faulty wiring being the reason for the fire. "You're saying his daughter burned down their house?"

"I'm not saying any such thing. That's what the Fire Marshall concluded. She was playing with matches in her father's den and managed to catch the drapes on fire."

Dom was dumbfounded.

"His wife was one of those bourgeois wine heads. She had too much to drink and passed out on the couch. Virtually useless when it came to caring for her children, from what I heard."

Dom stared at Gwen with a blank expression, an expression that echoed his trouble in wrapping his mind around the whole sham.

"Jacob got home from working late to discover his house on fire. Like any courageous man, he rushed in to save his family. Brought his wife out and went back for his kids."

"Were the children still in the house?" Dom managed to ask having wrenched his tongue from disbelief. Dom steeled himself for the worst.

"A firemen found them huddled together in their tree house out back," Gwen said with relief, as if she had found them herself. "The poor dears were frightened to death. The boy grabbed his sister when the fire started and they escaped to the backyard. I suppose as the fire consumed their house they found refuge where they felt safest."

"That being their tree house," Dom chimed in, sounding as relieved as Gwen.

Gwen gave Dom a tight grin with a slight head bobble before she continued. "Jacob didn't know his kids were safe when he rushed back inside. The rest is too tragic for words."

"That's terrible," Dom said. Gwen nodded her agreement.

"I think the poor dear blames himself for what happened," Gwen said in a hushed tone, as if sharing a secret.

"You mean Jacob," Dom said.

"Of course," Gwen said, her voice returned to normal. "Who else are we talking about?"

"Why would he blame himself?"

"Who knows," Gwen said. "Maybe he believes if he worked less and was home more things would have been different. He was a workaholic. Take it from me, I know. I'm married to one."

"Was he really an advertising exec?" Dom asked.

"Oh yes! President of some big ad firm, um, um…"

"Apex," Dom said.

"That's the one! Money didn't matter in the end."

Dom shook his head in sorrow.

"I know," Gwen said in reply to his physical response. "He can't seem to let go; keeps living in a fantasy world that they're one big happy family."

"Shouldn't he be getting some sort of help to break him out of it?" Dom asked.

"He is," Gwen said. "He makes progress then slides right back down. Since he's harmless the people in the neighborhood let him be."

"Everybody knows," Dom said. "About his situation, I mean."

"Afraid so," Gwen said. "It's hard to keep something like that a secret, especially when you look like him, the poor dear."

"That's really sad," Dom said from the pit of his stomach.

"Life will do that to you," Gwen said. "Hurt you in ways you'd never imagined possible."

"That's terrible to lose your family that way." Dom thought of Rosario.

"Losing your family in any way is terrible," Gwen said. "But I agree that way is pretty bad."

Dom drank the last of his coffee. He politely turned down Gwen's generous offer of more coffee or coffee cake, citing his growing waistline as the reason. Gwen laughed and told him he had no reason to worry. Dom thanked Gwen for her compliment but couldn't take his mind off Jacob.

"I can't imagine what I would do if what happened to him happened to me," Dom confessed.

"Who could," Gwen said. "His wife divorced him after the fire you know."

"So much for till death do us part," Dom said.

"Um-humph," Gwen agreed. "Some people are as shallow as a puddle of water."

"That poor man," Dom said.

"The witch told him to his face that she and their children couldn't stand the sight of him."

"That's awful!"

"Not that they were a happy family before the fire. What happened to Jacob brought matters to a head. After he rushed inside a burning house to save her worthless ass, she turned around and did him like that. It's not fair. Not fair at all."

Dom was speechless, saddened and disappointed all at once. What Gwen had told him supported what his instincts had attempted. Instincts he quelled in favor of compassion.

"If his family did that to him after what happened," Dom said, "why keep living in the past, one that's not true at that?" Dom posed the questions more to himself rather than Gwen.

"What else does he have?" Gwen matter-of-factly stated.

"Did it happen over there?" Dom asked, jerking his thumb in the direction of Jacob's house.

"Did what happen over there, dear?"

"The fire," Dom said.

"Oh no," Gwen blurted out. "The fire was on the other side of town."

"If you don't mind my asking," Dom said, "how do you know all of this?"

"My cousin told me," Gwen said. "She used to live right across the street from them."

With dissemination of that last bit of information, Dom knew it was time to leave.

Gwen saw Dom out with Princess weaving around her feet. Dom thanked Mrs. Crawford for her business. Thanks Gwen graciously accepted.

On his way to the company vehicle to drop off Mrs. Crawford's paperwork and pick up the paperwork for his next PC, Dom found himself staring at Jacob's house. It was a beautiful house, picturesque, quaint, Americana. The kind of house he imagined his family would one day call home. That dream was still alive for his children and perhaps his second wife if he were so lucky. Dom couldn't take his eyes off the house or shake his thoughts from the man who lived there. His next PC was a couple of blocks away. *The wise thing to do would be to drive*, he thought, not because he was too lazy to walk but so to keep the vehicle in sight. Cars were stolen or vandalized even in upscale communities.

He chewed on the idea for a moment. His eyes bolted to the house. His thoughts resting with what had transformed into somber memories of his time with Jacob Marsden. Dom wasn't upset Jacob lied to him, or even that he had chosen not to peer through his deceit. What troubled him most was that his lies were untrue.

Happiness was his illusion. Jacob had manufactured the family he envisioned, stepped into that hallucination, and refused to leave. Had his life with Rosario been a similar illusion played out on a world stage? Was he any different to believe that his flesh and blood children were not characters in a charade of which they could all become victims should their mother decide to claim her maternal right? That house represented his nirvana. Jacob's family life was his dream. How easily it all could be snatched away. How swiftly the impenitent heel of life could ground his loftiest hopes and ordinary expectations into fossil fuel for the pitch flames of remorse.

Dom stared at the house, hoping it would give him a sign. A cosmic signal that some of what Jacob had told him was worth clutching. He scanned the gleaming windows and appealing doorway in search of Jacob. Groping for validation their humane connection had been real. The crisp autumn air nipped his ears and nose. Neither the house nor its occupant gave notice to relinquish his doubt. Dom hopped into the company vehicle after a dozen disappointing heartbeats. He started it up, convincing himself that parking nearer his next PC was the prudent thing to do. Dominic took one last longing look at paradise, and then sped away like a man racing against time.

Love and Death

"What'd you think?" Sheila asked.

"Don't know," Rob said.

They both stared at the rigid white, blue, green, red, and violet feathered parakeet in the size eleven gray shoebox coffin. His lavender eyes glassed over in his large head, his barrel chest stock-still.

"Debbie is going to freak," Sheila said.

"I know," Rob said. "Are you sure you didn't do something to Bailey?"

"Are you accusing me of murder?" Shelia indignantly asked.

"Debbie knows you hate Bailey," Rob said.

"Not more than I love my daughter," Shelia said. "Just because that damn bird was a noisy pain-in-the-ass didn't mean I wanted him dead, just quiet. At times like this I hate you but you're still kicking."

"Is that out of love for me or our daughter?" Rob asked with amusement.

"Both, and don't let the facts that you pay half the bills and are good in bed obscure—let's not lose sight of our immediate concern here."

"Roger that," Rob said.

"What are you guys doing?" a voice from behind them asked. Debbie startled them. Rob hid the shoebox behind his back as they turned to face their daughter.

"Honey, I have bad news," Rob stammered. "You might want to sit down."

"Give it to me straight, Dad, I can take it," Debbie said.

After a hard audible swallow, Rob belted out, "Bailey's dead." Both parents rushed to their daughter's side in anticipation of an emotional breakdown.

"I know," Debbie said as calm as a lighthouse in a storm.

"*You do*," Sheila said.

"I found Bailey dead in his cage this morning. I was late for school so I didn't have time to tell you. Didn't you see the lace handkerchief I used as a shroud to cover him?"

"Now that you mentioned it I did," Rob said. Sheila stared at Rob as if he'd suddenly grown a third eye.

"And you didn't find that strange?" Rob shrugged.

"I thought after dinner we'd hold services for Bailey," Sheila said. "If it's OK with you I'd like to bury him under that big Oak in the backyard."

"Sure, honey, that's fine with me," Rob said.

"Me too," Sheila echoed.

"Good," Debbie said.

"You're not broken up, sweetie," Sheila said.

"Of course not, Mom," Debbie said matter-of-factly. "I loved Bailey but he was an English Parakeet. Their life expectancy is six to eight years. Bailey beat the odds and lived for ten."

"Where'd you learn about Bailey's average life span?" Sheila asked.

"Biology class," Debbie said, "remember I did a research paper on English Parakeets."

Mystified, Rob asked his daughter, "How old are you?"

"Dad, just because I'm only sixteen doesn't mean I don't know a thing or two about life and death. Bailey had a good run. Sometimes you just have to let go." Debbie walked toward the stairs leaving the words, "What's for dinner, I'm starving," hanging in the air.

"Roasted chicken, green peas, and wild rice," her dismayed mother said.

"Cool," Debbie said before she disappeared upstairs. Sheila and Rob stared at each other in disbelief.

"She could be in shock," Rob said.

"A delayed grief response is possible," Shelia said. "Let's keep a close eye on her for the next few days."

Rob nodded his agreement.

"In the meantime, why don't you put Bailey in the garage until the funeral," Shelia said. "He's getting ripe."

Shadows in the Mist

Davis Gamble walks into a posh restaurant gleaming with silver and crystals, buoyant with joy and light, teeming with prosperity and sophistication. Davis is wearing a black tuxedo. The impeccably dressed and groomed host greets him with a congenial smile and eastern bow.

"You're usual table, Mr. Gamble," the host says, his voice a rumble like distant thunder. His handsome smile with teeth the color of ivory alights in his rainbow colored eyes.

"Yes, thank you, Gabriel."

"Very good, sir," Gabriel hand signals for a waiter to join them at the greeter's station that is bathed in a clear golden light. A snappily dressed lad responds in a literal flash with a staid look upon his fresh face.

"Please show Mr. Gamble to his usual table," Gabriel commands more than request.

The waiter smiles with eggshell white teeth as if infected by Gabriel to do so, rainbows appearing in his dark eyes. "Yes sir," the lad says, bowing to Gabriel as the host had to their guest. "Right this way, Mr. Gamble."

Mr. Gamble follows his waiter through a serpentine path around a wealth of tastefully arranged refined tables occupied by choice people of all vintages and tribes having a wonderful time. As Mr. Gamble passes each table, the occupants stop whatever they are doing and stare at him as if he were a neon sign on the side of a moving bus. They resume their fun as if Mr. Gamble had never appeared once he passes.

Mr. Gamble recognizes some of the people in the restaurant: his Uncle Chase, dead; his Aunt Ellie, dead; cousins Sarah and Jamaal, dead, a favorite high school teacher, Mrs. Walden, dead. His doting grandmother and playful grandfather, dead; a high school friend lost to suicide and another childhood friend victimized by a drive by shooting, dead. There were others raised from the grave that he knew from life. He can see they recognize him in their unblinking eyes, but none acknowledge Mr. Gamble when he waves or says hello. The dead and the living seem to share the same pulse in this vibrant establishment radiating with good cheer.

"Your table, sir," the waiter says, his smile dimmed from bright to pleasant, the rainbows in his eyes more prominent than ever.

Mr. Gamble takes in the table for two. Opal linen, long tapered candles set in crystal holders placed on opposite sides of a bouquet of blush roses and white hydrangea centerpiece. Fine pearl china, Victorian silver flatware, crystal stemware and glasses, embroidered cloth napkins corseted by figural silver napkin rings rounded out perfection. It pleases Mr. Gamble to the core. He sits. The chair is as comfortable and familiar to him as his childhood home. The waiter takes up a position near the right elbow of a glowing Mr. Gamble.

"May I get you anything to start with sir," the waiter says while expertly filling his empty water glass, "something to drink, bread, an appetizer."

"The usual," Mr. Gamble says.

"Very good, sir." The waiter leaves, literally vanishing after taking a few steps. Mr. Gamble rests his elbows on the table as he was taught not to do by his mother, folding his hands above his place setting where he nestles his chin in the cradle of his interlocked fingers. He glances around the room blazing with elation. People are savoring their meals and basking in the affectionate glow of agreeable company. Mr. Gamble notices he is situated in the center of it all, the virtual hub if you will. Recognition of such makes him flush with happiness.

The waiter returns with a gleaming silver tray. On the tray, he has toasted garlic bread, soft butter, a saucer of lemon wedges, clover honey and a silver pot of steaming hot chamomile tea. After depositing the sum of nutrients to their proper places on the dining table the waiter hands Mr. Gamble a leather bound, gold inlay menu. Mr. Gamble accepts the bill of fare without comment. Gold had been used to write the menu on papyrus. Mr. Gamble knows this in the same way he knows his name; in the same way he knows everything about this restaurant; in the same way he knows what to expect when he opens the menu that feels like electricity in his hands.

On the left side of the menu centered beneath the bold heading "EX-GIRLFRIENDS," Mr. Gamble relishes each name as if they are the air he breathes. Grace as beautiful and chic as her name; Trinity, fiery, independent and spontaneous; Sophia, brilliant, friendly and wise. The ex-girlfriend selections detailed their attributes and shortcomings. Physical attributes are not included since the purpose of each item is to remind Mr. Gamble of their intrinsic rather than extrinsic qualities. Character being one of the ingredients of love that lingers on the tongue long after the peppery spice of lust has faded.

Choosing a date from women so dear to him was not going to be easy. The list covers almost three pages. That always surprises Mr. Gamble. The list is much longer than he imagined reaching as far back as Faith, his first official girlfriend back in the sixth grade. Faith always made his heart flutter every time she smiled. While he cares for them all none amongst them inspired the depth of love that would fate them to wed.

As appetizing, as some of his choices are none of Mr. Gamble's "EX-GIRLFRIENDS" excite his companion palate. On the right side of the menu prepared with equal care is a more detailed much shorter list. Under the heading "EX-WIVES" are but two, Lenora and Justine. Theirs was a love he believed was destined to last a lifetime. His ex-wives had blessed him with two children each. Try as he might, he could not seem to give them enough of what they needed for sustained happiness. Marital harmony escaped them more than it stayed. Once he asked Lenora what it would take to make her happy. She answered with one heart wrenching word, "Divorce."

"Lenora," he says, handing the waiter the menu.

"Excellent choice, sir," the waiter says, waiting a few heartbeats before speaking again. "Shall I light the candles for you, sir?"

"Not until my date arrives," Mr. Gamble says, after a moment's thought.

"As you wish, sir," the waiter says, vanishing again after taking a few steps.

Mr. Gamble waits with eager anticipation. He knows it will be great to see Lenora again. Butterflies dance in his stomach and he desires to join in. An evening rehearsal plays out in his mind. Mr. Gamble opens with how glad he is to see Lenora and how amazing she looks. They will talk about their children. Discuss their separate lives. He will minimize as much as possible any discussion regarding Lenora's second husband without being petty, juvenile or crass. At some point during their dinner, he will apologize to Lenora for having not amounted to the man of her expectations. Mr. Gamble will ask her forgiveness. In his fantasy, Lenora will grant him absolution. Even go as far as to disavow any necessity to apologize. His hope extends to her bestowing upon him her blessings that their life together had been for the most part grand and that he was an excellent provider, father and throw in lover for good measure. Mr. Gamble will not ask for her return but silently maintain optimism for reconciliation. Lenora will have to pry open that door for him to step through and prove himself worthy of a second chance.

As the restaurant half-emptied, Mr. Gamble retains faith Lenora will show. He switches from lemon water and hot chamomile tea to bourbon on the rocks. By the time all other tables are empty he is drinking his bourbon neat. Gabriel comes to his table gliding as if wearing invisible skis.

"I'm sorry, sir, but we're closing." The thunder resonates in his voice. His smile is one of pity. Storm clouds and lightening fills his eyes. "I'm afraid you're going to have to leave."

"I understand," slurs Mr. Gamble as he staggers to his feet. With the utterance of Mr. Gamble's words Gabriel vanishes. After Gabriel the staff, the decorum, the place settings, tables and chairs vanish in that order. Mr. Gamble stands slump shouldered, head bowed alone in the midst of gray calm.

In less than the blink of an eye, Mr. Gamble is adrift at sea shrouded by dense fog. In the distance can be heard the mournful bellow of a foghorn. Against the wall of fog is pressed a faint light wave generated by a lighthouse beacon. Mr. Gamble is forlorn but calm and alert to every sound: the lapping of the sea against his ancient lifeboat; the creaks and groans of the wooden craft; the steady idle of the tiny outboard motor. He stands as he did at the restaurant, head bowed, slumped shoulders, frozen in that position for a minute or an hour. When he finds the strength to raise his head and focus his eyes all he can see is the steady pulse of beacon light against the thick lead gauze of gray fog.

A glass of warm bourbon dangles from his left hand a microsecond later; the TV remote firmly clasped in his right. Supine on his lumpy sofa, he surfs up and down the cable channels for something of interest, something entertaining enough to patch the void in his unfulfilled life. The

TV goes mute. The light from the TV grows brighter and brighter blinding him with the intensity of a searchlight that is much too close. He shuts tight his eyes. It does no good. The light penetrates his eyelids as if they were chiffon. He shields his eyes with his bourbon glass forearm. It helps dim the intensity but now he feels its radiant heat. Mr. Gamble gets up, drink in hand, dropping the remote on the floor. The remote does not make a sound. He staggers barefoot and half-dressed out of the front door of his house only to find himself back in the same fogbound lifeboat adrift at sea.

*　　*　　*

"A person encounters a being of human form, manners and speech. That person is surrounded by other persons who they know intimately, either through association of sorts or contact of the slightest. Everyone, including the person, is dressed or 'layered in skins of different hues' as the being puts it. 'What level of consciousness do you seek?' the being asked. I remember it all so vividly. I am person."

"We can see that," Nolan said, refilling his margarita glass with his fourth helping from the second sweaty glass pitcher of homemade strawberry, kiwi margaritas with a touch of cucumber. No one was enjoying his original drink creation more than Nolan. The dinner party of three young childless married couples had gathered in the living room to continue into the night what was a great time. Nolan and his wife, Melanie were our host, Tempest and her husband, Owen, and finally me and my wife, Lenora rounded out the remainder of the gathering. It was a relaxed affair of great friends dressed casually and behaving accordingly. The hosts were cozy in their love seat while the rest of us made ourselves comfortable on their roomy sofa.

"No, I mean I'm a person like me—like us—," I said, "aware but separate from the experience so to speak."

"Disconnected as if you were an observer," Tempest said.

"Not at all, I mean both experiencing and observing simultaneously."

"That would give me a headache," Nolan said.

"Sometimes you give me a headache," Melanie said. Everyone laughed.

"I'm just saying it sounds a little space cadet," Nolan said after the laughter died.

"That's why they call them dreams," Lenora said.

"That is not why they call them dreams," Nolan said. "Besides, there are all sorts of dreams, some are even called nightmares. This isn't going to be of the nightmare variety is it? If it is I won't be able to sleep tonight."

"Will you shut up and let Davis talk," Melanie said.

Nolan shrugged, "Who's stopping him?"

We all stared at Nolan. "Shutting up and enjoying my special margarita which no one has bothered to compliment me on."

"The margaritas are wonderful;" "Never had better;" "More than delicious, they're magnificent;" "Superb, bravo;" "May I have the recipe?" came the adoring compliments absent Melanie who waited to the last. "You've outdone yourself this time, sweetheart," Melanie said with syrupy sweetness that even made Nolan laugh at its insincerity. We raised our shimmering glasses in toast to Nolan's special margaritas. His friends and loving wife exaggerated their verbal expressions of delight after a satisfying sip. Melanie and Nolan kissed, and then kissed again before Owen shattered the spell.

"OK, we know where that's leading so break it up, you two." Melanie poured herself into her husband's arms. It seemed to set off a love reaction as Lenora did the same for me, and Tempest did the same with Owen.

"Go on, Davis," Tempest said. "I want to hear more about your dream."

"Really," I said, having lost my nerve, becoming uncertain and uncomfortable about whether it was worth continuing.

"Definitely," Lenora said. "Don't leave us hanging, honey."

"You didn't know about this dream?" Melanie asked.

"It's the first I've heard of it."

"Maybe I should wait until I tell my wife before sharing with anyone else. She does have spousal privilege." Lenora gave me a sweet kiss on the lips.

"Someone's getting lucky tonight," Nolan said. Lenora nodded her agreement.

"Don't make me beat the rest of it out of you with a pillow," Owen said. "Spill it!" After the laugher died, I continued.

"I encounter a person, a being of human form, manners and speech."

"You said that already," Nolan said.

"Am I recalling this dream or you?"

"You don't have to be redundant."

"How about showing our guest some courtesy," Melanie said.

"Guest *hell,* we're best friends. Courtesy is for acquaintances." Everyone laughed in agreement.

"We would like to hear about Davis' dream, Nolan, if you don't mind," Tempest said.

"All in favor," Owen said. Everyone said *"Aye"* including Nolan.

"That being the case," Lenora said, "please continue sweetheart."

"*Ahem*, as I was saying," I began eyeing Nolan whose mischievous grin mirrored mine. "He or she, I couldn't tell, but for purposes of telling this dream, I'll refer to this androgynous being as he. That person is surrounded by other persons he knows either intimately or through association of sorts. Everyone is layered in skins of varying hues. 'What level of consciousness do you seek?' the being asked my person."

"I've got a feeling I'm going to need this margarita buzz to help wrap my head around where this is going," Nolan commented.

"Oh brother," Owen replied.

"Really," Tempest said. "Are you really going to keep doing that?"

Melanie shushed Nolan. "Please continue," she said to me in an apologetic voice.

"Level of consciousness, I don't understand, I said to the being. There's something I need to interject here, something that just occurred to me. He had a certain way about him, a way of contemplating before he spoke as if waiting for the precise words to formulate before speaking."

"Like a lawyer in a courtroom," Owen said.

"Nothing so scripted or calculated. It was more like he was searching me for the right words."

"Now that's spooky," Tempest said.

"Not really. It felt perfectly natural."

"Why do they get to talk and I have to keep quiet?" Nolan asked.

"Because they're not being derogatory or obnoxious, dear," Melanie said. Nolan shrugged it off with a sip of his margarita.

"'How do you prefer to exist?' he asked me, 'on the grounded plane, spiritual plane or coexistence?'"

"Spiritual plane, I guess?"

"'Then you must shed your skins.'"

"Skins?"

"'Clothes you grounded ones call it.'"

"You mean take off my clothes?"

"'In a manner of speaking yes, but more like shedding garments of fear and inhibitions,' he said, then smiled at me like a teacher to a student who had given the correct answer to a challenging question. Only *he* had answered the question."

"What about those people, they're dressed. I pointed to the swarms of people all around us who didn't seem to notice we existed."

"'As you shed skins those souls will be left behind to hopefully learn one day what I expect you already understand.'"

"I . . . understand, I said."

"Sounds like an orgy in the making," Nolan said.

"Am I going to have to send you to your room?" Melanie asked.

"Alone?"

"You'll be playing by yourself tonight if you don't zip it until Davis is done."

"Zipped and locked," Nolan said, sipping his margarita.

"The person said, 'You're only surrounded by beings of equal resolve so have no fear of difference here. We're all the same.'"

"As my person peels away skins, things change instantaneously. Beings around me are wearing equally less. We—I and the person—and those of equal resolve ascend, passing through different levels until arriving at a place where no skins exist, bare for all and everything. There are far fewer on this plane but there is a peace and bliss and understanding unmatched or unfathomed by anything I have ever known."

"Whoa! This is cool!" Tempest said.

Everyone shushed Tempest, including Nolan.

"Sorry," Tempest said. Owen gave his wife a peck on the cheek and hugged her closer to let her know all was well.

"Who are you? I asked my companion guide as I had come to think of him. You've traveled with me from one plane to the next shedding skins as we go. Are you too seeking a higher consciousness?"

"'Not at all,' he said. Then who are you? I asked."

"'I am Consciousness. This is my realm.'"

"Off in the distance I recognized what felt like for lack of a better word, love. I mean it had no shape or features but a sense of subsistence and energy. I ran toward it as fast as I could. Once I felt it safe to do so I leaped. I fell for what felt like forever before I was close enough to reach out and grab it. Then I woke up finding myself hugging Lenora."

*　*　*

The radio alarm snapped on, filling their messy bedroom with the unmistakable silky a cappella baritone of Lou Rawls. *Should auld acquaintance be forgot / and never brought to mind? / should auld acquaintance be forgot / and days o' lang syne / for auld lang syne, my dear / for auld lang syne / we'll take a cup o' kindness yet / for auld lang syne.* Through bleary half-opened eyes, Davis looked over at his pillow mate who hadn't budged. Lenora continued her light snoring. Nolan's delicious margaritas had made for a comatose morning for the two of them.

"Rise and shine sleepyheads it's time for your wake-up call brought to you by your personal alarm clock here at Kay Dee Zee Tee," the DJ yelled bringing to a screeching halt a mesmerizing rendition of a classic song. "For those of you who were out celebrating a little too much last night, GET YOUR HUNGOVER BUTTS OUT OF BED. This is the real world calling people on the first day of the New Year of the rest of your lives, and times a wastin'!"

It was Saturday. The alarm sounding off was a mistake. Davis silenced the radio and fell back into dreamland.

Tripwire

In a heartbeat, between moments life can tripwire your world, cramming you into a seamless metal box labeled past and future. Past can erupt like enraged volcanoes or delicately descend like drifting seeds germinating from intimacy spawned by a familiar song, a tantalizing scent, a violent vision or foul taste. Future not yet flesh or form, preordained or mystery, meanders within layers of spectral fog yanked into revelation by the searing winds of present.

Victor Hubble strode along in his designer attire. His down soft leather shoes made his feet feel as though he were walking on clouds instead of erratic old pavement. With his handmade leather shoulder bag pressed against his lower back like a main parachute, he weaved his way through morning rush hour pedestrian traffic toward the Eldorado Towers and his high-rise corner office. His eyes were glued to his smartphone screen cradled in one hand as if it were a microchip infant while the other hand efficiently commanded the microelectronic toddler to execute his bidding. Victor was checking his emails and text messages. He avoided others of the morning rush hour crowd on the downtown streets as if an invisible energy field deflected people and obstacles from crashing into him.

Ingrid Weatherstone was trying to rid herself of the terrible habit of doing anything on her smartphone while driving. Besides being a dangerous practice she was attempting to find ways to secure more *me* time. With the constant demands of family, friends and work baying at her heels she found it near impossible to catch her breath. Her efforts were not going well. When a message came through from her inner circle she found them impossible to ignore. Having a hands free voice activated system in her car helped relieve her guilt. Every instance of regress, each lapse was categorized as justified; a necessity in order to keep the wheels greased on her hectic life.

Victor was a 24-7 employee. He lived, breathed and divined his position as if earth would cease to hold its place in the universe should his duties go unfulfilled. Victor never required Ingrid to get back to him promptly when he messaged her during off hours, although oftentimes she did. That made him believe she was as driven about her career as he was about his. He was right.

Ingrid had her onboard system read aloud her messages. It began with one from Brian, her husband forewarning her, Rika, their oldest child of eight was going to ask her mother if she could have an iguana again. Rika had seen the tropical lizard featured on a PBS Nature special and became enamored. Brian had told his daughter no for about the 50th time. For Ingrid the no count was about half that. Brian wanted to reinforce with Ingrid the reasons they were saying no. They had just gotten Rika and her younger brother, Simon, two charming beagle puppies four months earlier. If after a couple of years they'd proven themselves worthy pet lovers then maybe they would give serious consideration to Rika's iguana request if her desire hadn't petered out by then. If anyone needed a pep talk on the matter of remaining steadfast it was Brian. Rika had her daddy wrapped around her little finger on most matters and their daughter knew it. If it hadn't been for Ingrid putting her foot down, Rika would have her pet iguana by now.

Miranda sent Victor an email. His wife of four years was six months pregnant. All was well with their first baby for the time being. Miranda had been experiencing chronic back pain. The doctor ordered her off her feet for the next few days. The doctor's treatment plan was working. Miranda's back pain was gone. As an added precaution Miranda decided to take early maternity leave in case job stress had also been a contributing factor to her chronic back pain; a decision that pleased Victor. The down sides to being bedridden and jobless was Miranda had become stir crazy and bored.

Ingrid's girlfriend Hazel called. They'd been best friends since kindergarten. Hazel wanted to remind Ingrid about the surprise party she was throwing her brother at her house in a couple of weeks and wanted to confirm Ingrid was still in. Hazel was clearly nervous about the affair going off as planned. Planning was Hazel's strong suit. Part of what made her a brilliant architect. Maintaining her cool under what Hazel deemed as personal duress was not. Ingrid allayed Hazel's fears by reassuring her she would be with her every step of the way. As an added sedative Ingrid invited Hazel over for dinner. They could use the time to finalize Hazel's party plans and to catch up on the latest gossip.

Miranda's strange food cravings were back. She wanted Victor to pick up some items on his way home from work: corn chips, Neapolitan ice cream, sour pickles, root beer, honey mustard, donuts, cookies, cupcakes, pretzels, apples, kiwi, tomatoes, cucumbers, spinach, creamy French dressing, peanut butter, Marion berry jam, potato bread and ketchup. Victor of course would do as his wife asked. What gave his stomach a turn was watching Miranda eat those foods in all sorts of unappetizing combinations. A cupcake dipped in honey mustard and washed down with pickle juice. Whenever he'd try to persuade Miranda to put down the spoon of ice cream covered in corn chips and eat a banana instead, his wife glared at him as if Victor were a stranger interfering with something that was none of his business. Victor would try to avoid watching Miranda wolf down her nauseating feast which she did with gluttonous glee.

Ingrid listened to more messages. Most were from her boss. She made mental notes regarding each task and would address them as soon as she arrived at her desk. As a double check she would forward all of his messages to her office computer to make certain she didn't miss anything.

For the first time in Victor's adult life something other than work had become his top priority. Miranda could have held that mantel had she not been on the same page with her career. The near birth of their first child had forced them to re-evaluate their lives in ways neither had found necessary in the past. It was both liberating and terrifying at the same time. Liberating in a sense to know while their careers remained important there were other things in life that trumped those cards. Terrifying in the sense they were wholly responsible for the care and well-being of another human being. That sort of challenge isn't covered in classrooms, work hives or industry boardrooms. Victor hastily replied to Miranda's email accidentally cc'ing others in the process.

Ingrid swallowed the last of her cinnamon dolce soy latte immediately longing for another. She placed the empty stainless steel tumbler back in its cup holder when a new message came in from her boss. When the onboard system read aloud the email attachment containing his pregnant wife's odd grocery list Ingrid laughed. Victor had started to show signs of distraction and fatigue, foreign characteristics to his work performance; classic symptoms of a father expecting his first child. Wait until the baby's born, Ingrid thought with an amused shake of her head. That's when the real fun begins.

Victor began reviewing his notes for an international tire account his firm was after. The company had spread the word their previous marketing firm hadn't delivered and they were anxious to reclaim or exceed their market share. His marketing team had won the internal competitions for the account, now he was sharping his pitches to convince the client. A meeting was scheduled with the client at ten. He was ready. His team was ready. He felt good about their chances of making the client's final cut.

Ingrid chuckled to herself as she considered humorous responses to Victor's accidental message. Her boss had a great sense of humor, a quality that endeared him to his staff. Ingrid eyed her docked smartphone for a moment tittering as she contemplated on whether to send Victor a quick text. Even though she intended to dictate her response, Ingrid had a habit of looking at her smartphone when she did so as if to assure it was getting it right. Her eyes were diverted from the road long enough to run a Stop sign partially obstructed by low hanging tree branches.

Victor stepped off the curb reading a congratulatory text message from the CEO about a new account they had won thanks to Victor's tireless efforts, making him more oblivious than usual to his surroundings. With the current Regional Marketing Manager being bumped up to National Marketing Manager this was the sort of attention Victor knew would get his name on the short list to replace him.

Ingrid looked up just before her car struck a man wearing a suit, whose eyes were glued to his smartphone. The screech of her wheels followed a dull thud and sudden jolt as she witnessed his body being propelled clear of the crash. But for a moment's panic and indecision, Ingrid switched off the engine and dashed from her car to try to help the victim.

Victor entered the lobby of the Eldorado Towers a half-hour earlier than usual. He forwarded the congratulatory text message to his team with a personal note added, thanking everyone for all of their hard work in helping make that happen. Victor considered adding a few words to prime the pump for his pep talk before the big show at ten but decided against it. Some things were best done in person.

Two people had rushed to the victim's aid ahead of her. Ingrid apologized profusely to the man writhing in pain holding his left leg which appeared broken. A small crowd gathered around the injured man. Some voiced accusations at Ingrid being a careless driver. Some murmured about lawsuits and criminal charges. Only two people inquired whether Ingrid was alright. Someone had called 9-1-1. Ingrid stood by repeatedly apologizing mostly to the victim but also to her accusers.

Victor entered his office and fired up his shut down computer. As his company computer connected to their internal network and ran updates, Victor decided to head to the break room and treat himself to a cappuccino and croissant. He checked his smartphone for more messages, whistling as he went. Victor was surprised Ingrid hadn't promptly responded to his great news as she was prone to do.

A Day in the Life of Frederick Douglass

Frederick Douglass never set his alarm clock. He still managed to rise every morning at precisely five a.m. On a normal day, he would extract from the sliding drawer of his cedar nightstand a gold leaf picture frame containing a color family portrait of him, his darling wife and their four precious children dressed in their Sunday best. The glow of their tan skin was prominent against a plaster of Paris white backdrop. Their grins blazed for the Sears photographer who prompted their smiles. The sparkle in their brown eyes was genuine, as dazzling and authentic as the love in their hearts. When Maya committed suicide, it shattered their joy. No one knew why Maya took her own life.

As much as Ella, his wife, loved all of their children, Maya held a special place in her generous soul. Their eldest daughter, Maya, was not only a clone of her mother; she had her personality and gift of commonsense as well.

Ella had been the bedrock of their family. Once a light social drinker, Ella took hard to the bottle in order to anesthetize the heartbreaking loss of her most cherished child. Try as he might, Frederick could not wrench his spouse's hands from the toxic liquor that only deepened her despair. Frederick had to work in order to support their family. While at work, Ella wasted no time commiserating with her distilled friend. Alcohol was blamed for the car accident that cost Ella her life. His beloved had passed out while behind the wheel of their family car and swerved into oncoming traffic. The medical examiner said Ella had so much alcohol in her system that she probably felt nothing when it happened. If there were mercy in such misfortune, it was in that grisly fact.

Frederick lost two of the people he loved most in this world within six months of each other. A happy family of six had been whittled down to four by cruel fate. At first, all he and his three remaining children could do was survive the horrific ordeals. By holding fast to one another and with the help of family, close friends and faith they were able to cope. Strength ultimately emerged from the forest of devastation. They cleared paths of hope in order to move forward. Along the journey strength solidified into a mental resolve to do more than survive but to succeed. Doggedness became the rally cry of the Douglass household. Positive academic achievements emerged as the norm even through the often-disruptive challenges of teenage years.

Frederick was proud of his offspring, but he kept his boasting to a minimum. He was well aware of how people who went on and on about the achievements of their children were received. Braggarts were first perceived as nuisances that would escalate to annoyances to be avoided whenever possible. His were excellent children. He knew that and that was good enough for him. Bragging was not necessary. In spite of the dreadful death of their mother and oldest sibling, his children had turned out rather well.

Frederick Douglass soaked in the photograph that had resulted from a combination of the photographer posing them, and they falling into a comfort zone of their own. He on one side, Ella on the other, and their children sandwiched between. Maya and Ella had their arms wrapped fondly about each other. Their eldest rested her head affectionately on her mother's shoulder. They looked more like sisters than mother and daughter. His eldest son, Marcus stood proudly behind his younger sister Gale who was seated with their youngest Aaron nestled in her lap. Frederick had his arm genially draped over Marcus's shoulders. Gale hugged Aaron who clearly relished his sister's embrace.

Reflected in the clear glass pane of the picture frame was the face of a man who had battled depression and won. Now into his early sixties the lines of age had furrowed on an otherwise smooth copper face. His eyebrows, clipped nose hairs, morning bristle and hair was gray, a gray that still made its presence known even when cut close to the scalp. If asked, Frederick would say the gleam of his buckeye brown eyes had dulled over the years. Any observer would disagree. They would say that he had a look of serenity. He appeared a man at peace. That was the magic trick Frederick had mastered over the years, the ability to camouflage pain behind a tranquil mask. It had been forged out of necessity to protect his children from the normal distress he often felt from losing people he intensely loved. At some point, Frederick came to believe the facade was real.

Frederick gazed at the frozen timeframe of his family for approximately five minutes then tenderly kissed it before returning the blissful memory to its wooden tomb. He rose from the ashes and committed to his morning routine of showering, grooming, cooking breakfast, eating breakfast while reading the daily online editions of the local newspaper, *The New York Times* and *The Huffington Post*, filled his thermos with one of a variety of hot teas that he preferred over coffee, made his lunch that he packed into a lunch pail, flossed, brushed his teeth, dressed in his Home Depot work uniform that consisted of crisp khaki pants and shirt and comfortable work shoes, grabbed his steel lunch pail and stainless steel thermos and fluorescent orange apron with his nametag pinned to it, jumped into his car and was off to work.

After more than twenty years of the same routine, Frederick could sleep walk through it. The major aspect of his ritual that had changed in the last few years was the absence of his children. The freedom from responsibility of their well-being had granted him immunity from the morning rush. He had enough time to take his time. A relaxed morning afforded him all of the liberties he had dreamed of from a casual sit-down breakfast to reading his morning newspapers; the latter that with family, he might have been able to squeeze in on his lunch hour at work. Still he missed his children. While Frederick was happy and proud they were making good lives for themselves, he would trade his daybreak leisure for a few hectic dawns with his brood.

On his drive to work on a clear spring day, Frederick reflected on the place he had raised his family. Philadelphia was a big city. His wife was from Philadelphia. That was why they moved to Philly from the small town in Wisconsin where he and Ella had met and married. Frederick never liked big cities. Not because they were spread out, dangerous, polluted or congested. He disliked big cities because they were too big to get around in a convenient and timely manner. Frederick liked to walk. He had always wanted to return to a place where one could walk to many of the places they needed to go. A place where convenience was convenient and time was on your side. Relaxed, quiet and small town was what he wanted. That was the lay of the neighborhood he now called home.

Frederick was a card-carrying journeyman laborer who could do just about everything from clean up to working a crane. He was the one who expanded what had been a two-bedroom home into a five-bedroom home complete with additional bathrooms. He was forced to fan out further and further in order to find work as local construction jobs thinned out. Frederick would only accept jobs reasonably close to home for the sake of his children. Kind providence brought him a present. A Home Depot opened not far from where they lived. Frederick got a job as a freight team member. It proved to be a natural fit. His years in construction had groomed him for a place like Home Depot.

After his youngest graduated college and found a job, Aaron officially moved out. That left Frederick alone in that great big house. He decided to put it up for sale. Around the same time, he had heard through the work grapevine that a new Home Depot was opening in Maryland and they were looking for experienced people to join their team. His older brother, Sterling, lived near the site of the new store. Frederick and his family had visited Sterling on a number of occasions over the years and he liked the area. Sterling told Frederick he could stay with him for as long as he needed. Frederick's boss hated to see him leave but supported his transfer request. The transfer came through shortly after Frederick sold his house at a time when dwellings were going fast. Frederick Douglass was returning to small town America and he couldn't be happier.

Frederick sold or gave away everything that had no sentimental value, packed up the remainder of his belongings and moved. After staying with Sterling for only six weeks, Frederick closed the deal on a charming split-level two-bedroom house not far from Sterling. He paid cash for a place that was coincidentally a little closer to where he worked. His new home was a far cry from the five-bedroom dwelling in which he had raised three children. While at times he missed the pleasant memories the old house harbored, he traded sentimentality for the cozy comfort of his new home.

His children were disappointed when their dad told them he was selling what they regarded as their home, but over time, they had learned to accept it. The biggest drawback became the fact he no longer had enough room to accommodate the entire family when they visited. It sparked changes in venues for the majority of their family gatherings. Sterling, Marcus or Gale hosted the events in the past he had shepherded.

As he marched toward the front entrance of Home Depot, he slipped on his orange apron with the Home Depot logo and the slogan "We Put Customers First" before he made it inside. Business had become unstable for the last few years due to the severe downturn in the American economy. The crunch took awhile to get to them but it finally roosted as more and more people lost their homes. Upper management was forced to cut back on hours across the board. Some people were let go. There were rumblings that upper management planned to approach senior employees about early retirement in order to minimize the impending layoffs of less experienced workers who did not have as much of a financial parachute to survive extended unemployment. That was the line they were feeding everyone.

All of the senior staff knew what the company really cared about was cutting their expenses. By cutting loose, the more top-heavy senior employees it would better serve the corporate bottom line. Frederick had no problem with early retirement. He had done well for himself by applying a principal that his father had taught him. "Treat every dollar you earn as if it'll be your last and you'll learn to respect money." His dad's philosophy had taught him to think in terms of the three basic necessities of food, shelter and clothing making all else a luxury. It was an attitude his children had aspired to as well. A way of life, he reasoned, had been absorbed by them more through osmosis rather than by parental lecturing, which he had done a lot of during his time.

Most people called him Fred, fewer called him Freddie, neither shorthand of his name had he commissioned. He preferred Frederick. His nametag read that way. On those rare occasions, when someone was polite enough to ask him what he preferred he humbly told them so.

With a last name of Douglass, his parents decided to complete the hope of destiny by naming him after one of their heroes. Frederick Augustus Washington Douglass had studied the life of his namesake, a larger than life man whose accomplishments continued to impress him to this day. While he deeply admired and respected the historic icon, Frederick could not help but feel he constantly fell short of deserving such an honor. When attempting to follow in the footsteps of such greatness he found himself much too small to fill his shoes. He was an average student on his best days. As a debater, he seldom won, and even when he did, it made his head hurt to think that hard. He, Frederick, did not have the intellectual prowess, style or pluck of his historical figure. He, Frederick, preferred to try to get along with people rather than beat the drum of his personal convictions. He, Frederick, was easy going and did not like getting involved in affairs outside of the jurisdiction of his family.

Frederick had been a lot and sales associate, a cashier and freight team member at Home Depot. He knew something about every product his store stocked because he made a conscientious effort to do so. It was important for him to be the best he could be, not for Home Depot, but in anything he attempted. It had somehow been encoded into his DNA. For him it was a matter of dignity. Frederick didn't know how else to approach life. He may not have had the aptitude of his namesake, but he did possess his focus and pride for a job well done.

While he was deserving of his position as manager, it came to be more from longevity rather than his possession of any particular leadership skills. Frederick had been with the company longer than anyone had in his department, and he knew the place backward and forward. Nonetheless, he was respected by his subordinates and many of his coworkers if only for his encyclopedic knowledge of Home Depot products and their best applications, a database that had earned him the nickname "Yoda" from his coworkers.

The day progressed like a creamy vanilla milkshake being sucked through a straw with no new developments or unique occurrences. It was the classic definition of an average workday for Frederick. His freeway drive home with a thicket of traffic that flowed all the way to his exit fit that definition as well.

While Frederick lived alone he rarely felt lonely. Video chats, emails, phone calls and family Facebook pages somehow made him feel near his family and close friends. Besides his older brother and sister-in-law who lived only a few miles away, he had a wealth of friends some of whom, his neighbors, could be counted amongst them. In light of his social standing, his evening routine varied. There were times he had plans that would range from getting together with friends or family for dinner to a night out at the movies or bowling. Tonight his plans were to stay in, and Frederick was glad. In spite of a relatively easy workday, he felt fatigued and could not put his finger on why. He had already decided to turn in at ten rather than his customary eleven. He believed the extra hour sleep would be enough to refresh him.

On one of his days off from work, Frederick cooked enough food for a week's worth of dinners. At home, he microwaved one of those formerly prepared meals and ate it in the living room while he watched PBS NewsHour. With his store bought dessert, he enjoyed Jeopardy. After Jeopardy, he cleaned up after himself, took a hot shower and slipped into his cotton pajamas, bathrobe and favorite blue fuzzy bunny slippers that were a gag birthday gift from his oldest son. They served as a reminder of the time Frederick had given his children bunnies as pets and they decided to liberate them at a local park never to be seen again. At the time, Frederick was furious with them for being irresponsible and reckless. Now it served as one of those humorous intimate memories every family shared.

Frederick rarely watched TV past eight. He preferred his home be filled with the structured musings of classical music, the driving rhythms of jazz, or simply quiet, rather than chatter. Any of those agreeable elements along with a mug of hot or iced tea—dependent upon the weather—and a good book suited him just fine. Tonight he was in the mood for the piano stylings of Oscar Petersen.

He was in his comfortable recliner with his feet up reading *Dreams from My Father* when at precisely nine o'clock his smart-phone rang. Frederick had the ringtone set to sound like a vintage American phone for incoming calls. His three children called him almost every day, alternating who would call on any given day. When Gale called, he had the added benefit of talking to her husband, Martin, and their six-month-old son Bradford, his third grandchild. Gale had made a great choice in Martin. He was a good, hard-working, brilliant man who was destined to go places in his chosen field of international banking and finance. When his oldest son Marcus called, Frederick had the added benefit of speaking with his wife, Pauline, and their two children Wynton and Harriet. Wynton was three and only beginning to have a conversation of sorts with Frederick. At four months, Frederick was lucky to get a laugh out of Harriet over the phone.

Frederick turned off the digital music with his entertainment remote and reached over to answer the phone without checking the caller ID to make certain it wasn't an annoying solicitor.

"Hello," Frederick answered with the warmth in his voice reserved for people he loved.

"Hey, Dad," Aaron said. His youngest son had matured into a strapping young man who at a glance would give one pause to start any kind of trouble. To Frederick, Aaron always sounded like the teenage boy who went on for hours about his first real kiss with a girl named Brandie. Tonight was different. There was a weighty sadness in his tone.

"How you holding up?" Aaron said. The question took Frederick by surprise. Frederick felt he should know what his son was asking him about, but for the life of him, he didn't have a clue.

"What do you mean?" Frederick said.

"Today," Aaron said. "You remember what today is, don't you?"

Frederick shook his head before realizing he had to voice his answer, "No I don't."

Aaron took in a solemn breath, held it, and then released it with a heavy sigh. "Today is the day mom died."

Frederick was speechless. Aaron was right. Today was the morbid anniversary of Ella's death. A flood of painful memories surrounding his deceased wife and daughter came rushing back to him. Frederick had conditioned himself to remember Ella and Maya the way they were in happier times. The dreadful final images of them being laid to rest paralyzed him.

"I'm sorry," Aaron said. "I shouldn't have brought it up."

"It's okay," Frederick said. He thought for a moment. It was rare these days for any of his children to resurrect their family loss. Frederick had come to believe that it was something they had learned to live with. Aaron was the brightest of his three children. He was also the most sensitive. While his youngest didn't quite wear his heart on his sleeve, it didn't take much to discover it under the cuff. As a father, Frederick needed to be strong. It was time for his magic trick. If his son needed him as a sounding board, as all of his children had many times in the past, then he would gladly step up to the task. "Did you want to talk about your mother?" Frederick said.

"Do you?" Aaron said.

"Only to mention that I love and miss your mom and sister very much," Frederick said.

"So do I, dad," Aaron said. "But you hardly ever talk about them."

"What's there to say?" Frederick said.

"I don't know," Aaron said. "A word or two every now and then wouldn't hurt. At least let us know you still thought about them. Let us know you still cared."

"What brought this on, son?" Frederick said.

"I heard "Girl You Know It's True" on an oldies radio station today," Aaron said. "I was zapping when I stumbled upon it."

Frederick began to understand. Maya and Gale loved that song. Their brothers used to tease them about it. Especially Aaron who thought it was the dumbest song he had ever heard. Whenever it came on his big sister's boom box, she would turn it up loud and seek out Aaron. Aaron would run away from Maya with his ears covered by his hands screaming his head was about to explode from that awful noise.

"Was it the original?" Frederick said.

"Yeah," Aaron said. "God forgive me, I still hate that song."

"I understand," Frederick said.

"Remembering Maya made me remember mom, too," Aaron said. "Then it came to me that today was the day mom died."

"Are you okay?" Frederick asked.

"I'm fine Dad," Aaron said. "I worry more about you."

"I'm doing just fine," Frederick said with genuine reassurance. "As long as you kids are okay, so am I."

"If you ever want to talk about Maya or mom," Aaron said, "I hope you know I'm here for you. We all are."

"That's my line," Frederick said, trying to brighten the mood. It got a slight chuckle out of Aaron.

"How's your love life," Frederick said. "Have you met anyone I should know about?"

"Well," Aaron said perking up, "there's this one woman I've been seeing for a couple of months."

"Really," Frederick said. "That long, huh."

"Yeah."

"What's her name?"

"Angela."

"You've been seeing this Angela for a couple of months and this is the first I'm hearing about her."

"Dad, you can be kind of hard on romance," Aaron said. "I tell you that I might be getting serious about a woman, and you'll have a private detective looking into her background."

"I'm not that bad," Frederick said with a chuckle of his own.

"Every girl I've brought home since middle school, you've given the third degree," Aaron said.

"You can never be too careful," Frederick said.

"There's careful then there's paranoid," Aaron said.

"Now I'm paranoid," Frederick said.

"Just a little," Aaron said. Frederick could hear the humor in his son's voice. He felt the love of his smile over the phone. Aaron was exaggerating somewhat and Frederick could care less. He did keep a close eye on the people his children associated with, most especially those of the opposite sex. He had frightened away a number of suspect unions with his no-nonsense interrogations and threats of physical harm to the boys that dated his only surviving daughter. He wasn't won over by pretty faces or flirtatious behavior by girls who wanted to date his sons either. He raised his sons to be gentlemen. A gentleman deserved the company of a lady. Their mother and oldest sister were ladies and he was a gentleman. Their children deserved the same.

Their conversation remained fixed on Aaron. Frederick made certain of that. Whenever Aaron attempted to alter the focus to his father, Frederick quickly returned it to his son. By the time their chat ended, Frederick was current on the life of his youngest.

It was just past ten and Frederick was not sleepy. He no longer felt like reading or listening to music. He went to the dining room and fired up his laptop that was being recharged on the dining room table. While Frederick waited for his laptop to boot, he admitted to himself that his conversation with Aaron had both invigorated and depressed him. Normally, he would have moved on quickly from depressing thoughts of Ella and Maya. His morning ritual kept them at bay, a ritual he had kept secret even from his loved ones. The accidental reminder of Ella's death had driven a stake through his heart that had penetrated deep into the nexus of his soul.

He opened an explorer window and accessed the My Documents folder in the left pane with a single click of his mouse. A list of files and subfolders appeared in the right pane. He double clicked on My Pictures. Aaron, Ella, Gale, Grandkids, In-laws, Marcus, Martin and Maya appeared as subfolders. Frederick positioned his pointer over Ella. Agony combated longing to pity a past that could never be resurrected. The quiet was threatening. Frederick could hear his heartbeat, the inhalation and exhalation of each heated breath. The normally soothing tick . . . tock of the handmade pendulum wall clock his brother had given him as a housewarming present made the passage of time seem both a destructive and healing force. *What would be the result of opening Ella's folder,* he thought to himself. *How would history greet him after all of these years?*

He double clicked on Ella. A list of JPEG files appeared. All of them were prefixed with Ella followed by a hyphenated number that formed their assigned sequential order. Frederick took a slow breath and double clicked on Ella_1. A photo viewer program sprang open showing a picture of Ella that filled the screen.

Frederick gasped. He had taken that photo during the honeymoon portion of their marriage. The sight of Ella smiling back at him so full of life and promise made a grief well inside of him he had not allowed himself to experience for decades. Frederick tenderly touched the screen as he would Ella's face were she alive. His wife had always been the most loving and beautiful woman in the world to him. Ella was the only woman he had ever loved. Those sentiments never changed even as Ella trudged through her darkest days. His two deepest regrets remained: not being able to prevent Maya from taking her own life, and his inability to help Ella survive the ordeal.

Frederick had in aching time come to grips with the agony that one of his cherished children was gone without any explanation. Ella never could. Frederick was unable to convince his wife there was nothing they could have done to save their daughter. Maya's was a tragedy that came about while doing something that so many young people had done before her and lived. There were no indicators that their daughter was unhappy. If anything, Maya seemed her positive upbeat self. They received news that their daughter had hung herself in her sophomore college dorm room.

Ella could not look past Maya and embrace the three vibrant blessings within their grasps. For his wife the loss of their oldest daughter represented a sin that could only be repaid in kind. Alcohol was the means for Ella's suicide. Her heart had perished long before her death.

Frederick was a widower. That word had not been a part of his vocabulary when he thought of his deceased wife, but that was exactly what he had been for all of those years. A man whose wife had died, a man who had lost the love of his life and she was never, ever coming back. How had that finality escaped him? Was it because he had usurped his needs for those of his children? Had his feelings for his wife and daughter been aborted in the process? Why had it taken him this long to arrive at that razor sharp point of reckoning? Maya was gone forever. Ella was gone forever. All that remained of who they were was housed in the memories of the people who knew them, loved them, and the still life portraits of proof they had lived.

Frederick had all of the photos originally shot on film transferred to digital as a backup plan in case the originals were somehow destroyed. He stared at the seamless slideshow of his life before the death of his wife and oldest daughter. The tears were constant. His sobbing interspersed. When the photo procession ended, he felt exhausted, as if every bolt of energy had been drained from his person. Frederick shutdown his laptop and made his way to bed. The journey took the last of his remaining strength. He crawled beneath the covers and fell into a coma-like sleep.

Five a.m. came and went and Frederick did not awaken. The same happened at six, six-thirty, seven and seven-thirty. Frederick did not open his eyes until eight-thirteen the following day. He felt exhausted but cleansed. Without any formal ritual or exercise, he had experienced a purging or purifying of sorts. His feet touched down on top of his fuzzy bunny slippers. He slipped his feet inside. He removed the family portrait from its tomb. For the first time since their passing, Frederick felt a sense of gain rather than loss. He stared at the family photograph that he adored and smiled. He loved them all so much at times it made his chest ache.

While his wife and eldest were with them, he had let them know how much he cared in both words and deeds. There was nothing more he could have done. There was nothing more to be said. He had been blessed with having been an intricate part of their lives and no one could expect more. Frederick smiled at the photograph, kissed it and set it upright on the nightstand.

Sleeping past his customary five a.m. was not a problem since it was the first of his two days off. If he grabbed a morning shuttle flight, he could surprise his youngest by this afternoon. It was a gamble. Aaron lived the single life even though it appeared he had set his sights on one particular woman. Besides, it gave Frederick an opportunity to check out Angela for himself. It was a gamble worth taking.

Frederick hopped on the internet and booked one-way passage on the eleven-thirty shuttle flight to Harrisburg. He skipped his morning routine except for his morning shower and grooming, packed a weekend bag, informed Sterling and a couple of his neighbors by phone that he would be away visiting Aaron for a couple of days. They all assured him they would look after things while he was away.

Windsor Knot

My Uncle Tony stood behind me in front of the bathroom mirror. The top of my head crested at his sternum. He was a handsome man, a physically fit man with an intense burn in his bold brown eyes that mellowed to a warm glow for family and friends. He meticulously measured the wide part of my tie twelve inches past the narrow before he turned it over to me. "That's the first step," he explained, "in making a good Windsor knot."

"Next cross the wide end over the narrow end."

I did as he said. He made a minor adjustment before we continued.

"Bring the wide end up through the loop between the collar and the tie."

I did it.

"Now bring it back down."

Afterwards, he made another minor adjustment.

"You're doing great, Phillip; now pull the wide end underneath the narrow end and to the left back through the loop and to the left again so that the wide end is inside out."

Again, he made a minor adjustment after I was done. So went my lesson: "Bring the wide end across the front from left to right." Minor adjustment, "Pull the wide end up through the loop again." Minor adjustment, "Bring the wide end back down through the knot in front." Minor adjustment, "Now use both hands to carefully tighten the knot as you draw it up to your collar," major adjustment accompanied by a proud smile.

"What do you think, Phillip?"

His big hands rested on my young shoulders. I replied with a grinning nod. "You look great, Nephew, now let's do it again."

We repeated the lesson until I could do it without any assistance from Uncle Tony. He was forty-three. I'm sixty-three. That memory percolates to the top of my reminiscent stew. I retrace his instructions with my black tie in the dresser mirror, feeling Uncle Tony standing behind me, his big hands resting on my shoulders. His funeral begins at ten. I'm one of the pallbearers. I don't want to be late. My tears blur my vision.

Daylight

Evening surrendered to nightfall without a fight. Cloud cover and starlight, rain and sapphire, alternated throughout this vibrant gentrified community of brick houses, luxury apartments and condos and mixed-use urban design. Greenspace provided room for residents to roam through groomed natural environments custom fitted for their living and working spaces. Modern convenience was everywhere. Coffee shops, restaurants, juice bars and cafes, grocery stores and hair salons, yoga studios and boutiques, small businesses and corporate chains efficiently and expertly located for maximum exposure. All within walking distance or a short bike ride. If you needed something you couldn't find in your neighborhood then it was no more than a quick drive or public transport away. Most of those same items could be located on the internet if you were averse to vehicular traffic, expensive parking or public shopping in general. The human animal pampered and spoiled and settled into the ultimate fusion of the agricultural, industrial and technological systems with a hint of rustic thrown in.

Night was serene in this comfortable neighborhood on an average Wednesday in August. Urban sounds were minimal and nonobtrusive. This was not unusual for this area of variegated race and wealth residents. A place that may be termed as a multi-culturally diverse community. Something often preached in America but very seldom practiced. While people of all sorts traverse the neighborhood at all hours, it was as if this part of the world had made a pact with the city Gods to permit urban day chaos in exchange for peaceful nights. And there is nothing like tranquility to grant voice to ones innermost concerns.

*   *   *

Brandon Taylor
9:32 p.m.

Brandon Taylor could not sleep. Two months, one week and four days ago, Brandon had turned twelve. With it came his first giant steps toward manhood in the forms of puberty and personal responsibilities. Puberty speaks for itself. The changes in his body were a shock he was still adjusting to. Once his voice finished making all sorts of funny noises when he spoke, it had dropped an entire octave. Sometimes when Brandon spoke, he didn't recognize his own voice. Girls he had been attracted to as friends for their personalities and like interests had taken on another dimension in his mind or perhaps he should say to his body. There was a physical magnetism he had never experienced before. Kissing had been something to make him want to gag. He made fun of smooching as being gross and stupid. Now he was curious, even anxious, to try kissing, especially with Amber.

Amber was one of his best friends. Now Brandon was beginning to see Amber as something more than a friend. He began to see her—dare he say it—as his girlfriend. It was a term Brandon had always found laughable when his older brother, Ramello, and Liana his sister in the middle, teased him about Amber. Now he not only liked the idea but fully embraced the vision. Although Brandon didn't know in the slightest what the difference was in Amber being his friend as opposed to his girlfriend. Judging from how Ramello and Liana behaved with their opposite gender friends, holding hands, gross kissing and cuddling were certainly involved.

When Brandon shared his feelings about Amber with his mom, she said he was transitioning from a platonic love into a more physical attraction toward Amber. His mom being a clinical psychologist and an adult lost him sometimes. She went on to explain what she meant, which didn't help clear his head, using expressions like "biological selection and evolution, mating and courtship, human psyche" and "choreographed by nature." For his purposes of understanding they were artificial terms of some versions he had heard in his Sex Ed and Biology classes. If anything, his mom only thickened the fog. In the end, Brandon did remember her saying what he was experiencing was perfectly normal which made him feel better.

Amber and he talked about any and everything before puberty including what they had learned about human anatomy and sex education in school. For some reason, now that it was actually happening, puberty was not something he felt comfortable discussing with Amber anymore.

Brandon shared his puberty experience with not only his mom but also his dad, Ramello, and his closest male friends. He discarded the internet input finding it less helpful, providing more content than substance for a twelve year old. Brandon had gotten a lot of straight answers from the people he talked to. Some of the answers intrigued him, others frightened him and still others went right over his head. He was still trying to piece together the puberty puzzle.

Now that it was actually happening, it seemed surreal. Like the air we breathe or a plant grown from seeds. All of the scientific explanations of how and why these properties exist do not prepare one for their realities. Deprive the body of air and we suffocate. Neglected plants will not thrive. These truths can only be fully comprehended through involvement. Knowledge only predicts outcomes but does not train. To live one must experience life. Most of the people Brandon talked to concluded as did his mom that what he was going through was completely normal for a young man his age. Brandon had no choice but to accept that puberty was an awkward coming of age, life experience, he would have to muddle through as best he could.

Brandon questioned a number of things about himself lately. Where did this physical attraction come from? When did kissing go from being something he and Amber made fun of as being gross and stupid to a mutual curiosity? He admitted he thought Amber was pretty, and he liked her smile and her voice and her laugh and how smart she was. Why did things have to change between them because of puberty? It all seemed weird to him.

Accompanying his adolescent challenge was that Brandon was entering a new school in just a couple of weeks. He was eager with anticipation and a hint of anxiety, ready to venture into the great unknown. As the day drew near, he was too excited to sleep. Brandon couldn't wait to see what high school was like. New students, teachers, classrooms, cafeteria, auditorium, gym, all of it made him feel like he was embarking on a wonderful adventure.

The name of his new school was Quadrivium Academy High School. A private all-boys school. Amber was going to Blessed Teresa's Catholic High School a private school for girls. Owen and Mason would be joining

Brandon at The Quad. Derick didn't have good enough grades for a scholarship and his mom couldn't afford the tuition. Derick was going to Waldman High School. A good public school but not a college prep school like The Quad and Teresa. While that meant he and Derick would no longer be school buddies, they would still remain good friends.

Brandon was blessed with athleticism but only chose to use those gifts recreationally. Being a disciple of Aikido kept him off the bullies' radar after a few self-defense demonstrations against those who meant him harm. Brandon loved to learn. He loved being in a classroom headed by a teacher driven to teach her pupils. He had been labelled a geek and had no problem with that classification. Yet he didn't look the part. He didn't wear glasses. He dressed affordably but well within the acceptable fashion sensibilities of his peers. He was a notch below good-looking but cute enough girls found him attractive and he was witty and charming when he chose to be.

While Brandon was not brash, he wasn't the least bit bashful. He dove right into any situation for better or worse. He spoke his mind when he felt it was appropriate, defended himself and those he cared about whenever necessary, and never settled for less than he believed he deserved. His mother had described her youngest child as having a quiet confidence. Just like your father his mom went on to say. Brandon relished that assessment since his parents were two of his heroes.

Brandon, Amber, Mason, Derick and Owen would socially be considered middle of the road teenagers. They possessed both book and street smarts. They were not junior thugs or playas in training but they never knowingly allowed themselves to be victimized either. While peace was their way, physical violence was not beneath them. Their acquaintances ranged from some of the most popular jocks and cheerleaders to those bringing up the rear in artists and nerds. With their closest friends they shared more than passing hellos and brief small talk as they did with acquaintances. Close friends comprised the people they ate lunch with, shared juicy gossip, and hung out with at school functions and breaks. Those were their communal peers, their peps, and their schoolyard posse. They were the populous of their middle of the road school universe. And Brandon was going to miss the comradery.

Brandon would miss Amber most of all. Brandon had always liked Amber. Nothing eventful sparked their friendship. On the first day of school, Brandon saw Amber from across the school playground. He marched right over like a man on a mission and introduced himself. Amber told Brandon her name, they shook hands as they said "nice to meet you" at exactly the same time. They laughed at their twin greetings and their friendship was born.

They saved the seat next to each other on the school bus without the other asking. Endured the teasing of their schoolmates who poked fun at their relationship with laughs and good humor. Remembered each other's birthdays, favorite songs, shows, colors, video games, movies and more. Kept private each other's secrets. Visited each other when they were sick. Volunteered delivery of schoolwork when an illness had one of them down for the count. Brandon was quick to anger when anyone had anything bad to say about Amber. Being just as quick to chime in when they possessed praise. Each cheered the other when they were blue. Bolstered their confidence when life dealt them a gut punch. Best friends are an extension of family his mom believed. Brothers or sisters or cousins from another mother. While Brandon felt that way about Mason, Derick and Owen, there was something more to it when it came to Amber. A special something he had been trying to nail down as of late.

Brandon always enjoyed doing special things for Amber. Stuff his dad and Ramello referred to as being a gentleman. Like holding the door open for Amber, carrying her books, walking her—escorting as his family mentors called it—home or to class. Brandon enjoyed going fun places with Amber like the movies, amusement parks, museums, beaches, concerts, the zoo, shows and festivals. He simply liked hanging out with her. Amber was good company as Liana would say. Brandon couldn't agree more.

Amber was one of his best friends with little difference from Derick, Owen and Mason except for the gentleman thing and her being a girl. *Being with Amber is like basking in the constant warmth of an eternal sun. Is this what love feels like?* Those thoughts came to Brandon when he was with Amber one day. Wading through his mind like a breaststroke swimmer in a cool pond on a hot summer day.

The question of love shocked Brandon. So much so, he stopped and stared at Amber as if she had grown another head. While Brandon enjoyed poetry, he never fancied himself a poet. He had thought about how he felt about Amber before. Love was definitely a word he would have used to describe his feelings. But love as a friend or love as in a boyfriend-girlfriend relationship way? Never had the question been so blatant. Never had the answer been so clear.

"I'm going to miss seeing you at school every day," Brandon said.

"We'll still see a lot of each other," Amber said, punctuating her statement with an innocent peck on the cheek.

Brandon took her hand. It was the first time they had held hands in earnest that he could remember. Brandon was confident it would be far from the last.

It was the first time they had held hands in earnest that he could remember. Brandon was confident it would be far from the last.

As they continued their stroll, Brandon felt relieved he hadn't told Amber the truth about what he was thinking. He believed one day he would. That day just didn't feel like the right time to share. He felt justified in his decision in the same way he felt the changes in his body. Brandon nervously fumbled through his rehearsed speech to ask Amber to be his girlfriend on a clear summer Thursday in late July on their way back from the Aquarium. Brandon had purchased a charm bracelet for the occasion. He planned to present it to Amber whether she said yes or no to his proposal. She said yes. He had no idea how he would have reacted had she said no. He was so happy he didn't have to find out.

When Brandon mentioned the idea of using his own money to buy a charm bracelet for Amber to his dad, his dad was all in. He even offered to chip in a little extra cash if needed. When asked by the jeweler what each of the pendants Brandon had chosen meant, Brandon explained: "The heart is a symbol of our love. The tree represents the beauty and depth of our relationship. And the cat is because Amber loves cats."

Both his father and the jeweler had big smiles when Brandon finished his explanation. Brandon had seen that smile on his dad before. It was one of pride. Brandon guessed the jeweler was smiling because she found what Brandon was doing to be cute. Her smile resembled his mother and big sister's when they felt the same way about him. Brandon was caught between reactions of joy and embarrassment. Ultimately, joy won out.

Brandon got down on one knee and delicately placed the personalized silver charm bracelet on Amber's left wrist as part of his proposal. Amber jumped around with excitement for a bit, calming down enough to throw both arms around his neck. Amber kissed Brandon again only this time on the lips. *That wasn't gross at all,* Brandon thought. *At least not with Amber.* They were officially a couple. Now all he needed to do was figure out what being a couple really meant.

Owen and Derick felt nothing but relief on graduation day as if they had just finished a grueling mountain climb. Amber cried tears of mixed emotions as she shared her reasons with Brandon while he tried to comfort her with hugs. Amber was happy to be graduating. Sad to be leaving. Mason felt the same as Amber. Mason was sensitive in that way. Being a young man, he was conditioned not to shed tears in public. Instead, Mason stole away to one of the boy's bathrooms and did his crying hidden away in one of the bathroom stalls. Brandon knew because Mason's eyes were red when he returned. He never called Mason out on it. Brandon doubted he was alone in noticing.

Brandon was conflicted on graduation day as well. Like Owen and Derrick, he experienced relief in what he had accomplished without it feeling like as much of a chore. Like Amber and Mason, he was sad to be leaving minus the tears. Men don't cry. That was the mantra of the men in his household. What most of his male friends believed. Most females in his life disagreed, including his mom, Liana and Amber. Their arguments were rational. But they were not men. He was becoming a man. While Brandon didn't think less of any man who cried for him shedding tears was unacceptable, with the possible exceptions of being in excruciating physical pain or the death of a loved one.

He and his posse had attended Morrison Elementary together since the first grade. Eight years of developing an intimate relationship with familiar people and surroundings. Brandon was going to miss Principal Goodman, Vice-Principal Yee, Mrs. Angaza his Guidance Counselor, Nurse Rivers, his favorite teachers and cafeteria personnel and the maintenance workers he encountered during weekend and afterschool projects and events. The halls, the classrooms, the multi-media center and computer rooms, the gym and assembly hall, the recess areas, study halls and playground, the library and music room and everything in between. He was sorry to leave. Brandon was going to miss Morrison like he would miss a second home. Like he would miss a good friend he knew he was destined never to see the same way again.

*   *   *

Nevaeh Moore
Thursday, 12:07 a.m.

My parents are middle-management stars. They carved out a good life for my little brother, Aaron, and me with those skills. Nothing vital was ever absent from our lives. Richard and Edith Moore are not only excellent at their jobs but satisfied with their stations. I, on the other hand, have always seen myself at the top. My mother has repeatedly lectured me, and my father concurred, that in business if you want to be at the top than it's best to start near the top. Otherwise, you'll find yourself stuck in the middle. Not because it's impossible to work your way up the corporate ladder. It was simply unlikely to occur.

Sage advice for a natural born leader like myself. While I gained treasured experience as a laborer, administrative assistant, supervisor and middle manager in high school by working part-time and summer jobs including working with my mom and dad for a summer, I had no intention of settling for anything less than executive management. I will be forever grateful to my parents for their tutelage. Working alongside my parents gave me vital firsthand real world insight at how to run a business. Those lessons will last a lifetime.

My summer college job resume leaned exclusively toward my ultimate objective of executive management. I interned as an executive assistant for the first three of my undergrad years. I landed those goldmine positions by focusing on small companies and nonprofit organizations in dire need of qualified upper management skills but could not afford to pay top dollar. A different approach from most of my colleagues who were understandably interested in making their mark with large businesses and corporations.

As with most small companies and nonprofits, it was common to wear a variety of hats. Being flexible and responsive helped me further develop my business intellect and people skills in a way classroom education could never match.

The summer after I graduated summa cum laude with my BBA, I landed a dream job as an intern with an up-and-coming products and services industry as V.P. of Marketing and Advertising. The previous V.P. had quit and they were looking for fresh brains outside of the company to nurture. Working at Drillmaster gave me an opportunity to work with Matthew Colegate. A marketing and advertising genius, who happened to be president of my division.

I have always had a firm grasp on the financial and operations side of business. Those elements were like common sense to me. Marketing and advertising had been more ethereal. Matthew brought it down to earth. "Marketing and advertising at their core in a supply and demand society" he said, "is to create a psychological or emotional need, want or desire where one may not have previously existed. Focus on those objectives and the way will become clear."

His ability to gracefully blaze those trails rubbed off on me. Matthew could sell moss to a rock. He changed how I viewed business from a selling prospective. The way had become clear if you will. It came as no surprise to everyone who knew Matthew when he started his own marketing and advertising firm. Satellite Elitc. It's now one of the world's largest and most respected. So much so, it is my number one go to marketing and ad firm when I need help bolstering sales.

As I said before, my parents provided well for their children. That also applied to our futures. They had generously set aside funds for Aaron and I to have fully paid top of the line educations. My 4.0 high school grade point average earned me numerous academic scholarship offers including all of my Ivy League choices. My parents insisted I take my college fund money regardless. I used a small fraction of it for college living expenses. The rest became seed money for my now lucrative personal financial portfolio. I have never worked because it was necessary as so many of my colleagues were forced to do in order to afford higher education. I worked because I wanted to.

Once I earned my MBA, again summa cum laude, the only job offers I considered were from fledgling businesses and established companies hungry for fresh talent to fill their anemic upper leadership positions. I did my research. I knew exactly who they were. I accepted a V.P. of Operations position with Solaris. A young one-hundred million dollar international solar energy company poised for continued success with unlimited growth potential. The opportunity and money were perfect. Predictably, I was successful.

Modern business is a dynamic and sometimes volatile adventure. One must be ready to adapt to changing winds which is one of my many fortes. So when the President of my division accepted a CEO position with a noncompetitor, I was ready to pounce. He was leaving not because he didn't like his job. It had become necessary for him to move on in order to move up. I and three other capable more senior candidates went to war over his vacated position. I enjoy a good scrum. Dirty or clean, I battle to win. If you're weak stay out of my ring. If you're strong step to the center because we're going toe-to-toe. I secured the presidency because the chairperson liked my fresh ideas, focus and energy. I surpassed my predecessor's accomplishments in no time.

I am repeatedly told that I'm a business genius. It's true of course, modestly speaking. What is less well known is my eye for mature talent. What I mean by talent is obvious. People who are gifted and or knowledgeable or both in specific areas of expertise. I'm not a believer in micromanagement. Thereby, I give my people the tools and resources to do their jobs well and room to do them. Building teams and managing people is where executive leadership excels. My expectations are high. I expect excellence in a timely and budget conscious manner. That's where maturity comes in. Mature employees have an innate prideful work ethic. This is not predicated by age but instilled in them from some source when they were very young, like my parents did for me. They don't need babysitters. They take full responsibility or as I like to call it "ownership" in their position and projects and do whatever it takes to see them through.

I have a great eye for that kind of talent and am rarely wrong. In the few instances I found myself in error, they were warned thrice then fired. I reward my people when they succeed or exceed expectations. Punish them when they fail. Working hard and working smart. I practice what I preach. I am the leader and a member of our team. The cliché a chain is only as strong as its weakest link is as true in business as it is anywhere else. Without that robust structure, without my dedicated team, I would falter and fall. Whenever possible, I try to show them how grateful I am for their commitment.

You may have noticed I possess an enormous amount of confidence. Swagger as my peers might say. While I'm not arrogant about it I don't hide my self-assurance either. At times that's a problem. If that problem is with a subordinate, I pull no punches in letting them know their negative behavior will not be tolerated. While I'm not quick to fire someone, I don't lose any sleep over it either. When that same situation exists with my colleagues or a superior, I deal with it head on. I don't give the proverbial inch. Yes I have been called the B-word on a number of occasions. Suit yourself. Although I prefer B.A.B—Bad-Ass-Bitch. A term my equally successful sisterhood coined to describe our kickass business personas.

With a brash attitude like mine you may think people dislike me. Quite the opposite is true for most. Part of what makes me great at my job is my ability to get the most out of my teams and to work well with others. I've never shied away from constructive criticism and believe it or not I *can* take a joke. But there is a line that must be maintained when you are the boss. Without that clear demarcation order cannot be maintained. Without order chaos ensues. In business chaos is your enemy.

One of my sisterhood girlfriends, Amanda—another natural business leader—is one of the world's youngest chairpersons. Her high school brainchild for women undergarments and shapewear had ballooned into a quarter-billion dollar business in just under seven years. With part of the Belle capital she acquired four moderately successful companies that showed real growth and earnings potential. Her enterprise had officially gone from being a prosperous company to becoming a thriving corporation. She needed someone trustworthy with a proven track record at the helm of this expansion. My business is making money. Business was phenomenal and about to get better.

The offer of COO was an extraordinary opportunity and I grabbed it. I'll start my new position in a week following my return from a two weeks' vacation on the island of Fregate with Desmond. That was my plan. What was happening to me now wasn't part of it.

I'm pregnant. It wasn't planned or even believed possible with the amount of safe sex Desmond and I practice. I had given my body a break from the pill because my breasts had become sore as a side effect. Desmond and I had unprotected sex twice during that period. They were spontaneous moments when all reason left us and passion presided. The first of which, coincidentally, was on the night Desmond introduced the question of marriage. By the time I discovered I was pregnant, it was too late for the morning after pill.

I don't feel ready to become a parent. Not shocking news since most mothers I know had felt the same way with their first child. My chairperson girlfriend felt that way. Now she's married with twin girls and she's only three years older than me. The difference being is she more or less planned it that way—all except for the twins' part. Her family had become her main priority. Yet she still manages to remain an amazing business leader and entrepreneur.

As laser focused as I am on my career with my personal life I have more of a lackadaisical approach. Getting married and having a family are not priorities. In fact, they are on the back burner as my mother would say. Aaron and his wife have already given my parents their first grandchild with a second on the way so the pressure's off there. It will happen if and when it happens. Those events I have left to fate. This pregnancy had come a couple of years early. My early target age for giving birth was thirty-one before accepting the Belle COO position. Now I was even considering pushing having a child back a few more years.

Aside from my family and sisterhood, my boyfriend Desmond is one of my most trusted confidants and advisors. He is also the father if that wasn't obvious. Desmond loves me. I know this not only because he tells me but he constantly exhibits it in deeds and manner. I wish I felt the same about him. I do care for Desmond. A great deal in fact. Whether my caring will manifest into love, I can't say with certainty at this point. I've never seen Desmond as the man of my dreams. Come to think of it, I've never imagined a dream man. I've never given any serious consideration to the type of man I wanted to spend the rest of my life. My career remains my goal. No other visions had an opportunity to breed. Being married and having children were never my fantasies. I was already living my dream.

I have been in love before. Twice in fact. Once to Jackson, a young man I surrendered my virginity to in eleventh grade. Another time when I was a college sophomore to a college senior named Cole. Both relationships ended in heartbreak for me. I hadn't realized how needy and insecure they were. Neither could accept my being in love did not trump my academic and career aspirations. My pinpoint focus on my studies and career goals coupled with my strong, outspoken personality seemed to drive them away. Since changing who I was not an option, I licked my wounds and moved on. From those experiences, I learned how to compartmentalize love and sex into the appropriate places in my life. Does following your ultimate dream sometimes mean another must die? If so, so be it.

I met Desmond at an executive leadership conference in Hartford, Connecticut. We laughed at the fact our offices were only a few blocks apart but our paths had never crossed. Desmond is funny, good-looking, personable, and I would soon discover brilliant. We shared the same philosophies on what it took to make a successful business. Our minds were in parallel on how to handle our employees although we differed in management styles. Desmond is more of a hands on micromanager overseeing even the smallest details. We debated when to trust instincts over logic, neither of us winning the other over to our side. When to be a hard-ass and when to lighten the reins. Desmond had inherited his family's neighborhood bakeries. He successfully dragged their business into the modern age by selling to national grocery chains and creating bakery outlet stores. While his business bottom line would be considered mildly successful compared to mine, he was doing what he loved and making good money at it.

What sets Desmond apart from any man I've ever been attracted to is he embraces my power and thereby who I am. My needs seem to always come first with him. He truly is a strong and independent man who is not intimidated by women of equal or superior favor. After having met his mom and grandmother, I can understand why. The problem is—if there is one—I've never seen Desmond as Mr. Right but more like Mr. Right Now.

Desmond asked me a couple of months back what I would say if he were to ask me to marry him. He framed it in that whimsical way of which he is a master when he's feeling out a situation. To my surprise I told him I'd think about it. I turned it around and asked him what he would say if I asked him to marry me? Without hesitation he said he would say yes. We smiled at each other, kissed and then dropped the subject. Desmond hasn't actually proposed yet but I have a strong feeling he is going to soon. Probably while we're on vacation. I'm still thinking about what my answer will be.

My girlfriends think I'm in denial about Desmond. A lingering fear from two broken hearts prevents me from taking the plunge into love. They could be right. When you're chronically busy there's not much time or energy left for self-analysis or couch time with a shrink.

I have always dreamed different than most of my female peers. Wanting it all never included marriage and children for me. While other little girls dreamed of lavish weddings, I dreamed of having a corner office with an unobstructed breathtaking view. While other little girls had tea parties with their dolls, mine were involved in board meetings and hostile takeovers. My family accepted and encouraged me for who I am. Some of my peers berated and belittled me for those same qualities. My family helped me believe in myself. The haters made me strong, motivated and independent.

When discussing the pregnancy scenario with my college girlfriends the choice had always been clear-cut for me. To have an abortion. Actually being pregnant made the fictional argument disintegrate in the fires of reality. In our hypothetical debates there was always early detection. The embryo had not become a fetus and thereby any pregnancy less than seven weeks was fair game for safe termination. At only two weeks my body had developed a connection to the embryo. My child was forming. What I knew for certain is the longer I waited the stronger that connection would become.

I hadn't told anyone about my pregnancy, not even Desmond. That was not going to change in the immediate future. Making a decision to have an abortion had been so much easier in theory as are most of life's challenging questions. In all of my executive decisions, I harbor no fear or doubt. I trust my instincts as well as my mind. I am willing to sink or swim based upon my choices. This choice was at the other end of the spectrum. I'm not one who had any interest in exploring the existential questions of life. This situation—if such a small word defines my condition—requires I search my soul for the answer.

I believe in the sanctity of life as strongly as I believe in a woman's right to choose. There is no doubt in my mind I will be able to have children when I'm ready. Love is an unpredictable variable of course, but I have no problem usurping cupid for parenthood. If love has not entered the picture when I'm ready then a sperm donor substitute will do. Desmond would be perfect in that capacity if he were still available which I doubt he will be if I turn down his forthcoming proposal. Would I say yes to secure him in the positions of surrogate sperm donor and father? Absolutely! Would I feel guilty about it? Not in the least. I will make Desmond a good wife and be an excellent mother to our children. I've learned from the best in both departments. To some this may sound cold and calculating, but to me it is merely a veracity of life. Time moves on and circumstances change. One must learn to adapt and adjust their best laid plans in order to accomplish their goals. Business has taught me that.

I have a loving, caring, you could even say doting family. I am content for the moment in that area. From all of the research I've done, having an early abortion would not hinder me from having children in the future. Still, I don't want to terminate this pregnancy out of convenience like discarding a piece of furniture because it doesn't fit into my decorum. A single high-powered woman executive having a child in America no longer raises many eyebrows amongst the enlightened sectors. A single high-powered female executive having a child in a company in transition, however, may be valid cause for Belle, Inc. to rescind their lucrative offer. That argument also makes accepting Desmond's proposal logical. Add to my personal circumstance a couple of professional bullet points: one being this is a critical juncture for Belle, Inc. Second, what if Belle, Inc. decides to go public?

While the verdict is pending as to whether that would apply in this particular case, I'm willing to bet Amanda, the presiding judge herself a mother and dynamic business leader and also one of my dearest friends, would understand and make whatever accommodations I might need to aide with my transition. Many a successful business has floundered and failed by expanding to fast. I'm the best at preventing that from happening. I will do everything in my power to make Belle, Inc.'s transition a successful one. And Amanda knows it.

My doctor said she could make all of the necessary arrangements. It could be done in a private facility secure of murdering religious zealots and kept confidential. All I need do is call and give her the go-ahead. I still haven't decided whether to make that call.

*   *   *

Marlon Jamison
Thursday, 4:06 a.m.

I never fancied myself a military man. I already possessed discipline and focus by the time I reached eighteen. In part because of my upbringing. My dad was a military man. And I was an Army brat along with my baby sister, Gladys and my little sister, Joya. My dad lived, breathed, walked and talked professional soldier. An Army man through and through. Had it not been for my mother he would have been a lifer. She had had enough of Army life and wanted out. Mom insisted dad chose. A decision he confided in me that he never regretted.

Another reason the service had no appeal for me was because two of its main selling points I already had. Maturity in the form of becoming a man, and discipline. Maturity and discipline felt natural to me. They are a big part of who I am. The skins I'm most comfortable in. My mother always said I behaved older than my years. There was no denying that truth. The armed forces claimed me nonetheless.

Had I a choice I would not have been in the service. In combat we found ourselves scrambling to survive most of the time rather than an idealistic march toward glory and freedom. About two-thirds of our unit were soldiers by choice. The rest, like me, were drafted into the military. It was my duty and I did it to the best of my ability. My feelings about Vietnam one way or another seem insignificant now. It was what it was. I played the cards I was dealt and lived to tell about it.

During my tour in 'Nam, I discovered a number of ghastly firsthand defects about mankind that both awakened and scarred me for life. Characteristics I would have preferred to remain blind to or at the very least naïve. Horrific theater of war events were branded into my brain, tattooed on my soul. The most deplorable tapestries of butchering and mayhem one could ever imagine. Violent death is never pretty. I suppose one could say death in and of itself rarely is. In war, in extreme combat, practically every form of death one could imagine bubbles to the surface. What I witnessed in the jungles of Vietnam both shocked and frightened me. The vast majority of my infantry peers felt the same but none of us would have ever admitted it. Our egos would have it no other way.

Strangely that recognition of fear and shock was a good thing. It proved we still held fast to what was good in each of us. Even amongst the most dreadful carnage of organized chaos there were acts of virtue and kindness. Like seeing Corporal Davidson comforting a crying infant whose mother was part of the bloody debris of a decimated village that had been carpet bombed. Or our infantry unit helping rebuild a South Vietnamese village that had been plundered and burned to the ground by the North Vietnamese Regulars. Simple reminders of the best we could be even while mired in the quicksand of vicious conflict.

War does truly bring out the worst and the best in us. Test our character and resolve. Honor and integrity become more than words pinned to the lapels of what makes a good soldier. They are dared into action in combat. Qualities that are tested under the most severe conditions imaginable. If you can trudge through the belly of the beast and emerge with those virtues intact than you have embodied what it means to be a good soldier. You not only do honor to the uniform you wear but are truly a person of sound character and good principles. I can honestly say that through ever gnarly twist, every grisly turn during my tour in 'Nam, I did my best to live up to those lofty standards.

I leave it to my brothers-in-arms to decide whether or not I achieved my goals. I received the Distinguished Service Cross and the Silver Star in honor of my service. I was honorably discharged and I would be lying if I said I wasn't proud of those accomplishments. One thing I discovered which in retrospect doesn't surprise me. In combat there are few heroes, most are survivors. I consider myself amongst the latter.

Unlike me, my father had joined the armed forces. He enlisted in the Army at sixteen. Encouraged by his parents to seek a better life than the one they had sharecropping, which his parents regarded as having no life at all. The service was his means of escape. My paternal grandparents believed in education even if they hadn't been fortunate enough to receive much education themselves. They made sure dad, Uncle Winslow and Aunt

Janine, dad's older brother and younger sister, got as much "Learnin'" as possible. All and all, his amounted to the equivalent of an eight grade education by the time dad entered the service. Once he completed two tours of duty in the Korean War, dad set his sights on continuing his classroom education. Through hard work and determination and assistance from the Army dad earned his high school diploma and went on to earn his BS and MS in Civil Engineering.

Being an engineer was something my father had always wanted. He became a member of the US Army Corps of Engineers. During peacetime the Corps was in high demand for building and maintaining infrastructures both domestically and worldwide. Dad loved peacetime work and was never prouder of his time in the service than when he had the opportunity to make positive contributions. The only downside was he didn't like being away from his family for long stretches of time. That's why when mom gave him the ultimatum, he understood and conceded to her demands. His family would not be required to make the same sacrifices he had made.

Civilian transition was initially a little rocky for my dad. I never suffered from posttraumatic stress disorder. Somehow, I was fortunate in that regard when it came to PTSD. My dad did. Except in his day they called it battle fatigue. Most of his issues came from wartime flashbacks and nightmares and short bouts of depression. Talking to his Vet friends only helped so much. His battle buddies didn't have any more answers than he had to dispel those demons. My dad was a proud man but he was never too proud to ask for help when he needed it. He took full advantage of his VA benefits. The shrinks and counselors helped but he refused to take any medications for his condition. He only drank socially and never saw the bottle as an escape for problems he believed needed to be met head on. Dad had discovered Tae Kwon Do while serving in Korea and immersed himself in the martial art form for the remainder of his life. Dad did not simply embrace the physical aspects of Tae Kwon Do but its trinity of mind, body and spirit. Time and patient. The angels he thanked for seeing him through.

My father and I talked military from time to time although not as much as one might think. Possibly because we shared so many other common bonds that our joint time in the Army only amounted to one of them. We would get together and reminisce on our first days in service. The trials and tribulations of boot camp. What instructors we liked and those we hated and the fact not one of them fell anywhere in between. Completing basic training, our first days as soldiers and the pride we took in wearing the uniform. What it was like during our first deployment, the bad food, short supplies, comradery and infighting, the best pranks and entertainers, those were the lighter moments of our military lives. The ones that made us smile and laugh out loud. The ones that allowed us to burrow into far less pleasant territories of hostile enemy action that would haunt us for life.

Dad never shared his combat experiences with me before I went to Vietnam. Perhaps he was trying to protect me or maybe he thought I simply wouldn't understand. Afterwards, we compared notes. Although we fought in different wars the horrors of combat had not changed. We talked about our first, best and worst firefights. What we did to pass the time and forget during those rare moments of downrange. The units we served in and the soldiers who comprised them. At times we were somber as when we reminisced over good friends and fellow soldiers lost in battle. Other times, we were sarcastic and filled with playful or black humor. We shared photos that reminded us of who we were and the ghost of our past. We praised our good leaders and trashed those who let us down. We talked about how much we missed home and the people we loved when on tour. How those memories kept us focused, strong and alive in our pins and needles world.

Service and patriotism and sacrifice were reasons to raise our glasses. We found moments to toast peace and family as well. There is a sacred bond of brotherhood for those who served in the military, especially those who have served within the same branch of service. That bond can also extend across generational lines. A hard earned comradery, an intimate understanding of what it takes to make the sacrifices to do what we did.

My father was a master sergeant by his second tour in the Korean War. I made corporal and was content with my rank. His units spent the majority of their time on the front lines as did mine. Dad not only had to battle the North Koreans during his time but an ongoing internal struggle against domestic racism amongst the rank and file. In that regard, dad had a tougher go in the military than me. I asked why he stayed. Why did he tolerate prejudice? Why deal with the maltreatment from his fellow soldiers?

"I never tolerated maltreatment or bigotry from anyone," dad said. "Standing up for yourself was something I firmly believe. It was my duty as both an American citizen and for future generations to stand my ground and fight those fights." A trait mom and dad had passed on to their children.

My father was living history of why life was better for me in America. I was always proud of my dad. As a father, he set high the standard I have tried to uphold. As a soldier, his sacrifice, his commitment, his unheralded contribution for the betterment of a nation who at times regarded us as second class citizens was a legacy, that in my own way, I hope I have carried forward. Only my children will be able to answer whether my attempts have succeeded.

My parents are gone. We lost mom six years ago in a fatal car accident that wasn't her fault. A few months after my father retired from his state civil engineering job of thirty years. Mom had just come from a travel agency. Mom and dad were never big on using the internet. They preferred dealing with flesh and blood people whenever possible. Mom was loaded down with travel information on all of these great places to visit. My parents had been making plans to see the world for what seemed eternity. It was a dream about to come true for them.

A man driving much too fast missed a stop sign because he was talking on his cellphone and not paying attention to the road. There was a savage collision. He broadsided my mother. The emergency room doctor who gave us the fatal news said mom's injuries were extensive. The paramedics had done all that they could on the scene but broken ribs had punctured her lungs. They were too late to save her. Mom literally drowned in her own blood. It was the first time I had ever seen my father cry. The second time was at my mother's funeral. Fortunately for the driver, he was convicted of involuntary manslaughter. I say fortunate because if he hadn't been convicted my father would have killed him.

Dad was devastated. Spiritually, he seemed spent. Of all the deaths he had witnessed, of all the losses that had occurred in his life that he endured, losing mom was the one that broke him. Depression weighed on his shoulders like a two-ton backpack. Family and friends, civilian and Vets, feared for his life because he was in such dire distress. Bit by bit we helped pull dad out of his pit of despair. First we were able to convince dad that continuing on was something mom would have wanted. Then we were able to convince him to do it for his children and grandchildren. Finally, I believe through more of a will of his own rather than anything we did dad was able to stand on his own two feet again. Dad returned to practicing Tae Kwon Do a couple of hours a day after months of lethargy. He adopted a healthy diet and was the picture of physical good health. There were times we could tell dad missed mom. Sadness seeped in from shared memories. Mom's birthday, their wedding anniversary, their first meeting and first date, the birth of their children, their very first kiss. Thanksgiving and Christmas could be particularly challenging. They could bring dad down real low. Once

Joya, Gladys and I grew up and moved out, my parents loved to host those holidays in their home to bring the family together. Gladys, Joya and I insisted dad stay with one of our families during those holidays after mom passed. Surrounded by love and receiving plenty of warm attention. It always seemed to cheer his spirit.

How could dad not feel melancholy from mom's passing and still be human. Mom and he had been together for fifty-two glorious years, in dad's words. He truly loved mom more than life itself. Dad learned to live in the moment and appreciate the small blessings of each day. That was his way of soldiering on. That was his way of honoring mom and respecting his family.

We cocooned dad in as much love and attention as adults with families of our own could. The gaping hole in his heart for mom never healed. He never remarried or dated or had any lady friends although a number of women showed definite interest. Dad lost his desire to see the world. Without mom by his side the world meant nothing to him.

Dad followed mom almost five years to the day of her passing. A fatal arrhythmia took him away in his sleep. There was no way to predict it according to the doctor. The condition struck dad down as sudden as a sniper bullet during a firefight. Death came quick and painless. His journey home and reunion with mom was complete, in my opinion. His last few years of noble suffering had come to an end.

I started my Tae Kwon Do training with my father when I was five. I believe his early teachings contributed mightily to my early maturity and positive prospective on life. I have taught Rebecca and Bayden, my daughter and son, and they have been teaching their children. One of a number of traditions dad has contributed to the Jamison legacy.

I'm having exploratory surgery this morning to discover the depth of colon cancer I have. I'm not afraid. I can handle it whatever the outcome. Being battle tested exposed that aspect of me to myself. I can handle anything as long as it only involves me. What I can't handle well is when it involves people I care about. I don't want those I love to suffer in the least due to any personal hardship that may come. I'm worried about Candance, my wife. She's a strong woman who understands what I'm up against. If it's for the worse, there is no way I want to put her through this ordeal. Candance deserves better. I feel as strongly about Rebecca and Bayden. Children should never be burdened with the care of their parents.

Candance is a pediatrician. My wife is meeting me at the hospital. She was called in due to a patient emergency that has prevented her from accompanying me. I don't mind. It cuts down on uncomfortable silences and dialogue while minimizing the anxiety Candance is feeling that she is so bravely trying to mask. We have agreed not to discuss my colon cancer situation any further than the exploratory surgery. We don't want to get ahead of ourselves. We've been able to keep what's happening with me a secret so far from our children although we suspect they know something is wrong. Both the endoscopy and CT test have revealed my cancer is minor. My doctor and surgeon and Candance all concur. This surgery is more of a precaution serving as a removal of what little cancer does exist and to explore whether there is more than tests have revealed. I'm confident their initial diagnosis is correct. The surgery is routine and should present no problems. But thinking of my parent's passing and my military combat experience reminds me life holds no guarantees. I want to make certain all of my paperwork is in order before I go under the knife in case that time happens to be near.

MY LAST WILL AND TESTAMENT. Bold, centered and capitalized across the top of the page. No truer words have ever been written. The summary of one's final demands and requests of whatever accomplishments and desires of one's life. Reviewed, signed and dated. I appreciate a couple of my Vet buddies acting as witnesses and keeping it on the DL. I've made a few minor changes to the original to include some personal items I want my grandchildren to have. Other than that it's the same, making certain Candance is well taken care of and Rebecca and Bayden remain heirs to our estate.

As I sit here staring at my last will and testament, memories of my parents weigh heavy on my mind.

"Nothing beats preparation when it comes to navigating misfortune and disaster," dad used to say.

As I contemplate my own mortality, I wonder how my own family views me as a husband and father. I owe much of the man I am to dad. To both my parents. Sentiments I made crystal clear to them while they were alive. Candance and I have shared the fact we complete each other. Corny and clichéd but nonetheless true. Our children are a little more self-centered than I would like. Something I expect they will eventually outgrow. For now it is their way and I can't blame them for being who they are. I do fault myself if I have failed to teach them about the rewards of teamwork and charity as I have learned from my parents and the service.

If an impending cancer battle looms, how do I allay the fears and distress of those who care most about me? I don't have a firm grasp on the answer to that question yet. Perhaps by letting them know I've lived a good life. I harbor no regrets and consider myself the most fortunate man to have ever walked this earth because of them. I will always be with them in spirit as I have in life. Celebrate my life. Do not despair in my passing over.

It all sounds good while life beats strong in my chest. Will I have the courage when my moment arrives? YES I WILL. And I'll find a way to let the people I love know come what may, I'll be alright, and so will they.

*   *   *

In the whispering hour at the doorstep of dawn some droopy eyed residents began their morning rituals of readying themselves for the world. Others either pranced or prodded themselves into their daybreak routines. Some pondered their day and what challenges lie ahead. Others simply sought to get their bodies and minds in motion.

Neveah set off on her morning run in the clear blue promise of another hot and humid summer day no closer to a decision about her pregnancy. Wearing his annoying bike helmet and ridiculous bright orange safety vest as Candance would have wanted, Marlon pedaled his city bike to the hospital feeling good about his chances. Desmond sat on his wooden porch steps texting with Amber waiting on his parents to finish cooking breakfast for the family. He and Amber were finalizing their exclusive plans for the day. Neveah encountered both Marlon and Desmond during her run. She exchanged good morning greetings with Marlon as they passed each other going in opposite directions. Neveah smiled back at Brandon who happened to look up with a smile as she was jogging by. Brandon was actually smiling at something funny Amber had texted.

UFOs and God

Aunt Carol was my father's younger sister and his only sibling. My Aunt Carol and Uncle Mason had three children, Owen, Eden, and Cole, respectively ages eleven, eight, and five. They were our favorite cousins belonging to our favorite aunt and uncle. When my father died in military combat and my mother followed him a year later more from a shattered heart than the car accident that actually killed her, my Aunt Carol and Uncle Mason welcomed twelve-year old me and my younger sister Quinn into their home without hesitation. We were family and never felt a twinge of imposition in their care.

My Uncle Mason was a serious and thoughtful man, steeped in the old-fashioned Christian work ethic. My Aunt Carol had a sharp, insightful, playful wit and a vivid imagination. No one brought out Uncle Mason's silly side faster than the love of his life. Aunt Carol would say or do something outlandish that would cause my favorite uncle to laugh out loud, often cajoling him into joining her for some hilarious skit of storytelling or into trading snappy quips with each other and we children. If laughter did not ensue from Uncle Mason, then a smile and gentle shake of his head were the minimal results of her efforts. Their dynamic was perfect. Uncle Mason was the roots and Aunt Carol was the tree, and we were the fruit that benefited from their nurturing.

My favorite aunt came to believe in UFOs and aliens. She developed that belief system from her near reverence of the TV show the X-Files. The same show fostered in her an acceptance of conspiracy theories. It seemed that many of our adult conversations came to center around one of those three areas of discussion. I would attempt to steer our chat toward more mundane topics such as children, health issues, family gossip, fluff news or even the weather. But somehow UFOs, aliens, government or corporate conspiracies seemed to win out. I had learned to stay away for the topic of religion since my dear aunt had come to believe that religion was the greatest conspiracy of all.

My Aunt Carol wasn't crazy. She simply allowed her overactive imagination at times to will out over her intelligence. I, myself, believed that UFOs and aliens were possible. The difference between me and my darling aunt were that I could care less whether they existed. My feelings were if they did—and they were more intelligent than us—we'd know soon enough. I wasn't going to sit around obsessing over what they looked like, what their motives were, who already knew about them or why their existence was being kept secret from the rest of the world.

Conspiracy issues were a whole other kettle of fish. Every occurrence that fell a bit outside the norm was regarded as fodder for creative speculation. Over the years, I had learned not to interject logic into these debates. Aunt Carol's existential reasoning could extend beyond the farthest reaches of our universe. She was fully committed to whatever idea or theory we were discussing at the time. Extensively arguing with her over the matter merely frustrated her. As her health deteriorated from age related diseases, I found it best to be her sounding board. I would interject an "uh-huh, really, you don't say, I don't know about that, are you sure, wait a minute would you explain that again" and other such innocuous comments to convince my precious aunt that I was listening as opposed to doing something else. Such as keeping an eye on my children, surfing or texting on my cell or watching TV. On occasion I had to put up a fight or Aunt Carol would get wise. If my beloved aunt was ever aware when I had mentally checked out during our otherworldly discussions she never let on.

My Uncle Mason lent her a patient ear, but offered no insights or debate about her deductions or assertions. Uncle Mason accepted what Aunt Carol had to say as interesting or intriguing opinions. Down deep I believed my choice uncle was as apathetic as I was on the subjects. He simply did not want to hurt his wife's feelings by telling her so.

My cherished aunt championed UFOs, aliens and conspiracies with her inner circle through much of her twilight years. A couple of members of our family wanted to have Aunt Carol committed because of her eccentric outlook. Being working class they called her crazy. The majority of us defended her. We made it clear that with all of her discourse Aunt Carol never harmed anyone in order to support her odd views. In other words, Aunt Carol was all talk. The majority won out. Those who argued for institutionalization were more concerned about themselves than my favorite aunt. Aunt Carol only felt comfortable discussing her far-reaching beliefs with a minuscule group of family members or like-minded people. Whether that was due to a general lack of trust or simple paranoia I never learned. If word got out about Aunt Carol, those image conscious family members would have been social media embarrassed.

Aunt Carol was not one for hospitals, doctors or regular checkups even as age demanded more maintenance and vigilance. Her suspicions about alien implants and unauthorized medical experiments made it challenging to overcome her misgivings. When she was rushed to the hospital by Uncle Mason for suffering from severe abdominal and back pains, it was cause for serious concern. When she was diagnosed with inoperable pancreatic cancer it came as a numbing shock.

There was nothing the doctors could do but make her comfortable in the end. Aunt Carol wanted to die at home. She also wanted to end her life on her own terms. All of our family was gathered around her bedside on the day Aunt Carol was to have doctor-assisted euthanasia. Aunt Carol told us she loved us and not to feel sorrow at her passing. She stated with conviction that she had lived a good life. Aunt Carol beamed through the pall as she spoke of how proud and happy we had made her, and that her family was the greatest blessing she had ever received.

There was no talk of UFOs, aliens or conspiracies. It was as if those unconventional themes had dissipated in importance; stowed away in a steamer trunk like toys locked away after play. Near her final moments Aunt Carol made no mention of heaven, reincarnation or past lives. My favorite aunt smiled, and with a glint in her twinkling brown eyes, she drew her last breath. It was the only time I had witnessed Uncle Mason cry.

Cancer halted Aunt Carol's steaming locomotive far too soon for any of us. While my precious aunt was a bit askew at times when it came to real life, she had a bountiful heart and a good ear when it came to people. My aunt loved people—the good, the bad, and the ugly. She had a gift for bringing a smile to the most downtrodden or opening the hearts of those who were set cold against the world. And when she passed away many of the people she touched joined our family to pay homage to her legacy.

When I visit Aunt Carol's grave it is not in mourning. I miss her. I always will. But Aunt Carol had seeded so much of who I was as a person. Many of her positive qualities shaped me into the professional and personal success I had become. If there is a God then my beloved aunt deserves a place in his kingdom. If God turns out to be the greatest hoax perpetrated against humankind, then I hope a UFO filled with compassionate aliens shuttled her off with them to a better world than ours. If they had, I could see my Aunt Carol give me a knowing smile and a clever wink with a final, "I told you so."

Locusts

Thurgood Boyd drove north along a stretch of Washington state highway at a clip exceeding the posted speed limit by a few miles. It was the Third of July and he had made great time. Early morning was clear and bright with a sun that promised to sear. Thurgood was listening to Bob Marley's "Buffalo Soldiers," missing his recently departed dreadlocks. He had traded his dreads in for a buzz cut that revealed a healthy scalp. Gone too was his coarse black beard grown during his solitary time hiking and camping in Bitterroot National Forest. He missed his fiancée, Mae, who couldn't join him because of her graduate school commitments, but little else. The absence of a beard unveiled his twenty-five-years old baby face. His skin had tanned from amber to dark caramel. His brown eyes were clear. His hands were callused from meeting his survival needs and doing that which he loved, both observing and enjoying nature. His six-three frame was made lean and strong from the three months long experience that lasted from mid-spring to midsummer.

To his east and west was abundant forest rich with mature western hemlocks. The highway medians alternated from short green grass to native colorful plants. Thurgood was enjoying the scenery, blue sky and sun, when on the east side an unexpected sight caused him to gasp. It was an environmental and conservation tragedy. Shock, dismay, frustration and anger swept through him when the carnage of clearcutting came into full view. A stretch of tree stumps provided their own grave markers for miles.

Flashbacks of the deforestation he had seen in the Amazon and West African Rainforests came to mind.

Was it previously protected forest wrangled from the government by an unscrupulous and insatiable lumber industry in order to meet the wants and desires of the few? Was it timber theft, stolen right from under their noses? Thurgood knew with the forces employed to protect the forest and wildlife being undermanned and underfunded, illegal logging was a lot easier to accomplish than most people could imagine. In the end, it was another example of shortsighted humankind pillaging natural resources. *We've become the locusts of this planet,* Thurgood thought. *Feeding on everything and leaving little to nothing in return.* Thurgood made a mental note of the location. He would check in with local authorities to discover the fate of that tree cemetery as soon as he could.

The more he thought about it the more frustrated he became. *Why did we insist on behaving like fools? Arrogance, brought on by God knows what, brought on by man knows what. We do seem to be a suicidal breed. As if we seek to punish ourselves for some innate injustice in being what and whom we are. Through human conceit and gluttony, we're killing our mother. How does commonsense battle avarice and supercilious whores whose insatiable egos outweigh sound judgment?*

Thurgood accelerated in an effort to speed past the graveyard. He and Mae had wanted to go green. They had strongly considered getting an electric or hybrid vehicle but the roads they traveled didn't give them much choice. Being impractical would have been an understatement. Their option of necessity gave them great gas mileage while leaving a minimal carbon footprint. It was the best they could hope for until the demand for alternative energy not only became feasible but profitable choices.

*   *   *

Everett Boyd's old bones never felt so weary. They had risen with the sun, he and his wife, Ida, which in this part of the world in the heart of summer had meant 5:17a.m. Thirteen minutes before the clock alarm was set to go off. Dawn dragged them into their morning ritual of preparing for another day on the farm. For Everett that meant a subconscious routine of marching to their barn through the early morning mist to hand milk Bertilda their dairy cow; Ida had the same out of body experience feeding and watering their chickens and gathering eggs from their henhouse. Afterwards Ida washed up. She made breakfast while Everett fed and watered their

Anatolian Shepherds, Rufus and Gracie. They went about their morning routine not in their usual somber state of mind but with a sense of gloom and regret. Everett came in through the back door and took off his dirty leatherwork boots. A practice his wife instituted for the family because she was tired of them tracking dirt on her clean floors. By the time Everett washed up and shaved, it was time to eat.

"I'm going to visit Dora for a bit," Ida said while they were eating. "Catch up on the latest gossip."

Everett nodded. Dora was the wife of another small farmer just up the road. One of the few small family farms left in the area.

"Tell 'em I said, hi."

Ida nodded.

They were the only words spoken during breakfast. When they made eye contact, Ida threatened to burst into tears. She had been crying off and on since the final decision had been made three days prior. Both knew they had no other options. Neither found solace in that unbending truth.

It began a long time before his, beginning with his great, great, great grandfather. Land Thaddeus Burch Boyd originally homesteaded was taken from him because of his race. The rich white landowner who wrested possession of his land allowed him to stay if he agreed to sharecrop. Fortunately for Thaddeus the man was not only mean and greedy but also stupid when it came to money. The landowner lost it all through horrible investments and lavish spending forcing the bank to foreclose.

Thaddeus Burch Boyd had somehow managed to put away enough money to buy his place back once the landowner went bust. With the help of a trusted white sharecropping friend, Thaddeus gained control over his parcel. His friend bought up the land Thaddeus had been farming along with his own. His friend then clandestinely signed over ownership to Thaddeus while making it appear Thaddeus was working for him. Despite the bank's racists policies excluding Negroes from owning property they let it go when they eventually discovered the ruse over two decades later. To disclose the truth would not only have been a source of embarrassment but would have been bad for business for a trusted financial institution to admit fraud was going on right under their noses. By the time Thaddeus passed the farm on to his oldest son, Carter, his great, great grandfather, they were clear to own the farm outright.

After breakfast, Everett changed out of the bib overalls he wore earlier into a comfortable pair of jeans and a short sleeve white T-shirt. He plucked the red and white mesh cap embroidered with the gold U.S. Farmer logo from amongst his limited collection of caps on the expanding beech wood rack and slipped it on. Everett laced up his leatherwork boots parked just inside the back door next to his wife's and headed toward the barn.

His skin mirrored the dark caramel of his grandson, Thurgood, only with a leathery texture. His eyes were an opaque brown. Ida cut his hair and he liked it as near as bald as he could get it for this time of year. In autumn and winter when he would let it grow, it was white silver. He was a big man by anyone's account. Barrel chest, plank wide shoulders, powerful limbs and hands as large as catcher's mitts. His size belied his warm personality and gentle soul, a soul that was reeling with despair.

Everett saw Ida leaving the farmhouse from the barn where he tended their horses. His wife had changed out of her morning attire of comfortable jeans and work boots and one of Everett's flannel shirts that fit her like a nightshirt into a pair of white summer slacks, a flowery print short-sleeved blouse, white sandals and a straw sunhat. Her skin was the color of raisins and her eyes dark chocolate. Her Afro-textured hair was thick, rich, and gray as steel, refusing to lie down no matter how much she brushed it. Her body was old but strong like her husband's from decades of hard sometimes-backbreaking work on the farm. After cleaning the kitchen, Ida headed for their car with Rufus at her side. Gracie was with Everett. Rufus always did favor Ida just as Gracie always favored Everett.

Ida sat in the passenger seat with the door wide open. She vigorously petted Rufus talking pet baby talk to him, which he enjoyed. Ida kissed Rufus on top of his head and said something to him that sent him happily along. Rufus barked twice as he pranced across the green space between the farmhouse and barn looking around as if searching for something. Gracie rushed to the barn door and barked twice to inform him where they were. Rufus sprinted to join them. Ida slammed shut the car door and drove off toward the farm road. Everett and Gracie watched her leave from the barn. Rufus sauntered in still jubilant. His wife had opted to visit a friend rather than tend house as she normally did. He understood. Everett didn't expect Ida back any time soon.

*   *   *

Thurgood estimated he had witnessed the desolation of about 3,000 acres of forestland on his road trip from Colorado to Washington. On the drive he had noticed not only the devastation of clear cutting, but arid farmlands, shrinking wetlands and forest, polluted water and air. He could see from what proceeded to his west and what lay ahead how the delicate balance of nature had been changed. Beautiful, mature, tall western hemlocks that had densely populated about 1,000 acres were gone. Gone with it was the protection and nourishment of dependent wildlife and insects. Another ecosystem reduced to a minimalist environment that retained nothing to stop the runoff from heavy rains that were common in the area during late autumn and throughout winter. A wasteland of what it once was born of a voracious and selfish criminal act.

Having earned his doctorate in Agriculture, and his bachelor's in Wildlife Conservation, Thurgood had worked summers as a park ranger, conservationist, environmentalist, and farmer. There was evidence of the same shortsighted deeds everywhere he went. Few seemed to harbor either appreciation or respect for nature. They treated natural treasures like reserves for their spoils to be raided at will with the insane expectation they would forever be available to fulfill their ravenous wants or desires. Seldom had they the foresight to comprehend ecological limits, unwilling to learn their lesson until the evidence lay at their doorstep. It was always too late by that time.

His middle name was Marshall. His parents had named him after one of their heroes. A man they considered one of the pioneers and architects of the American Civil Rights movement, a movement that had achieved tremendous successes in humane progress against diabolic opposition. His parents had been active participants in the charge toward people progress. They had attended the 1963 march on Washington. Protested and rallied in nonviolent movements throughout the land and helped with voter registrations in areas that could have easily gotten them lynched for their efforts. They were the future of America. In a larger sense, they and the world were not backing down from tyranny anymore.

Thurgood often heard their personal stories of triumph and despair. He swelled with pride knowing his parents had battled on the frontlines risking it all for a better future for his generation. He also bristled with disappointment that a number of those hard fought victories in American rights and liberties were being systematically dismantled since the Reagan years. Oppression had revamped itself and taken center stage again. Aided and abetted by those who didn't care or were in denial regarding the continuing subjugation of human rights that initially sparked those flames of dissention, loitering like a boiling plague of racism and sexism in our nation's bones exasperated by the throes of economic calamity.

As part of that conservative onslaught, the plight of Black farmers in America echoed that notorious trend. Black farmers were losing their farms at an alarming rate. Having been victimized by both social and systematic racism and discrimination over the centuries, which included even the United States Department of Agriculture, their struggles to survive has had to hurdle more than the erratic stumbling blocks of natural forces.

Agriculture had become big business. With his work and research experience along with his education, corporate farms were eager to hire him. Thurgood had other ideas in mind. One of them he wanted to discuss with his granddad.

*   *   *

Everett moved Bertilda and their chestnut stallion and mare into the corral. Storm and Lightning were accompanied by Gracie and Rufus who were in a playful mood. Storm and Lightning weren't workhorses. The days of using horses for farm work were long gone as far as Everett was concerned. They were fine examples of American Quarter horses. Storm and Lightning were purely for recreational purposes. He and Ida liked to ride. Once done cleaning the stalls Everett washed up again and decided to take a walk around his farm.

He started out heading across the green space that he had mowed a couple of days earlier between his farmhouse and the barn. He moved past the henhouse and the barn and then looped around the corral. As was his habit, he checked on the chickens, Bertilda and Storm and Lightning along the way. All was well for the moment. Everett continued his walk.

Gracie and Rufus decided to join him. It was going to be a hot one. Everett could tell. He was already starting to sweat under his cap and in his tan cotton T-shirt. Everett made his way down to the first field. It was his habit to rotate crops in order to maximum yield and replenish the soil. That was particularly important for an organic farmer like himself. He walked across the field where he had planted carrots last season. It had been another excellent crop and harvest as had been the wheat, potatoes, beets, onions and corn he had raised on his other parcels. Unfortunately, the prices at the markets for his crops were far less than what he had anticipated.

As senior member of the local organic farming community, many of the local farmers came to Everett when they had agricultural issues they couldn't resolve. Everett was often able to give them sound advice to remedy their problems. That didn't mean Everett had all of the answers, and he wasn't ashamed to admit when he didn't. Everett was considered the best farmer in the area.

"You should become an agricultural consultant," Ida said. Spoken in the warm afterglow of early morning lovemaking.

"I'll consider it," Everett said.

"Don't consider it, honey. *Do it.*"

Everett nodded. Ida kissed him, snuggled against his chest, closed her eyes with a satisfied sigh, and left him to his thoughts.

Everett was seriously considering the possibility. Maybe even write a book on organic farming. If he did become a consultant, writer, or both, he would target family owned organic farms. He wasn't interested in sharing his experience and expertise with anyone else.

Everett knelt down on one knee and grabbed a fistful of soil. He had tilled his fields over the last couple of weeks in order to keep the soil vibrant as his father used to say even though he did not intend to plant anything. It was rich dark soil ready for planting. The friable texture, the sweet near chocolate smell made it pulsate to Everett. As if the energy and breath and even the soul of the earth was alive in his hand. Everett studied it with a forensic gaze, examining the soil for any discrepancies or abnormalities that might adversely affect fertility. Gracie and Rufus sniffed the dirt in his hand. They weren't impressed. They seemed more interested in his attention. Everett allowed the soil to spill from one hand to the other like water flowing from a cup returning the soil to the earth where it belonged.

He stood, dusted off his hands, wiped them cleaner on his jeans and stared out over the land. Everett had grown-up on the Boyd farm. He and Ida had raised their children here. Six generations of farmers had worked this land. Since Thaddeus Burch Boyd, each succeeding generation had not only prospered by the Boyd farm but also expanded its size and produce. The gift to grow things was a blessing he never took for granted. From dusk 'til dawn he was a farmer. This was his life and he was damn proud of it.

*   *   *

Thurgood and Mae had been living together for almost two years before they became engaged. Wedding plans weren't yet underway but their initial inkling was to keep it simple, intimate and inexpensive. If they could get their moms to go along with their thinking then all would be well. That was a tall glass of hope to swallow and they knew it.

Mae could not be persuaded to join him in surprising his grandparents for the Fourth of July. Mae couldn't disappoint her family in Idaho again after having chosen Thurgood's family over her own for Thanksgiving and Christmas. Thurgood and Mae drove up from Colorado together. He dropped Mae off at her parent's house, spent a day with them and then hit the road.

Thurgood hadn't seen his grandparents since he helped on the farm the summer following his college graduation a couple of years back although he talked to them all of the time. He had graduated with honors in both the studies of Agriculture and Wildlife Conservation. Thurgood had been considering taking over the family farm but had kept that thought close to his vest until he could work out the financial details. He planned on bringing up the possibility with his grandfather during his visit.

For the temporary hands hired to help tend and harvest the crops it was labor. For Thurgood it was pure joy. He loved being out there doing what he could to assure successful crops, the open space, the open air, the sun and sky, everything about being on a farm felt right to him. While he never expected his grandparents to retire from a life they loved, he did have a proposition for them. Sell the farm to Mae and him.

Mae had come from a farming family. Also a staunch conservationist and environmentalists, farm life suited her fine. Let them take over the entire operation with the provision his grandparents could stay on for as long as they liked. Thurgood even had plans to build a separate house for him and Mae so his grandparents wouldn't have to move an inch. He'd already done some preliminary work on financing and discovered they had enough in savings and investments to have little trouble securing a loan for purchase. All that was left was presenting the idea to his grandparents.

Black farmers were scarce enough as it was. Having an opportunity to keep one in the family would be great. This was not the sort of thing you discussed over the phone; this was a matter for "face-to-face" as his father would say. What better way than to pay a surprise Independence Day visit to discuss the subject.

*   *   *

It all happened as fast as if they were sliding down a greased pole. The farm was doing fine right up until the financial collapse. Dire economic conditions combined with a drastic increase in local corporate farms that had come to recognize the profitability in organic farming were devouring the market. Despite the fact, the productivity of small farms often exceeded larger ones. They had the market by the throat with monopolizing ownership of almost all outlets aside from farmers' markets and co-ops. Everett discovered how much of a chokehold corporations had on the market firsthand when selling his crops over the last few years. What the market bore was bargain basement prices that never covered his expenses, time or labor costs. Small farms like the Boyd farm were being forced deeper and deeper into debt in order to survive.

He and Ida had expected to be able to ride it out as they had done so many times in the past. This time was different. They were able to manage at first. Their cash reserves vanished more quickly than they estimated due to the chronic recession. Access to money and supplies shriveled up almost overnight along with their credit lines. They were finding it impossible to compete even with government assistance. They weren't alone. Small family owned farms that once thrived in the area were falling into the same pit of depression created by the recession and corporate takeovers.

Urban sprawl was also becoming a factor in the collapse of some small rural farms but it played less of a component than did its corporate farm competitor. The Boyd farm was too distant from what one might call modern world conveniences such as shopping malls and superstores. Everett was certain the developers were a front for a corporate farm entity; one that would continue to grow organic crops on his land and why not? All that was missing was money and they had plenty of that.

Even the off farm work Everett and Ida would occasionally take on to supplement their income had vaporized. Neither Everett nor Ida dared ask their children for help. In part, it was pride. In part, it was the knowledge their children were struggling in this tough international economy like the majority of people around the world. They had made it this far on their own. He had expected they could make it the rest of the way. By the time Everett realized they couldn't, their debt had piled up too high for redemption. The last thing they wanted was to become a burden to the people they loved most. Now it was too late. Even if their children could and did help, their financial hole was deeper than a dry oil well.

Their bank was losing patience they would ever make good. There were no more options available. Foreclosure was looming just over the horizon when along came developers with fat pockets who were ready to buy. They were far from the first. The Boyd land was prime real estate. Only now had the necessity to sell became a factor. Everett had to give his banker, Caroline Hobson, credit.

"How'd you get such a good deal, Caroline?" Everett asked. He and Ida not believing their eyes as they stared at the fat bottom line figure.

"By keeping a tight lid on your outstanding debt so developers couldn't lowball you," Caroline answered with a lively, confident smile. Reminding Everett of what a brilliant and spirited child she had always been.

Caroline was their friend. A friend as good as her dad, Virgil Hobson, was who had managed the locally owned bank before her. One of the few banks left in the county that had shunned being engulfed by big banks thanks to her leadership. Caroline was part of the extended small farming community. If there was anything more Caroline could have done to help Everett and Ida hold onto the Boyd farm she would have.

Everett was the only black farmer left in the area. Fewer and fewer family farms were surviving in the new economy. Fewer of those were black owned farms. While a number of farms would love to have him work for them, he couldn't see it. He'd been his own boss for far too long. Not to mention he was feeling his age. Retiring didn't bother him. It was losing the farm that cut him to the quick.

Storm and Lightning had been with them since they were foals. They were as much a part of their farm family as their shepherds and Bertilda. He and Ida saw to it that Storm and Lightning only had the best just like Gracie, Rufus, Bertilda, and their chickens. The same could be said about their farm overall. If you expected the best then only the best would do.

Since Everett knew he wouldn't be able to hold onto their quarter horses and dairy cow where they were going, he took the best offers in cases that applied. A reputable horse rancher had offered him a fair price for their ponies, as well he should Everett had felt. They were in excellent condition. He knew the people who owned the ranch and knew he was leaving Lightning and Storm in excellent hands. The same was true for Bertilda who was being sold to a local dairy known for their humane treatment of their cattle. He was going to miss them nonetheless. It is said of love that absence makes the heart grow fonder. That's not true of family. With family absence makes the heart yearn for more. Gracie and Rufus were going with them. Their handful of chickens were to meet a less hospitable fate. They were to be slaughtered and eaten at a farewell barbeque hosted by the local organic farming community in the backyard of their local church.

Where exactly they were going to settle was still a mystery. They had visited a variety of places over the years and one thing they knew. City life was not for them. Everett and Ida were country folk. It was the life they knew and loved. All of their children lived in cities. Living close to their children and grandchildren seemed unlikely for that reason. Moving to a place in the area was out of the question. The last thing he and Ida needed was a constant reminder of something that would crush their spirits.

Ida and Everett foresaw the day when they would be too old to run the Boyd farm. About five years before the economic crash, they had tried to interest anyone of their children into taking over with no success. None was enamored by agricultural life. It was too much work for too little payout is how they felt. Everett tried to engrain in them how owning land was important, and farming the land was the closest thing to God on this planet. They didn't buy it. By consensus, they encouraged their parents to sell the Boyd farm and retire. Their nephews and nieces echoed the same refrain.

Everett and Ida loved the Boyd farm. It was their home. Everett was hurt and disappointed, most especially in his children who didn't think of the Boyd farm as theirs. Legacy and tradition meant nothing to them. Everett blamed himself in the case of his own children. He felt he had failed to infuse in them the same sense of pride, honor and importance of being a farmer that his parents had instilled in him. After six generations of farming the line was about to be broken and he felt personally responsible.

With his brother and sister having passed on that left him and his bedridden older sister suffering from Alzheimer's and diabetes; he was the last of their generation. Only one child seemed to care whether the farm survived. Thurgood had worked the land with him and shared his love for it. Thurgood appreciated and respected the farming life and took pride in the profession. His grandson had his gift, the one with the ability to see the land as he saw it. Everett had no idea how he was going to tell Thurgood. It was going to break his grandson's heart.

"Don't worry about your farming equipment," Caroline told them. "I can get you a fair price."

Everett and Ida trusted Caroline to do just that. The farmhouse, garage, barn, henhouse, pump shed and all the rest were included in the purchase. Caroline had thought of everything.

No one else in the Boyd family was aware of their plight besides Ida.

Despite the vast majority of his own kin being on board for him to sell the Boyd farm, Everett couldn't imagine some part of them wouldn't regret the news. Being in the red was not a burden he wanted to leave his children. At least this deal would allow them to vacate the Boyd farm in the black. That's a lot more than most independent farmers could say when it came time to foreclose.

The deal had been concluded. Today was the day he would make it official. Today the developers and Caroline were coming to bring him the final papers for his signature. It was the reason Ida did something she had never done when healthy. His wife neglected their house in order to visit friends. Ida couldn't bear to watch their home being turned over to strangers. Everett couldn't blame her. It crushed him to know he would mark the end of their legacy. Thinking about it made him sick. It felt like nausea attacking itself. Everett stared out at the Boyd farm seeing his world through rain blurred windows.

*   *   *

Thurgood passed an expensive looking car heading in the opposite direction on the paved two-lane farm road that ran along the perimeter of his grandfather's farm. He recognized the woman behind the wheel as Caroline Hobson, his grandfather's banker. The three men in suits were strangers. They were all smiling.

From the farm road, Thurgood turned onto the Boyd farm. He could hear the crunch of gravel from the road. His grandfather was standing on the porch with his hands stuffed into his back pockets staring off into the distance. His granddad turned his attention his way moments after he made his turn. Everett Attucks Boyd was a mountain of a man even from a distance. Thurgood saw Storm and Lightning trotting around the corral enjoying the sun. Bertilda watched the horses play as she moseyed over to a better grazing spot. Rufus and Gracie raced across the greenway toward the farmhouse once they noticed his car.

Thurgood's excitement ballooned into giddiness. He was not only thrilled with anticipation at seeing his grandparents, but elated at the prospect of owning his own farm. As quiet as his grandfather had tried to keep it, the family was well aware of his financial situation. Thurgood's offer would remedy his woes and keep the Boyd farm in the family.

Everett watched Thurgood all the way. Thurgood pulled up in front of the farmhouse stopping at the foot of the steps. Thurgood power downed his passenger window and looked up at his grandfather standing at the top of the steps. A rush of hot air instantly eradicated the air conditioning. He beamed a smile at his grandfather expecting the same in return. The miserable look on his granddad's face shocked him to the core. If Thurgood wasn't mistaken, his grandfather was crying.

Echoes

Mason Hammer opened his weary brown eyes to the pale peach colored ceiling that needed a fresh coat of paint. It was daylight, morning to be exact. Mason knew these things from the first gray light of dawn filtering in through his closed blinds and drawn summer curtains. Final confirmation came by way of the gentle backlit 6:13 a.m. glow from his nightstand radio alarm clock peeking out over the latest mystery novel he was reading. Without preamble, Mason pulled back the spring blanket of his queen-size bed and rolled onto his buttocks. His broadcloth pajamas had seen better days. Neatly arranged on the hardwood floor was a recent birthday gift from Lily, his teenage daughter. Mason slipped his bare feet into the cozy fleece of suede, cinnamon moccasin slippers. For a moment he sat there, slump shouldered, staring at nothing, appearing to gather strength.

"It's time." The thought came and went like a chill through his leaden body; like a whisper in a storm. He stood after a deep breath, walked over and slipped on the new plaid, terry kimono robe hanging from a brass hook mounted center high on the back of his bedroom door. The robe was a gift from his adult son, Evan, as part of a coordinated birthday theme with his half-sister.

When Evan and Lily were little and desired sleepovers, Mason relinquished his bed to them while he slept in the smaller guest bedroom. As his children grew older but were still up for the occasional sleepover, Mason altered the arrangement so that one of them would sleep in his bed, which they prized, and the other slept in his guest bedroom. To make matters fair, Mason alternated between Lily and Evan dependent upon who slept last in his bed. During that time, Mason spent the night in a sleeping bag on the living room floor or stretched out on his couch. It had been years since his children had wanted to sleep over. He missed those days.

Mason moved unconsciously. He continued that way as he strolled from the master bedroom, down the hall, past the only full bathroom in the house and down the second floor stairs. At the landing for no particular reason, Mason felt compelled to stop. He stepped up to the polished wood banister that came to his waist and looked down at the living room of his small two-bedroom house. Mason didn't mind the size of his home. In fact, its size was a big part of what endeared him to the place. It provided him with enough space to live comfortably and was easy to maintain. Mason took in his living quarters for a moment. The living room encapsulated best his tastes and philosophy. He favored elegance over flash, refinement over trend, and while his budget only allowed him to indulge in modicum, he made the most of it. Mason endeavored as Channing wrote, "To live content with small means."

What he saw both pleased and disappointed him. What pleased him most were the knickknacks and family photographs, including those of his children and their moms. He felt the same about his choice pieces of art. What disappointed him, pained his soul like a nail in his heart, was the fact that his possessions had come to represent the sum of his accomplishments, the focal points of his ambitions. There had to be more to life than the quest for things. At the moment, Mason couldn't quite grasp what that *more* might be.

He continued his journey to the kitchen. At six foot and sporting a middle-aged spread befitting his age, his kitchen appeared to be built for one. Any attempt at two or more adults managing their way around the food prep areas made for "a cozy arrangement" as the second woman he loved and failed to find the courage to marry had kidded.

Mason dumped two healthy scoops of Maxwell House coffee into the removable filter basket and closed the lid. He filled the glass carafe to the "2" marking with tap water and poured it into the coffee maker's water reservoir. Mason could hear the water began its flash boil moments after he turned the coffee maker on.

At sixteen, Evan commented that Mason's old school coffee maker looked like the kind you'd find in a cheap motel room.

"How do you know about coffee makers in cheap motel rooms?" Mason asked.

"Um, uh, we stayed at a couple when we were on vacation," Evan stammered. Looking around as if searching for a place to hide.

Mason checked his story with Naomi, his mom, and it didn't pan out. Naomi said she would never allow her children to stay in a cheap motel. Knowing his mom as Mason did that sounded about right. Instead of confronting Evan about the lie, Mason decided to have a talk with his son about safe sex. Mason remained patient but persistent. His persistence paid off as Evan eventually confessed to being sexually active. Mason asked his son to promise him that he would always use protection. Evan made and kept that promise.

Years later Naomi thanked Mason for his intervention. His mom and stepdad weren't able to get through to Evan about the importance of safe sex. For some reason Evan listened to him. Mason speculated not living in the same house had somehow convinced his son that Mason was someone he could trust, even if he was an authority figure. The result made Mason proud he could contribute to his son's well-being.

As Mason waited for his morning elixir, he placed his hands flat on the kitchen counter and leaned forward like a man with too big a burden to bear. He remembered the moment as if it were yesterday. Mason was called into the manager's office, given the spiel about cutbacks, business shortfalls, and a poor economic climate and sent packing with a modest severance pay and benefits to the end of the month.

Since the axe fell, Mason had been diligently seeking work for over three desolate years. Never had he seen the American job market so arid of living wage opportunities. Optimism and hope had fallen off to despair and depression. He would do his internet routine of checking his emails, company websites, Craigslist, job websites, unemployment job websites and newspaper classifieds. He would stay at it for hours. Mason had easily applied for more than three thousand positions—many of which were far afield from his forte. Despite his best efforts, he was only able to ferret out a handful of interviews and no job offers.

His final unemployment benefits extension had run out two months ago. He had already been forced to leech half of his meager savings in order to supplement what his unemployment didn't cover such as dental and medical costs. Once the portion of his savings that Mason was able to salvage after his bank collapsed was exhausted then he would be forced to cash in his anemic IRA that had also suffered considerably due to the financial cave in. If nothing broke for him in the meantime, Mason didn't know what he would do. He was still years away from qualifying for social security if he would ever become eligible at the rate they kept shoving back the eligibility age. Mason Hammer had witnessed the American Dream transform into the American Nightmare with no end in sight.

About midway through his senior year of high school, Mason decided to join the Peace Corps upon graduation. The idea came to him after stopping by a Peace Corps office on a whim he'd happened to be passing. The recruiter was polite, articulate and passionate about his cause. He managed to convince Mason that he could make an important difference in the world if he joined. Mason left with a fire in his belly to do just that.

Mason approached his parents about joining the Peace Corps. His father howled with laughter at the suggestion. His mother snickered.

"What you wanna do that for, son?" his father asked, wiping tears from his eyes with the white handkerchief he kept stuffed in his back pocket. After his laughter died to a lingering smile he said, "You ain't never been away from home longer than a week."

"And you got homesick being gone that long," his mother added, the laughter in her eyes making her smile almost maniacal.

Once his parents composed themselves, they launched into their opposing argument by first commending their son for wanting to make a difference. They told him he had a good heart and his intentions were noble. It made them proud to see he had compassion for the plight of others. Then they skillfully shifted their case to explain how important it was for him to get his college education and begin building a career. Then, they said, once he became established he could take a leave of absence to do whatever he wanted. They stipulated the pros of their case to convince Mason that once financial stability took hold he could do far more for people in need than a broke kid out of high school. His parents managed to douse that flame in his gut in a matter of minutes. Mason bought their argument. Ultimately, the idea of joining the Peace Corps became as lost to him as his childhood comic books.

Mason had been all over the globe he was proud to say since then. He discovered he loved to travel and made it a point to visit different places every year. Besides taking his children with him on a number of trips, he managed to convince his parents to join him twice, once and for all eradicating that homesick kid label they had sewn on him. Even though he hadn't traveled except to visit family in the States for the last three years, he still kept his passport in good standing.

College life didn't agree with Mason at all. He dropped out the second semester of his freshman year. Mason enrolled in a technical school where he earned his associates degree in Civil Drafting and Design. His family was heavily disappointed by his decision but eventually lent their support for his drastic focus change from Business Management when they found they couldn't change his mind.

This was before the age of PCs, drafting and design programs, and the internet. When Mason began his career all drafting and design was done by hand. When drafting and design software became a reality, Mason kept abreast of his field's technologies and became an expert in multiple platforms. Even that knowledge along with his vast experience base wasn't enough to salvage his job, or, apparently, find him new opportunities. It was no secret. Companies were searching for younger, cheaper talent, in hopes of longevity and the expectation of lower insurance and benefits costs. Retraining was another issue with older employees that employers didn't want to tackle. That didn't apply in Mason's case since he could step into any drafting/design platform and was ready to hit the ground running, to use an industry cliché. Mason couldn't do anything about his age nor would he want to, but he was flexible when it came to his asking price, benefits and insurance. No one seemed to want to give him the opportunity to prove it.

Mason never married. The often-bitter relationship of his dysfunctional parents as he saw them created within him a marriage phobia. Mason believed his parents remained together for the sole sake of their children. Although his only proof was their constant bickering and sniping at one another that far too often led to screaming arguments; couple that with the disastrous unions of his older brother, Gavin, and his younger sister, Kaylee that ended in acrid divorces and his taste had soured for the institution for life.

Even love couldn't conquer his fear of matrimony. He loved few women from puberty up to his current mid-fifties. The two he loved most, Naomi and Makayla, he could never find the courage to marry. Haunting, nagging thoughts of marital doom and costly vinegary consequences that could follow in a divorce made Mason break out in an asthmatic cold sweat as if he were having a panic attack.

He poured himself a steaming cup of black coffee. Mason never took to lattes or fancy brews. To him a straight cup of Joe in the morning really hit the spot, although a few years back he did switch from the classic morning roast to the heartier South Pacific Blend.

After a moment of savoring the robust aroma by waving his Steelers' cup under his nose, Mason took his first sip. It made him smile. This morning was going to be different. This morning instead of having his usual bowl of cold cereal with vanilla soymilk, a glass of orange juice made from concentrate, and two slices of buttered wheat bread toast smothered in strawberry jam, Mason decided to make himself a Greek omelet. Being a good cook who was comfortable in the kitchen it wouldn't take him long to whip one up.

He set to work gathering the items he needed. Before long, a perfect Greek omelet was being served along with a glass of concentrated orange juice and two slices of buttered wheat bread toast smothered in strawberry jam. Rather than eat in the study to begin his daily job search, as had been his practice, Mason sat down at his dining room table and enjoyed his breakfast.

This neighborhood had been a new development, a shining testament to a thriving economy when he purchased his home. In an astoundingly short period after the financial collapse, the erosion of the economy seeped into his community. Homes once pristine showed signs of neglect, some up for sale, others abandoned by their owners with no new legal occupants in sight. Mason tried not to think about those who were already impoverished when the economic crisis hit. Their fate had gone from bad to horrid. He witnessed the devastation up close and personal whenever he did volunteer work for shelters. Seeing children in that circumstance was always the worst.

Mason confessed to himself that he didn't miss the work only the money, benefits and some of the people. Working in the engineering field had once been a passion and joy. With the completion of each new project, Mason felt a genuine sense of teamwork accomplishment. Somewhere along the line, it became simply a job, a grind, a means by which to pay the bills, a business of cranking out work in a fashion no different from an assembly line. His best friend, Cooper, had come to refer to the condition as being a "work zombie." Ironically, he found it necessary to throw himself back into the voodoo in order to survive.

Unlike most parents, Mason didn't regard the news of becoming a father as good. His children were the results of having unprotected sex. Mason had been monogamous and he trusted his lovers to be the same.

Both were on the pill. Both encouraged Mason, who was adamant against having children, that having unprotected sex with them would be okay, not that they needn't to do much convincing. Naomi and Makayla put the heat in hot as Cooper put it and Mason agreed.

When they told Mason they were pregnant, he was upset. He asked how such a thing could happen with them being on the pill. They tried to explain the pill was not one hundred percent and there were times their bodies needed a break. He accused them of entrapment. The more they denied it, the angrier Mason became. When they refused to abort the child, Mason became furious and presented it as evidence his entrapment allegations were true.

His refusal to marry his loves broke their hearts but did not damage their resolves to have his child. Mason stayed with them throughout their pregnancy, fooling himself into believing he was doing so to try and change their minds. His helping out in any way possible didn't register that he was sending the opposite signal. To his reasoning, he was doing so in order to help them execute what he considered an extremely foolish idea. Yet whenever the possibility of putting the child up for adoption was put on the table by both Naomi and Makayla, Mason would have none of it. No child of his was going to be placed in foster care as long as he drew breath. No one could convince Mason to embrace what these women had to offer, surrender to their love and his own. Mason cried upon seeing his son and daughter for the first time, in part from joy, in part from anger, in part from fear. He was angry he wasn't able to prevent one of the things in life he feared most, fatherhood.

While Evan and Lily weren't a result of marriage, it didn't mean Mason didn't love them any less. Evan was a senior at Northwestern. Lily was a musically gifted high school junior who was well liked for all of the right reasons. Mason still loved Makayla and Naomi as they did him and they got along well as friends. His exes, as Mason playfully referred to Naomi and Makayla, moved on once convinced Mason would never marry them. Neither mother denied Mason access to or time with his children. Mason surprised himself in how good a dad he turned out to be. It didn't surprise their mother's in the least. They even went as far as to give the children his last name with his blessings. Child and mom (Mason called it that instead of spousal) support was completely voluntary on his part and never demanded by their mothers. Once Naomi and Makayla married, Mason continued to pay child support at his own insistence.

"It's time," he thought. It was more like someone else's thoughts. The voice inside his head, the one he didn't recognize. The one who rendered unsolicited opinions, philosophies and advice had emerged. The sarcastic he, the one with curt responses to all of life's challenges was withering. A sober more pragmatic, endearing voice had emerged. He was evolving from seeing life as a bitter comedy to a somber tragedy. The voice, this other voice, this other he, did not surface like a bolt from the blue. Its appearance wasn't sudden like an indigestion apparition or age related enlightenment. Its emergence was more subtle, starting faint and distant like sonar bouncing back from a distant land or the outer edge of an echo from a deep ravine.

Early on Mason ignored the strange voice; his more dominant voice berating it like some obtrusive brat. The voice persisted on occasion, nudging aside the person he knew, the comfortable he. There were moments when the voice would resonate through his normal mind chatter with a rebel thought, a foreign idea. Still his dominant voice controlled, made the decisions whether to heed or desist this uninvited guest. Wisdom like politics and religion is a matter of prospective. One size does not fit all. The voice persisted. The echo became louder, having its say without permission to speak from his most intimate conscience.

Break time was over. Mason cleared the table, rinsing the dishes and flatware in the kitchen sink before putting them into the automatic dishwasher. He refreshed his coffee, which was almost gone with half of its original and headed for the study.

Mason sat down in his old-fashioned executive vinyl office chair at his sturdy renaissance carved oak desk. The black flat screen monitor reflected his silhouette. The tiny blinking green light at the lower right of the monitor informed him it was sleeping but very much alive. Mason had placed his PC in standby mode and forgotten to turn it and the monitor off at the end of his job search day as he typically did.

He awoke his PC, giving it a few seconds to settle into his desktop. An old black-and-white wedding photograph of Owen and Bessie May Hammer appeared as his desktop background. Mason had found it along with a few of its photo album buddies stored in one of the dust covered boxes stashed away in a storage unit that none of the children knew their parents had. It had been two years before his firing, five years in all since his parents died. Mason was puzzled why his parents remained married after their children had moved out. The volatility of their relationship remained intact. He, Gavin and Kaylee saw it in full force every time they visited or his parents visited them. When Mason talked to his siblings about their mom and dad, they were clearly able to accept them as they were, unlike Mason who sometimes wished for people less hot-tempered and more agreeable to be his biological legal guardians. Neither their parents nor their acrid divorces had turned Kaylee or Gavin against love or marriage. Both were looking forward to giving the experiences another spin on the dance floor. Why had he become so jaded? Why had he been the one who spit in the winds of unbridled romance and marital bliss?

The photos had revealed to Mason people that he didn't know existed. In many of the pictures, his parents appeared content, even happy with each other and their offspring. Seeing his parents happy made him ask what happened. What happened in their lives between that time of joy to the far too often moments of verbal abuse, yelling and screaming, drunkenness, and through Mason's eyes and heart, hating each other? What happened to the flame of love that glowed like hot embers in their eyes? Mason had the photos he'd found scanned to digital so that everyone in his family could have a complete set. Mason surprised himself when he decided to keep a copy on his PC.

His parent's wedding anniversary had been a few days ago. Mason found himself feeling sad they weren't around to congratulate and celebrate. They had been married sixty-three years. On the day his father died in the hospital from a sudden stroke with his mother right by his side, his mother suffered the same fate almost immediately after her husband passed. It wasn't until after their transition, when Mason saw his parents laid to rest, quiet, serene, still as glass, that he realized something. No matter how irritated his parents were with each other they rarely took it out on their children. Perhaps in their souls they were always at peace.

Mason logged onto the internet. "It's time." There was that voice again. The one inside his head; the one he couldn't identify. The one he couldn't shake.

Time for what?

You don't recognize me?

Isn't it obvious? You're inside my head. You know I don't recognize you.

Let me give you a hint, Evelyn Bradford on the front porch at her parent's house.

Eve was the first girl I kissed back in the fifth grade. What's your point?

Correction, Eve kissed you.

That's not the way I remember it.

That's the way it was.

Whatever man. The voice chuckled. Mason let it pass.

Here's another. Your parents treated you and your little league team to pizza and root beer after your team was humiliated in the championship game.

Yes they did. Still, what's your point?

What they did made you happy and proud. Which wasn't easy considering how down you and the other Eagles were.

Yeah, they did us a solid. What are you laughing at?

When's the last time you used phrases like 'did us a solid' or 'whatever man'?

I don't know; back when I was twenty, twenty-one maybe.

Try high school.

Okay high school so what.

Your parents did a number of things that made you proud.

Again, what's your point?

Final clue, if you don't get it after this you're denser than lead.

Gavin used to say that to Kaylee and me whenever we couldn't figure out something he thought was easy. He'd call us lead head. Kaylee didn't mind but it used to piss me off.

All in the family.

What's your final clue?

The summer before you entered middle school, you and Cooper stole some candy from a convenience store just to see what it'd be like. The two of you felt so guilty that you considered taking the candy back to the store but were afraid the store manager might have you arrested.

We gave the candy away instead. Cooper and I never told anybody about that. We swore ourselves—

To secrecy from here to eternity.

That's right. There was a silence in his head, a stillness that was rare and for the moment disturbing. His reasoning voice, the voice of his familiar was shell-shocked.

You're me.

Of course, I'm you. What other clunk head would be bouncing around inside your head.

But you're not me.

In a sense that's true. I'm you up until the time you graduated high school. I'm the kid you left behind.

Where've you been?

Waiting . . . hoping . . . praying you'd hear me again one day.

I didn't know I was neglecting you.

There wasn't any room for me in your life anymore.

But you're me.

I was.

My life's gotten along just fine without you.

Has it?

It has. Why should I listen to you now?

You need me now more than ever.

Why now? Why try to take me back to you?

I can't do that. Only you can make that call. I'm just trying to help.

Help how?

Give me a chance and you may be surprised at all of the good things the second half of your life has to offer.

I always was an optimistic kid.

And cynical about love and marriage; I never could break you out of that funk.

Can you blame me after the example mom and dad set?

They did their best, and that wasn't half-bad. You, Kaylee and Gavin turned out okay.

My feelings about marriage are never going to change, not at this stage.

We'll see. Never hasn't come and gone yet.

So what should I do?

Listen.

To what, what am I supposed to be listening for?

You know.

If I knew then I wouldn't be asking.

It's time.

The musky sweet smell of fresh soft rain came through the cracked opened window of his study. Closing and locking it another thing Mason had forgotten to do before dragging himself off to bed last night. He saw his reflection in the window glass. Mason looked tired and beaten. Not in the way of someone who had given up and was prepared to move on, but more in the way of a person who had come to the realization that the system had failed him and would continue to do so as long as he traveled this path.

That uncomfortable silence again settled onto the landscape of his brain. This time, Mason breathed it in like pure oxygen, easing his mind into a cool comfortable place. For a moment, Mason stared at his home page "Favorites" tab. This was where he stored the links he needed to begin his daily job search. He clicked inside the "Search" box. The cursor blinked awaiting his input. He typed in P-E-A-C-E space C-O-R-P-S and hit return.

The Zany World of Al, Nitro, Dynamite & Their Dog Blaze

While laughing hysterically at The Omen IV, noticing how much that demonic child resembled my daughter Dynamite when she was that age, I heard the familiar sound of a deflagration explosion. I wiped my teary eyes on the ragged sleeve of my Clockwork Orange T-shirt, stopped the video, rose from my comfortable couch and strolled to the open front door to see what had happened.

My Dodge Ram pickup was spitting flames from everywhere. An exquisite fire if there ever was one. No doubt ignited by diazodinitrophenol near the fuel line. Dynamite and her friends stood around mesmerized by its apocalyptic grandeur, wicked smiles on their faces. One of the kids gave Dynamite a high-five. A couple of others saluted her with thumbs-up.

Needless to say, I was upset. Just this time last week, I ordered Dynamite to refrain from torching any more vehicles for the next six months. The Ram made it three in the last five. My car insurance payments were already higher than those flames licking the niter sky. Not to mention her mother, Nitro, and I, had warned her not to play with explosives without parental guidance.

"Dynamite," I yelled across the street, not asking how the Dodge wound up in the middle of Cinerary Park, "stay back from those flames!"

She took a couple of tiny steps backwards. The other kids nonchalantly did the same.

"Where's the dog?" I asked. She said Blaze was in the house.

Blaze loves playing with fire. That was how he got his name. Vehicle fires are his favorite. His one failing was he had a tendency to stick his head into the flames. Which explains how he lost his eyelashes, whiskers and sense of smell.

I checked Dynamite's room where Blaze liked to hangout. Our bulldog was lying on Dynamite's bed watching MTV and gnawing one of Dynamite's mutilated Barbie Dolls. He stopped chewing for a moment to acknowledge me with a bark and a pant. I smiled, waved and left.

On the way back from checking on Blaze, I ran into Nitro in the dining room just after she had ascended from the basement. She was wearing her sexy blue welder's outfit. There were TNT smudges on her face. Her red hair was tied in a ponytail with a black powder fuse.

To see her that way made me crazy with desire. I put my arms around her and gave her a volatile French kiss. She smelled of ammonium nitrate. An aphrodisiac if there ever was one. I pulled her close. "Not now," Nitro said, shoving me away. "I don't have time. I'm in the middle of assembling a land mine for the company picnic. Which by the way, *Alfred Bernard Nobel*," she went on to say, "are you going to attend this year?"

I frowned. I could see it coming. Nitro was about to go on a roll.

"Did you call the fire department?" she asked.

"Not yet," I told her.

"Don't," she said. "Let the fire burn itself out. That way Dynamite won't get the satisfaction of booby trapping a fire truck like she's done the last two times this has happened. Lucky for us no one's gotten hurt. Kids today, where do they get these crazy notions? I simply don't remember us being so irresponsible. Do you?"

"No, dear."

"I certainly hope you intend on giving your daughter a good tongue lashing about this?"

"Yes, dear."

"Better than the last two, I'd expect?"

"Yes, dear."

"Good," Nitro said, turned and walked away. I watched her until she disappeared behind the basement door, wanting her more than ever. I shook off the craving to pursue my little toasted marshmallow and went back to check on Dynamite.

The kids had inched closer to the incinerating vehicle. I yelled at Dynamite that she was to come in the house as soon as it burned out. She flicked ashes from her cigarette, returned it to the corner of her mouth, thick with purple lipstick, and took careful aim with her armed crossbow. Firm but gently she squeezed one off. Just the way I taught her. The arrow lodged in the wooden doorframe to the right of my shoulder. Her juvenile friends laughed, coughed and choked on black smoke and booze. She leered. I yelled, "Nice shot! For that, you're not only getting your explosive's allowance taken away, but your firearm privileges are suspended for a month!"

She frowned and threatened to launch another salvo. I crossed my arms atop my potbelly and waited. She lowered her crossbow. As an afterthought I added, "You can forget about getting those mercury fulminate fuse caps you wanted for your birthday too!"

"Aw, dad," she griped, "that's not fair! Because of one stupid fire?"

I raised my hand. "Another word from you young lady and they'll be no more plastic explosives lessons!" She started to speak then apparently thought better of it. "And what did I tell you about smoking near a gasoline fire? Now, for the last time, step back away from those flames!"

Dynamite took an exaggerated backward step along with her friends who were temporarily subdued. For a moment, I enjoyed the fiery spectacle. I had to admit, that kid was an artist. I breathed deep the toxic aromas of burning rubber, plastic and leather filling the living room before returning to my couch to watch the zany antics of that wacky Omen IV kid.

War

The night was still, the sky, clear and starlit. Heavy air lingered, maintaining a chill; chest high foxholes covered a callous desolate landscape giving it the surreal appearance of being populated by giant prairie dogs. Helmeted heads popped in and out of those human excavations returning gunfire at an inexorable enemy. A deafening deluge of artillery assault ripped through all who participated. Exploding shells hurled men skyward, making them grotesque participants in a macabre trampoline act.

Commanding voices rang out "Cease fire! Cease fire!" Sounds of destruction shredded the air with a crescendo then dissipated as fiery ripples from the center of a gasoline pond. The firing halted in descending waves. Silence blanketed the land like a morbid spirit. Odors of gunpowder, scorched earth, decaying corpses, human waste, and bedraggled bodies molested men's nostrils. The dreadful cries of those in physical and mental anguish reverberated off the eardrums of soldiers only to echo in their minds. Wars amongst nations were made from these ingredients.

It took time after the ceasefire was ordered before the survivors began to relax. From some foxholes came the hushed tones of conversation. An occasional outburst of laughter could be heard above it all creating a sadistic blend of suffering and glee. Some occupied foxholes they had not dug themselves. James was one of them.

The 22nd Brigade converged with the 58th, 74th, 96th, 97th, 168th, and 176th battalions at the scheduled rendezvous point, the last within six hours of the first. The 74th, 96th and 97th were Negro battalions. The remaining infantries were white. These men were unified by American military strategists to form the 35th Infantry Division.

The German army had defeated American forces at Bizerte and Tunis and was continuing south along the Tunisia border. It was the mission of the 35th Infantry Division to provide a human barrier along the Kasserine Pass and prevent further penetration by the enemy into allied territory. Behind a winding wall of barbed wire were dug two wide lines of trenches. The first was booby-trapped with explosives. The second contained infantry volunteers. Seventy-five meters behind the second trench were foxholes deep and wide enough to accommodate two men. Once tanks and artillery were in position all was in readiness.

There had been a briefing of command personnel prior to an address to the troops by the Division Commander five days earlier. It was not simply a military pep talk. An urgent tone crested upon every syllable: "Every American soldier will work in complete cooperation with his fellow soldiers during this crucial period," General Perkins demanded. When his speech ended, each congregated with their own: white soldiers with white soldiers and Negro soldiers with Negro soldiers. Separately they waited.

The battle lasted nearly three days. James scurried to a friend's foxhole to borrow a pack of cigarettes during a brief lull in enemy assault. The assault resumed on his way back to his own foxhole. James vaulted into the foxhole nearest him for cover. When his feet touched down, he fell forward only to have something cushion his fall. That something was a dead soldier.

James remained frozen in a kneeling position near the corpse. He had encountered dead American soldiers before, whites as well as Negroes. In the past, the grim reaper had always been a quick merciless beast striking during battle while every speck of James' being was focused on personal survival. That had allowed James time to adjust, to keep the ravenous dogs of panic at bay. This time they had him by the throat.

Distant rumblings from an exploded shell slapped James back to his senses. He leaned over the body and cautiously checked its pulse. The soldier's gelid eyes stared stolidly at him. James had time to reflect on those vacant eyes now that the battle was over, wondering how many more times he would be forced to witness eyes such as those again.

James looked around the battlefield. His gaze steadied upon the body of the dead soldier. The rigid corpse lay peaceful in the place James had laid it. The soldier's back was to him so he could not see his eyes. He thanked

God for that before continuing his visual patrol.

Fatigue took a foothold once he was satisfied the battleground was secure. James sat on the hard packed bottom of the foxhole and eased his weary back against its jagged wall. His cumbersome metal helmet pushed backward from his forehead exposed grimy beads of perspiration to cool night air. James unzipped his army jacket and instinctively reached into an inside pocket for a cigarette. He discovered a smashed pack of Camels still unopened. He tore open the pack with a grunt, extracted a bent cigarette, placed it between his chapped lips and lit it. James took a deep draw and held it for a few seconds. When he exhaled plumes of white smoke jettisoned from his wide nostrils like discharge out of ebony steam whistles.

His muddy brown eyes surveyed the desecrated ground within whose bowels he rested. The wooden match James used to ignite the crooked cigarette flickered harmlessly on the dirt floor projecting a dim light on the opposite wall. His gaze halted. His forehead wrinkled as he focused his night vision on a curious sight. It appeared to be a plant peeking through the crusty earth. As he crawled toward it for closer examination, he heard the rapid pounding of heavy footsteps coming toward him. James grabbed his rifle. The footsteps grew louder. He crouched against the side of the foxhole he had been previously resting in. The footsteps were upon him when suddenly they stopped. A man leaped into the foxhole. James took aim. He recognized the uniform. The soldier stood stock-still. The two men stared at one another for what seemed the longest few seconds in history.

James slowly lowered his rifle. The soldier audibly exhaled but did not move. A few minutes passed before the soldier was able to gain his composure, apprehension fixed in his eyes. James apologized for his actions. The soldier shook his head in suspicious acceptance. The two men shied away from each other's stare, hearing only the rhythmic thump of their own hearts.

It disquieted James, this eldritch peace. All forms of calm he had known flashed through his memory. None paralleled this eerie tacit noise. The chill of such foreboding formed abstruse words inside his head, words as foreign to him as the Germans. *This is all that exists within the musty confines of a grave,* James thought, *expect no more.*

"Why in hell are you running 'round in the dark jumping in foxholes?" James shouted at the soldier. "Don't you know that's a good way to die?"

"This is my buddy's foxhole." The soldier paused, looking around as if his friend were in hiding. "Where is he?" he asked.

James thought before uttering, "The soldier that was in this foxhole is dead."

The intruder's head fell back against the unforgiving dirt wall unveiling the helmet's shadow from across his eyes. Tears streaked his sooty face. James wanted to say something. He knew exactly how it felt to lose a friend in combat. No words could compress the new void created by his irretrievable loss. As was always the case, it would take time. James squatted and stared up at the stars, looking away from the soldier. Again, a morbid silence hovered over the land, this time not to be broken until the light of day.

James awoke squinting. Daylight had crept upon him while he slept. It took a minute for his eyes to adjust. His neck, legs, back, and shoulders were stiff from sleeping in what amounted to a squatting position. James saw the soldier across from him once clear vision was established. His dirty face irrigated with clean wavering lines.

Moving so not to arouse the soldier, James stood and stretched before having a look around. Aside from the removal of a number of the dead soldiers, everything appeared much the same as last night. It was standard procedure after a battle to place corpses in body bags, tag them, and pile them in an assigned area until they could be shipped home. A duty normally regulated to Negro soldiers. James was not assigned mortician duty this time. The soldier's friend was one of the tagged remains.

James remained standing if for no other reason than being tired of squatting. He noticed the sky. Gloomy dark clouds abounded. The air was cool and dormant, an invisible weight of murdered souls. "Nothing changes in this godforsaken land," James murmured to himself wiping, his runny nose with the filthy sleeve of his field jacket. *When's this damn war going to end?* His thoughts continued where the murmuring left off, *seems like I've been fighting forever. It must take years to perfect killing human beings, not the act, but the acceptance. Still don't have the hang of that part yet but I will; got to if I want to survive.*

Hunger interrupted his thoughts. James eased over to his backpack and quietly rustled through it for a can of emergency rations. The iron or Armour rations as they were commonly called consisted of three small cake mixtures of cooked wheat and beef powder, and three chocolate bars. They were all he had left. Negro battalions were not issued any of the far more nutritious reserve rations. They were told that was due to short supply. As were the more sustenance trench rations, of which they received one. Buffalo soldiers soon learned that shortage did not extend to white infantry who had been issued a helping of each. A few of the men in his unit believed they should have been grateful for what they received. James disagreed. He believed they had fought and died like everyone else wearing an American uniform and they were as deserving of those meals as white infantrymen. The majority of his unit had sided with him.

James washed down his iron ration with cool water from his canteen. His palate had become accustomed to the cake mixture long ago. While it was a poor substitute for home cooking, his stomach welcomed it just the same.

While James leaned against the foxhole wall, eating, he used the time to analyze his new mate. The soldier appeared somewhat pale. James could not be certain of that particular observation. To him most white people looked pale. Yet he had heard them speak of this paleness amongst themselves. It apparently occurred when they were ill or in shock. They called it losing their color. What color? While that drain of color they spoke of was evident in corpses, James was hard pressed to spot it in the living.

One thing he knew for certain, this was the most unusual thing that had happened to him since he joined the army. The very idea of him and a white soldier occupying the same foxhole was unimaginable. *Life sure is strange sometimes,* he thought. *You never know what's going to happen next.*

The soldier groaned awake. James refrained from his train of thought. He shed his relaxed expression and replaced it with a defiant countenance. This was his war face. The face he used when doing battle with his enemies at home or abroad. Although he was not fond of his war face, it had become an integral part of his true self. A character he had created for the sole purpose of generating reservations in the minds of his foes. The soldier was white. At minimal that made him suspect.

The soldier gained consciousness at the time James finished eating. His eyes, like James', took time to focus. He slouched forward, resembling the posture of a drunkard staring somberly at something only he could see.

James had returned to his visual patrol, anticipating any sort of trouble. Lack of movement by the soldier made James glance in his direction. The soldier sat as lifeless as an abandoned marionette. It was obvious to James he was suffering from shock. Realizing it would not be necessary, James relinquished his war face. What the soldier needed was an instant friend. He would have to do.

"Are you hungry, Private?" James asked.

The soldier's lips formed the word no. James responded as if he had heard him.

"Can't blame you for not wanting to eat this garbage," James said. "I'll bet the army puts slop the pigs won't eat in these cans. At least nobody can accuse them of wasting money on real food."

The soldier did not respond.

"What's your name, Private?" James asked.

The private stared vacantly at James before he faintly answered, "Johnson . . . Billy."

"Carver, James. Most people call me Jim when they ain't calling me other things."

Billy faintly nodded as he sluggishly moved to stand.

"How long you been in this man's army?" James asked.

"Ten months," Billy said with a heavy sigh.

"Drafted?" James asked.

"Enlisted," Billy looked out over the battlefield. James noted that Billy did so unconsciously, a product of his combat experience and infantry training, no doubt.

"Me too, still can't figure out why I did such a damn fool thing," James said with a shake of his head.

"Where is he?" Billy asked, turning to face James. The question startled James. He had hoped to ease into a discussion of the dead soldier by getting the private to talk about home or a girlfriend or family or his peace plans. The private stared him down, his eyes vacuums sucking away James' resolve.

"Hate to tell you this, son," James said, "but he's probably in one of those body bags."

"I'm not your son," Billy said, his voice as sharp as a bayonet.

James smarted from Billy's remark. American forces had forced the German military to fall back. Billy stared at what was until last night the front line. Suddenly Billy screamed, "Those goddamn chicken shit sons-of-bitches! They had no right! Damn those Nazi bastards! Damn them all to Kraut hell!" Billy pummeled the wall of the foxhole with a ferocious flurry of punches. The punches quickly diminished to faint jabs that faded into spent tapping. His head fell forward against the dirt wall as he sobbed, "Those bastards, those goddamn Nazi bastards!"

James watched. He reflected upon friends he had lost to violent death because of this unholy war. James knew all too well the rage Billy felt, blaming their unjustifiable deaths on the murdering soulless Germans. "Why the hell did he have to die?" Billy whimpered as if there were some reasonable explanation. James did not attempt to answer such a question. This was war. There was nothing more to know.

The arrival of afternoon brought with it a welcomed leap in temperature. The dark clouds dispersed, permitting thick shafts of sunlight to pour over the land. James removed his field jacket while Billy wore his tightly zipped as if the chill remained. Both men sat on the foxhole floor with one leg bent and the other fully extended. A German sniper had killed a lieutenant and wounded three enlisted men. Everyone had been ordered to stay put until the sniper could be flushed and terminated.

The conversation became fluent between Billy and James. Billy rambled on about his deceased friend, how they became acquainted, the gradual building of their friendship and the adventures they had together. There was a break in the conversation when James stood and took a short step toward Billy. James stopped directly over the private, bent over and looked down near his head.

"I don't believe it," James said.

"What?" Billy asked.

"I don't believe anything can grow in this hell hole," James said.

Billy turned his head to see. He squinted before his eyes grew wide with surprise. "Is it real?"

"As far as I know," James said.

"What is it?" Billy asked.

"I'd say it was a plant," James said with a hint of sarcasm.

"No shit!" Billy said.

James glared at Billy. "Well, *Private*, if you know that much then maybe you can tell me something I don't know?"

Billy stared quizzically at James. He seemed transfixed on the area around his shoulders. James watched Billy work his way to attention then snap his right hand to a traditional salute. "Private Johnson requests permission to speak, sir?"

James was stumped. Other white subordinates had addressed him as sir before but none with sincerity. James scrutinized the private for inklings of disrespect intended by the gesture. Billy waited at attention, his eyes staring straight ahead.

"At ease, Private," James said.

Billy placed his feet shoulder length apart and clasped his hands behind his back.

"You'd better sit your butt down before that sniper gets a bead on you,"

James said. "I'm a sergeant not an officer. I work for a living just like you."

"Yes sir," Billy said and then did as he was ordered.

"No sirs about it. Call me Jim. At least while we're stuck in this hell hole together."

Billy nodded. "What about that plant, Jim? Any idea what it is?"

"Too soon to tell," James said. "Maybe in a couple days I'll be able to figure it out."

"Hope we're not stuck here for that long," Billy said.

"Could be worse," James said. "We could be fertilizer for that bud."

"Guess you're right," Billy said.

"Where're you from Billy?"

"Williamsport, Pennsylvania," Billy said.

"City boy, huh."

"Williamsport? Shoot no," Billy said. "It's a little town on the west branch of the Susquehanna River about eighty miles north of Harrisburg. Not much to it but I like it."

"Why'd you join the army?" James asked.

"I wanted to do my duty."

"Yeah, me too," James said.

"Some duty," Billy said. "They give us guns and tell us to kill the enemy for freedom and glory and God. They leave out the part about the enemy having identical motivations to kill us."

"It's a hell of a situation," James said.

"That it is."

Each man lit a cigarette, neither offered the other their burning match.

"You're from the South?" Billy asked.

"It shows?"

"Accent," Billy said, "you've definitely got one. Where in the South are you from?"

"Little place outside of Macon, Georgia called Peach County."

"I've never heard of it."

"Not surprising," James said.

"Are you a farmer?" Billy asked.

"Fruit grower," James said.

"Don't talk like I'd imagine a southern Negro would," Billy said. "You sound educated."

"That's because I am," James said.

"Why would an educated Negro want to join the army? Don't get me wrong Sergeant, but I heard . . . maybe I'd better not say?"

"Go on," James said. "I've probably heard it before anyway."

"This is what I've heard mind you," Billy said with reservation. "Coloreds are lazy shiftless inferiors who can only be trusted with the simplest tasks."

"That's a lie!" James yelled.

"Mind you, Sergeant," Billy said, putting his hands up as if he were about to surrender. "I'm only repeating what I've heard."

"What do you think about *what you've heard?*" James said with a hissing whisper, intentionally correcting the mistake of having raised his voice.

"I can't say really," Billy said. "I don't know much about you people."

"You people," James mumbled.

"Sir?" Billy said.

"Nothing," James said, "go on."

"The only coloreds I've ever encountered were porters or bootblacks or maids, Negroes of that caliber," Billy said as he lowered his hands. "Even then I didn't interact with them much—except for small exchanges of pleasantries now and then."

"I'm here to tell you none of those statements are true," James stated with conviction.

"I'm only passing along what I've heard," Billy said.

James quietly considered what Billy had said. The private had echoed the lies often told about his people without apparently giving it any thought. Common sense should have told him you don't kidnap lazy people from another land and expect them to be productive. No manner of punishment will change the true nature of a person if that is who they are. To transport human beings like abused chattel across an entire ocean to clear fields, plant and harvest crops, construct towns and cities and in short help build a nation, is not the character of a lazy people. It most certainly is not the earmark of people who had already built nations in their homeland without any intervention from Europeans or Americans.

"What school did you attend?" Billy asked.

"Tuskegee Institute," James said clearing his mind.

"I've never heard of it," Billy said.

"Have you ever heard of Booker T. Washington?"

"I can't say I have," Billy said.

"He started the school," James said.

"Went to St. Joe's myself," Billy said. "It's a very good school. Have you ever heard of it?

"I have," James said.

"What was your focus?" Billy asked.

"Agriculture," James said, "yours?"

"Education, a hell of a lot of good our degrees are doing us in this pit," Billy finished with a smirk.

By now, James had settled into his previous spot in the foxhole. Billy had apparently snapped out of his distraught frame of mind for the moment and was behaving—at least James assumed as much—like his old self. Billy's domination of the conversation allowed James to feel less need to do more than interject a "yeah" or "no" with an occasional sentence thrown in to disguise his fading concentration. James' mind kept drifting until it finally floated off completely.

"Are you listening to me, Jim?"

"Huh?" James heard himself say, not fully comprehending why.

"You haven't heard a word I've said for the past five minutes," Billy said. "Where's your head at?"

"I was wondering how my wife and boys are doing," James said.

"You've got kids?"

"Ezekiel and Joseph," James said, "ages two and four."

"That's great!"

"My family's staying with my folks." James paused for a moment and sighed. His words came with more deliberateness. "The most beautiful peach trees on God's green earth are in my parents' orchard. Belle of Georgia peaches are what we mostly grow. In the summer, those trees are dripping with plump ripe peaches ready for the picking. Let me tell you there ain't nothin' better than the sweet smell of Georgia peaches riding a summer breeze. About this time of year, when we were little, my brother and I would hang out in the orchard once our chores were done, and pluck a few peaches for ourselves. We'd be perched beneath one of those trees eating and talking for hours. Hated to see evening roll around because it meant we'd have to leave our little piece of heaven and go home to eat supper. Not that we minded going home, especially to eat supper, we just didn't want to leave. Not to mention we'd stuffed ourselves so full of peaches we could barely eat another bite."

James stopped talking. He looked sharply at Billy as if the private had appeared out of nowhere. Billy was smiling.

"Don't stop," Billy urged, "I can almost taste those sweet Georgia peaches.”

James couldn't continue. He felt embarrassed having exposed so much of himself to a white man. Without explanation, he declined to speak any further about his reflections.

“When I was a boy,” Billy began, “my parents and I would sit in the living room after dinner. Mom would be chewing dad's ear off about the latest gossip while she crocheted or knitted. Dad sat in his chair reading the newspaper, sipping coffee and making silly faces at me when Mom wasn't looking. I'd almost bust a gut trying to keep from laughing out loud.

“When Dad finished his newspaper, we'd usually walk around the neighborhood and talk about everything under the sun. I'd walk at his side immersed in every word my father said. He'd always stress something by saying: ‘Son may the good Lord strike me down right where I stand if what I'm saying isn't the God's honest truth.’”

Billy allowed a warm smile to replace his exuberant one before continuing. “I've got a peach of my own waiting for me back in Williamsport. Her name's Judy. Judy Arlington and she's a looker. We're engaged. We would've been married by now if I hadn't let my father talk me into joining the army. Worst advice he ever gave me. She said she'd wait. I hope she does. I hope I live through this damn war to make it home to her.”

Billy's smile evaporated. James had listened to what Billy had to say. He was astonished to hear a white man speak so openly about himself to a Negro. James had never been in any sense close to any white person. Considering how he had been mistreated by most whites he encountered, he assumed a lack of intimacy was something undesirable by both races.

The sound of heavy footsteps broke James from his train of thought. Billy and James grabbed their rifles, squatted, and anxiously waited. James poked his head out of the foxhole. He saw several American soldiers darting about the battlefield. They would stop at the mouth of a foxhole, deliver a verbal message, and then scurry on to the next. James was quick to alert Billy that the footsteps belonged to their comrades. As they sat awaiting the arrival of one of the armed soldiers, they looked at each other and grinned. Then for no reason at all they laughed. They continued to do so even after the soldier—notably startled by the sight of the two men together—arrived with the message: “Get ready to move out!”

“What about the sniper?” James asked.

“Never you mind, boy,” the soldier said to James. “He's been taken care of. You just do what you're told.”

Billy lunged for the soldier who was smiling in his direction. The soldier scurried backwards causing Billy to miss. James grabbed Billy, preventing him from going after the messenger.

"This man's a sergeant in the United States army, you pinhead prick!" Billy yelled at the grinning private. "Treat him accordingly!"

"My, my, aren't we a lovely couple," the grinning soldier said to Billy and James. "I'd love to stay and chat, ladies, but I've got business to attend to; maybe later."

The soldier darted toward foxholes north of where they were. James settled Billy down by telling him it was okay. Quietly the two men gathered their field gear. Reality had reared its ugly head. The possible fate that awaited them on the battlefield now loomed large. Fear returned but so did courage. An hour later obtrusive booming voices commanded the 35th Infantry Division to "Move out!"

James and Billy wished each other well. Billy thrust out his hand. James responded with both pleasure and surprise as he shook the hand offered him. While hoisting his field gear out of the foxhole, James noticed the plant.

"If that sprout can make it through this hell, then maybe we've got a chance," James said with genuine hope. It was a pleasant thought that managed to survive only a few seconds.

Crossing the Burnside Bridge

My wife left me two years ago. She took the kids. Don't know where. I haven't been contacted by an attorney about divorce. Her parents claim not to know of her whereabouts. No note, no warning, just came home after a twelve-hour day and they were gone. Everything except her and the children's belongings remained. A well planned quick escape. Then it was painful, crushing in fact. Now it haunts me like a nightmare I can't forget.

I had to sell our house. Couldn't stand living with seven years of family memories. Got a little two-bedroom apartment on the northeast side of town. It's convenient for shopping and using the city's bus transit system to go back and forth to work. Neither my faltered marriage nor my apartment is what I wanted to tell you.

I do consultant engineering for a civil firm located in downtown Portland. It had been another bleak eleven-hour workday. We'd lost three key people in our support area that week and help had been scarce. My diet consisted of pastries, fast foods, coffee, and an occasional beer. Life was not good.

Across from Pioneer Square, where I catch the bus, the 19 GLISAN came to a smooth stop behind the 12 SANDY BLVD. I saw the 19 early and boarded first. Behind me, a young woman boarded. I recall looking at her twice. She resembled the teenager currently on trial for the attempted murder of her mother.

After I showed the bus driver my monthly pass, I sat in a padded seat facing the back door. I removed *Bloodline* from my briefcase and began reading the story, "The Sky Is Gray."

The 19 proceeded down S.W. 6th at a stop and go pace. When the bus made its right turn onto Burnside, it was three-quarters filled with passengers. A young man reading *Robocop* disembarked at the stop just before the Burnside Bridge. I moved quickly to the vacated two-seater and scooted over as far as possible toward the window.

Dense silver clouds danced with black clouds above the Willamette River. That's when I first noticed the threat of storm, when we were crossing the Burnside Bridge. The Willamette was majestic. Mild ripples rolled across its olive-green surface. Traffic on the bridge was congested. Homeless people lingered in front of restaurants, bars, and storefronts. I saw no one along the riverbanks. I found that odd. People were usually walking, or jogging, or sitting along the bank enjoying the view. I remember thinking, "Calm before the storm."

The bus stopped at the corner of Burnside and Martin Luther King Jr. Blvd. A young Filipino, with a lit cigarette dangling from the corner of his mouth, stepped from the curb and crossed the street out of view. My book no longer interested me. I returned it to my briefcase, and then looked around the bus. People were mesmerized by their smartphones, reading, staring out of windows, straight ahead, down at the floor. A few brave souls glanced around at other passengers. No one was talking. Everyone had found a way to withdraw from interaction. I looked at the sky. Dark clouds ahead, above, behind. It was going to rain.

We went through an underpass just before the Sandy Blvd., East Burnside fork. I missed the bridge. I wanted to stay there and watch the river. Ask hushed questions about it, my wife, my children, and the world in general.

A teenager dressed in black got on the bus. His footsteps were loud and heavy. He wore steel-toed construction boots (for style, not labor, I quickly surmised). Other seats were available by this time, beside more attractive traveling mates, but he sat next to me. He grunted, and then sighed. He attempted to edge over. At six-foot-three, there is little legroom for me in bus two-seaters. I didn't budge. Even if I wanted to, my knees were already wedged against the back of the seat in front of me. He nudged me. I didn't move. I stared out of the window. His hair was in a long, straight ponytail, hanging out of the open back end of a black baseball cap. He had a silver ring through the center of his nose and an earring in his right ear that was an upside down cross. These things I could see from my peripheral vision. Just as I could see, he was irritated at me for not moving.

I took in the young man next to me by pretending to glance around the bus at nothing in particular. His staring at me became a glare. He looked away. When two-seaters became vacant, he didn't move. He was taking this personally. I stared out the window and watched the world become a misty, dismal gray. My stubborn traveling mate moved to an abandoned two-seater cater-corner from me with a loud grunt, stretching one of his skinny legs out across the seat, leaning his head back against the window and closed his eyes. My mind stayed put. He would remain there until I got up to exit the bus. At four steps toward the front door, I heard him plop down in the seat I vacated. I looked back to see him grinning at me as if he'd just won a gold medal.

The Burnside Bridge in consort with the Willamette River had captured my imagination. It was there I had wanted to wait for the seconds to drift away. Suspend myself long enough to comprehend something which all of nature understands except humankind. No matter mass, bulk, or believed power, we are less than the river from which we crawled. I could sense a duet between the Willamette and bridge, *Go back to your beginning. Join with water again and become whole.*

"Do you love me?"

It was not the duet of river and bridge asking that question. The voice was not my own. Nor did it belong to my wife, son or daughter. For the remainder of that bus ride, on the walk home, and well into the evening, that final voice haunted me. I didn't hear those words again that night. The mystic voice invaded not my dreams. Dawn came with pensive eyes witnessing its splendor, and still the voice was silent.

My morning bus ride was common. A sparse ridership of drowsy, quiet passengers awaited their turn to disembark. I had the Ernest J. Gaines novel *Bloodline* with me but was in no mood to read. I wanted only to stare out of the window. From where the bus waited at a red light on the east side of the Burnside Bridge, I had a good view of the Willamette River.

A thin mist played upon the water. Under the Steel Bridge, a tiny tugboat waited near the east bank. Seagulls hovered above the water, one with the wind. A small motorboat sputtered upstream, past the sleepy tugboat and a mammoth barge coasting downstream. As we crossed the Burnside Bridge, I could see the west bank. A man and woman jogged in tandem. A brightly dressed bicyclist zipped past them in the opposite direction. Things seemed normal again . . . until the voice returned. A whisper inside my head: "Do you love me?" The voice was male, that much I could tell, but it was not mine. I could not answer. I needed to know who was asking the question.

My eyes found banal surroundings on the other side of the Burnside Bridge: buildings of varied colors, sizes and shapes . . . homeless transients . . . fellow proletarians . . . taxis . . . buses . . . cars. No familiar faces, nothing that rang of home.

All day I heard the voice. It grew louder and more distinct with each asking. Sometimes the question was asked quickly; other times slow and deliberate; once every hour at first; then every half hour. I refused to respond without knowing who the voice belonged to and why it needed to know.

At lunch, we watched the noon news in the lunchroom and debated life, as we perceived it. "Do . . . you . . . love . . . me?"

Was it God? Did the creator need to hear me avow my love? Had my doubt of divine eminence reached his kingdom?

"Do you . . . love me?"

I assumed stress had gotten the better of me. Still, *who* was an aching question I had no remedy? I left work at five o'clock that day, an early departure for me. The constant echo of that question would not allow me more than random moments of concentration. At the bus stop, my head was filled only with my voice, cascading thoughts of work, future and past.

By the time, the 19 reached Burnside and Sixth there was standing room only. At the foot of the bridge, we stopped to allow passengers to board. As we crossed the Burnside Bridge, it came: "Do you love me?" I looked toward the Willamette. Its waters were choppy, angry at the wind. I wanted to scream "No! I don't love you! Leave me alone!"

That would not have been true. The voice was intimate. It was as much a part of me as my blood. Yes, I did love the voice as a blade of grass loves the sun. As seedlings love warm, soft rain. It filled me with nourishing contentment I had not known since childhood. Made me, as we proceeded across the Burnside Bridge, smile at an elderly woman across from me who smiled back and averted her eyes. I stared past her out of the window and watched the angry waters until they passed from view.

The remainder of that evening was uneventful. Cooked, ate, watched TV, read *Bloodline*, showered, set the alarm, and went to sleep. I had to be at work by six the next day. In the dark, before sleep arrested me, I waited for the voice. It never came.

"Do you love me?"

The 19 waited two blocks away from the Burnside Bridge. The voice was loud and pleading, almost hysterical. How could I have not recognized it? Five years ago on that day, my father died of colon cancer. Along with my mother and brothers, I watched as my father dwindled into that man; his vitality robbed; all his vigor strangled; an emaciated man with a quivering voice and recessed eyes encircled with deep, dark rings. Hanging on because he knew it was expected of a person who had been a fighter all of his life.

Mom stopped going to see him every day. My father ordered her to visit him no more than twice a week. My brothers and I were given duplicate dictums. I was "hard-headed," the one always in some kind of fix. My paternal grandmother called it being, "Just like your father."

He fought me at first. Then he took to brooding. Finally, adversely, he tolerated my intrusions on one condition: I was to tell no one else in the family. Everyday I visited. I told no one. Neither did my dad although somehow I think mom knew.

"Do you love me?"

How could he ever have doubted it? During that time, my brother, Samuel, reminded me of an incident that occurred when I was ten. I received what my family called "a whooping" from my father for beating up a boy who tried to steal my lunch. I was paddled in front of the entire class, suspended, and sent home with a note. At home—after reading the note— my father beat me with an ironing cord. He never allowed me to explain my side of the story. My body had fiery welts that throbbed with heartbeats of their own. I told my father I hated him and would hate him for the rest of my life. I also said, through my bawling, that when I became a man I would beat him like he'd beat me. We stared at each other; me blubbering and shivering; my father stern and mute.

"Do you love me?"

He asked me on his last day if I loved him. I lifted him from the bed. There was a russet vinyl chair under the west window in his room. I sat down in that chair and placed him on my lap. He was wearing a diaper. His head lay to rest on my chest, a child making himself comfortable in the bosom of his son. I wrapped one arm around his spindly legs. With the other, I held his fragile frame close to me. His breathing was faint, nearly undetectable. I rocked him back and forth. He was my father and my child in the pallid evening light. I didn't resent him for his duplicitous existence.

It was always what was inside that mattered most to me about my dad. That was where his strength, wisdom, and courage resided.

I hummed to my father as I rocked him. I wish I could remember the song. Back there in the brine it is floating, waiting for me to discover it.

There were moments he hummed along with me. The nurse saw us in the corner of the room and quietly closed the door. He fell asleep in my arms. His breathing seemed that of a normal man, although I knew it could not be. I placed him in his bed gently as I could, kissed him on each eye, and left fully expecting to see him alive the next day.

The bus stopped at the head of the Burnside Bridge. I jumped out of my seat and disembarked through the front door. Darkness had begun its daylight retreat. The river's surface was clearly visible. It was sedate, seductive, pleasantly anticipating another round of being. My father's face appeared upon the dull surface of the water. Not the frail person I held in my arms in the VA hospital room, but the man who had carried me upon his shoulders.

"Do you love me?" The voice was steady and clear.

"Yes, Father. I love you."

His face brightened and descended into the depths of the Willamette River. Something touched my shoulder. I turned to find a man dressed in rags.

"You got any spare change, brother?" he asked, "Anything at all will do."

I gave him all of the change I had.

Wake Up

Thump!
Thump!
Thump!
It was quiet—*no*—it was silent in his family home except for the persistent *thump* of water drops from a leaky kitchen faucet striking the empty abyss of a stainless steel sink echoing throughout his house. Chris Lucas counted the beats between each drop. One . . . two . . . three . . . four, *thump*. One . . . two . . . three . . . four, *thump*. The rhythm was consistent. You could set a metronome to it. Counting drops for Chris was no different from counting sheep. Neither method helped him fall asleep.

Chris opened his eyes in darkness. He struggled to his right side and glanced at the clock. Harsh red numbers glared at him from the nightstand a hot breath away from his king size bed. Three-thirty-three, a glaring red dot to the left of the digits told him it was a.m. Chris could have awakened from a two-year coma and known it was a.m.

It was pitch black outside. Chris was in the dead of a Pacific Northwest winter, when days were so short it could fool a sundial. His alarm would sound at five-thirty a.m. Even then, a desperate hint of gray would wage a valiant struggle against the lumbering bear of night. He would thwart the gentle coaxing of sleep when the buzzer sounded, move his six-five, stocky, middle-aged body out of bed to begin his morning ritual.

Chris would first make his bed. Shower, shave, dress, brush what remained of his thinning silver-black hair, cook and eat a country breakfast, floss, brush his teeth, rinse with water, rinse with Listerine, pocket his wallet, cellphone and a clean, white handkerchief, grab his keys and briefcase, then be off to the office. There were times he set his routine to music in his head. He sang aloud each thought as it pushed him forward. Sometimes it came out as a spirited melody. Other times it droned like a dirge.

"What became of the man I loved?" Kelli asked after telling Chris she didn't love him anymore. Chris stood there dumbfounded by both the question and answer he didn't have. His wife's piercing brown eyes were accusatory, condemning the man before her to the man he once was. That was what he remembered. Not her marmalade skin, wide smile, powerful legs or full hips. Chris assumed Kelli was referring to the rebel he used to be who railed against the establishment and all it stood for. His answer then was that he grew up. Her response to that was that he stopped growing at all and had accepted a pot to piss in.

"Better a pot to piss in then ah . . . ," Chris couldn't think of a reply. Kelli stared at him in disbelief while his mind fumbled for a response.

"Chris," Kelli said, exasperated, "if you don't have a comeback for that, then you're further gone than I thought." Kelli walked away. "We'll be at my parents," she told Chris as she climbed into their magenta mini-van. Chris didn't try to stop her. All he could do was stare at Kelli through the driver's window as if some demon seed bent on destroying his life had possessed her.

"Don't call me. I'll call you," Chris heard Kelli say through the glass. "If you can pencil me in," her last statement a direct shot into the heart of one of their problems.

Money is a combative issue for most marriages. For Kelli, time was her sore spot. Chris didn't spend enough time with her or the children. Chris tried to convince Kelli of the necessity of his work schedule. Kelli wanted Chris to cut back on his ten to twelve hour workdays that far too often included weekends. Chris argued that in order for them to live comfortably and give their children the best opportunities in life, a full commitment to his career was necessary. Kelli wanted him to have a full commitment to his family and for Chris to place his job lower on his priority list. They could change their lifestyle as far as Kelli was concerned. Move into a less expensive home, cut back on extravagances as Kelli viewed them, necessities as Chris had come to accept. Chris saw his efforts as part of the bigger success picture. Kelli saw it as their albatross.

That had sparked the fires of discontent. Infidelity fanned the flames.

Mary Landis had been working closely with Chris on the Imperial account for six weeks. The longest they had worked together on previous advertising accounts was a week. Mary was an alluring thirty-something blue-eyed brunette who made no bones about her attraction to Chris. They had worked together on a number of accounts without incident. Chris set the boundaries, and the professional Mary, respected them.

The combination of incessant arguments with Kelli, no sex, and Mary's occasional flirtations took their toll. Chris gave into temptation. Kelli was waiting in his car in the hotel parking lot for Chris on his eighth night of infidelity in the last two months. Chris was stunned to find her there. He expected a scene. Kelli was controlled and icy.

"How long?"

"How long what?"

"Don't play dumb with me, Chris. I have no problem ripping out your throat and leaving you for dead in this parking lot."

Chris sat in silence. Shamefaced, head bowed, shoulders slumped, a life-size caricature of disgrace.

"Let's try this again. How long have you been screwing Mary?"

"This was the first time."

"Liar."

"It will be—it's my last—time."

Kelli nodded. "Promise?"

"Yes, honey, I swear. *I promise.*"

"Don't bother."

"Kelli, I'm really—"

"Shut up."

"I just want to say—"

"Shut, up."

"If you'll give me a chance to—"

"Shut-the-hell-up, Chris. Do you not understand what *shut-up* means? There is nothing you can say, at this moment, that will cool the loathing I have boiling in my gut for you right now. Or do I have to run you over with this car to get my message across?"

Chris shook his head. Afraid to speak. Afraid to move. For a pregnant moment, Kelli and Chris sat in silence staring straight ahead.

"Drive," Kelli commanded.

Chris did as ordered. Every time Chris attempted to rupture the silence, Kelli told him to shut-up in a voice that seethed with hatred. On the drive, neither could look at the other. At home, Kelli went to their bedroom. Chris made do in the den. Neither one slept.

The following morning, their final argument as a married couple under their own roof ensued. Kelli eased the mini-van out of their paved driveway. Chris could not shake the sense he was having a nightmare from which he would soon awaken. His sad eyed and long faced children stared at him through the back windows of the van. Erin, their six-year-old daughter, began crying. Simon appeared ready to burst into tears, but at the age of ten, his son no longer cried in front of his father. Both waved goodbye as if their wrists were broken.

It was after the mini-van turned out of their cul-de-sac that reality charged the gates. Chris ran after them. Two blocks away he stopped in the middle of the street. His children's faces disappeared along a serpentine residential street. His life went with them. Damp with perspiration, and panting like an overheated dog, Chris yelled at the mini-van that had left him in the whiff of its exhaust, "Better a pot to piss in than not having a piss pot at all!" That was the first time Chris thought of killing himself.

The alarm went off. Sleep had temporarily wrestled him away from his anxiety-induced insomnia. Chris rolled over from his left side to his right. He was tentative at first. Half-expecting, half-hoping Kelli would be asleep beside him. For twelve years, two months and a day, Kelli shut off the alarm when it sounded.

"Get up, Chris" Kelli would say in a voice weighted with sleep and unintentionally laced with sensuality. Then she would nudge him until he would tell her to stop. "Get up, Chris, then I'll stop," Kelli would say.

Chris would resist awakening for as long as he could. Kelli would win in the end. Chris would plod out of bed like an elephant disturbed from slumber and ready himself for the day.

Chris turned off the alarm and threw back the comforter. He was at a critical juncture in his morning routine. Sleep would reclaim him with a sledgehammer blow if he didn't stand in the next five minutes. An hour could pass in what would seem a few heartbeats should that happen. Chris lacked motivation. Security for his family and a stable future for his children had always been paramount behind his drive for success. What he wanted with their absence in his life was sleep or death.

Chris stared at himself in the bathroom mirror. He wore a Brooks

Brothers' suit, shirt and tie. The uniform of the establishment he had despised throughout his youth. The idealist, the instigator, the activist in him from time to time questioned his choices. What became of the fire of change that would purge the land of greed and arrogant power hungry demigods and place it on course for a free and just society? They were ambitions worth fighting for, even dying for.

Their first-born literally changed his perspective overnight. Their second-born cemented the deal. Moral and ethical compromises became necessary for economic survival. Creature comforts, safety, food, a healthy, nurturing environment took precedence over power to the people. Chris gradually became the sellout he had once despised. Kelli had left that man before she left the house. Adultery was the final push out the door.

Chris placed a hand on the single action revolver on the bathroom counter, as he had every morning since his divorce became final, for his Russian roulette ritual. Agony over what he deemed as the loss of his children and wife resonated in his eyes, rippled on his pallid face. He sang the last lyric to his morning ritual repeatedly to himself in the mirror. Each chorus grew louder. Tears welled in his eyes and rolled down his cheeks. He spun the revolver cylinder loaded with a single .45 cartridge. It mechanically clicked like a gambling wheel. Chris gripped the pistol like a man desperately hanging on to a lifeline. He pressed the barrel under his chin as he shouted the lyric at himself. His shout became a maniacal scream he could not control. His eyes were red from tears. The scream mixed with what had become deep sobbing. The decisive moment arrived. He could feel it tremor throughout his entire being. His throat became sore but he could not stop. Then with the brutal swiftness of a bullet . . . silence.

I Hate When She Calls

I'd given up trying to debug a new software routine I was writing for our engineering department when the telephone chirped. I expected my boss to be on the other end telling me what time to pick him up for our golf game tomorrow. To my chagrin, it was Inez. I hadn't heard from my ex-wife in months. I don't realize how alone I am until she calls. I miss her. I know that every time I hear her voice, but I don't want to miss her. What I want is to tell her to leave me alone. *Don't call, don't write, don't drop by or do anything remotely close to reminding me of your existence*, is what I thought.

"*How are you?*" is what I said, my voice dripping with sincerity as I put my laptop on STANDBY by closing its LCD.

"Wonderful!" Inez is one of those people who always sound perky.

"How've you been?" she asked.

"Good." I meant it. I was actually doing well until I heard her voice and all that changed. She resurrected the void in my life. I hate her for that, her and Alexander Graham Bell.

"What've you been up to?" I asked, not really wanting to know since whatever it was no longer included me.

"Oh the usual: work, staying fit, having fun when I can—which reminds me."

I can't count how often that phrase was followed by something I didn't want to hear. That time was no exception.

"Douglas and I went to Crater Lake last weekend. Have you been there?"

"Not yet." She knows I haven't. Just as she knows, I don't want to hear about what good times she's having with her second husband, *Douglas*. Why can't she call him Doug like everyone else, for God's sake?

"You have to go," she went on to say. "The view is breathtaking and the park is absolute tranquility. If you take that special someone she'll love you for it."

The closest thing to special in my life these days is my laptop, and I don't believe it could appreciate the scenic beauty of Crater Lake National Park.

"Sounds great," I responded.

"Douglas and I just love it. We're thinking about going again next month."

This was the part I dreaded the most, the invitation. As if I was supposed to forget about our six years of marriage when I see her, not reflect on our lovemaking, and Chinese dinners, and lovemaking, and cozy evenings alone, and lovemaking. If we could've gotten along outside of the bedroom as well as we did in chambers, maybe we'd still be together? Maybe I should get out more.

"Care to join us?"

When Inez and I were first married, our differences were intriguing delights, the computer geek and cosmic queen. Those endearing qualities gradually became sore spots that blistered then festered like boils. To Inez, I manifested into a predictable tiresome hardwired chip head. She became my whiny spaced out interstellar wing nut. In a last ditch effort to reboot our marriage, I attempted to surprise Inez with an impulsive move. I suggested we have dinner at the restaurant where I had proposed. Inez went along with it although I could tell she wasn't enthusiastic about the idea.

The restaurant was closed. According to the notice posted on the front door, it had failed to meet minimum health code requirements. In an effort to salvage the evening, I drove over to the Pelican Club where we had danced the night away in celebration of our impending nuptial. It had been replaced by a video arcade. Inez tried making light of the whole debacle. According to her, we could have eaten at the restaurant and gotten food poisoning; or the Pelican Club could have become a biker bar.

I was so embarrassed by my failure at reigniting our flame; I couldn't look Inez in the eyes for the next two days. Her take on the whole mess was that it was divine providence, along with some other mumbo jumbo about karma and astrology and incompatible enneagrams. Signed divorce papers were merely a corporeal formality to what was predestined in the stars according to Inez.

"I don't think so, Inez," I said in response to her question. "Work's got me pretty busy right now, maybe some other time." *Like when I find a girlfriend,* I thought.

"Come on, Harold, live a little. I'll bet your lady friend would like it."

"I'll think about it."

She did it to me again. There's no *lady friend* to ask and Inez knew it. Cicely was my last steady and we lasted all of three months. She said I was dull and needed to loosen up. No chance honey, I told her, this is as loose as I get. That's when she told me "*hasta la vista*" and "good luck."

"Ask her," Inez said. "Better yet let me. Give me her name and number and I'll give her a call. I'll get her to toss you out of that computer rut you dig for yourself."

She must have been insane. Have my ex-wife call my girlfriend—if I had one—to ask us to join her and *Douglas* on a weekend trip. What gonads that woman had.

"I'm not giving you her number, Inez," I told her.

"I promise I'll tell her all about your delightful qualities, and how she'd better snatch you up while she can." I wondered if any woman was gullible enough to believe character testimony from another woman about her ex-husband.

"The answer's still no." I tried sounding playful, hoping she wouldn't detect I was hiding something.

"Come on, Harold," Inez said.

"Nope," I said.

"Afraid she might like me and discover the mean things you've been saying about your ex aren't true?" Inez said with that teasing playful tone I adored.

"I've never said a mean thing about you that *wasn't* true, Inez."

Inez chuckled. "That's what you say now. Bet you sing a different tune when you're around your friends."

When I talk about Inez to my friends, it's mostly complimentary. It's been four years since our divorce. Each year has made it more difficult to remember any of her shortcomings; strange how talking to Inez seemed only to remind me of mine.

"Let me think about it," I said.

"You have two weeks. I'm putting you on notice."

"I'll talk it over with my *lady friend* and get back to you."

"It'll be fun! You still haven't told me her name."

I thought about who I might be able to bribe for a mercy date. Three single women from work came to mind. They owed me big for straightening out their home computer problems. "All in good time," I said.

"Keeping her a secret, huh?"

"You could say that."

Inez laughed. Her laughter sent warm shock waves through me like a straight shot of hundred-proof bourbon. I wanted to tell Inez I loved her. To make her understand she would forever be the only woman for me. To remind her of the good times we shared and how often those recollections were the chicken wire that held my life together. I could no more do that than alter the banal Harold she had come to loathe as a husband. So I did what I always do at emotional moments of truth, I maintained a cowardly silence.

"Why'd you call, Inez?" I asked, hoping to realize my ultimate fantasy that she wanted me back.

"I worry about you, Harold. There's more to this world than technology. If I know you, life is a bus you keep waving by." Her voice had altered to that all familiar pitiable tone I hated. It was as though she were speaking to a precocious child and not a man.

"I appreciate your concern but I'm doing just fine," I said. *Not*, I thought.

"Are you eating okay?" Inez asked.

"Yes."

"Getting any exercise?" *Very little* would have been an honest answer. The golf game my boss forced on me because his regular partner was out-of-town was the first exercise I'd have in months. "Oh you know. When I can," is what I said.

"I do know, Harold. That's what worries me."

"I have one mother. I don't need two."

"Sorry," Inez said.

"You mean you're sorry you ever got involved with a cyberpunk?"

"That's not what I'm trying to say. If you'd listen you'd understand."

"What exactly is it I'm supposed to be listening for, Inez, a tree falling in the forest?"

"It sure as hell beats surfing the Internet."

"How would you know?"

"I've been there, Harold, and it's boring."

"Not to me," I said.

"You're afraid of people. That's your problem, Harold."

"Just because I prefer cyberspace to those pretentious gatherings with your esoteric friends doesn't make me a hermit."

"Really," I said.

"Yes really!"

"When's the last time you've been out, Harold?"

"I'm out all the time."

"With friends," Inez said. "You do have living breathing flesh-and-blood friends, don't you?"

"Of course," I said.

Inez was right. I hadn't been out socially in months. Most of what I call friendships I've developed on social media. There was a wrenching pause. For a long moment, I felt as though we were husband and wife again. It's a cruel trick time plays on people heaping them with memories that can make you ache.

"Is that why you called, to harass me?" I asked. Something about the question made for instant regret. I heard Inez move the phone away from her mouth. It was probably my imagination but I could have sworn I heard her heart beating. Shortly thereafter, she said, "I'm pregnant."

I was dumbfounded. Inez announced the taboo topic. We had always wanted children. We tried everything. Our doctors assured us it wasn't biological. It just never happened. Not having children was another cosmic sign for Inez that ours was a union destined for failure.

"Congratulations." The word choked me with shame. I wanted to be happy for Inez, but all that crossed my mind was the selfish thought it was one more joyful thing I couldn't give her that *Douglas* could.

"It came as a shock," Inez said. "I mean, we weren't planning it or anything."

"How far along are you?" I managed to ask, my head still reeling.

"Three weeks," Inez said. "I've got a-ways to go."

"You deserve a child, Inez. I mean that. You're going to be a great mom."

"I didn't tell you to hurt you, Harold. I only wanted you to hear it first from me, so you wouldn't be surprised if you saw me one day looking like a beached whale."

"I've got to go—but I'm really happy for you," I said.

"Really, Harold?" Inez said.

"Absolutely!" I said.

"Get back to me on that Crater Lake trip when you have a chance. You might as well say yes because you know I'll keep hounding you until you do."

"I'll do that," I said.

"Promise," Inez said.

"Yeah, I promise." There was a pregnant pause. I felt empty and deserted. Even after our divorce, I maintained a lingering connection to Inez, one that refused to be severed.

"I'd better get going or I'll be late for my Yoga class," Inez said. She sounded sad. "It's been nice talking to you, Harold."

I had to swallow hard to clear the lump in my throat before I could speak. "It's been nice talking to you too . . . Inez."

I reached over and opened my laptop. For the first time, it felt dead to my touch. My laptop beeped to life. The screen flickered then radiated with my motherboard screensaver and desktop icons. I was a double click away from connecting to cyberspace. My world, a place I felt safe and confident. I logged onto the Internet. I needed a cyber buddy. I could sense Inez had something sentimental she wanted to say. The moment passed in awkward silence.

"Take care of yourself, Harold."

"I will," I said. "Take care of that baby."

"We'll talk soon?" There was a tremor in her voice. I knew she was crying.

"Sure," I said, failing to sound sincere.

Before I said the word, we both knew it was truly, "Goodbye."

What's In A Name?

I don't remember his name but I remember his story. That comes as no surprise. I'm great with faces but horrible with names. I've been that way all of my life. My wife says it's because I'm visually oriented. Being a family therapist—and a good one I'm told—that wouldn't bode well for me in my chosen profession. Since I have a great memory when it comes to conversations and experiences, that theory doesn't hold water. The problem is obvious. I'm simply bad with names.

We met in the hospital emergency room. Daiyu had broken her arm rollerblading. Daiyu hurt herself a lot when rollerblading. Most had been minor injuries up until then. I was waiting for my ten-year-old daughter to be fitted with her cast. She was a brave little soldier who insisted on going in alone. She's twenty-two now and as courageous as ever. I was the one consumed with concern regarding her well-being. That's the way it is in our family. My wife worries more about our two sons. I worry more about our two daughters.

I was searching for a seat with weighted thoughts of my oldest daughter on my mind. Foremost amongst them was how much discomfort was she experiencing and how to convince Daiyu to give up rollerblading. Ultimately she did, for skateboarding, surfing, tennis, snowboarding, soccer, volleyball, basketball and track. From none of which did she suffer any serious injuries. I'm eternally grateful for those grand blessings.

There was a man seated in the waiting area when we arrived. He was a large man, stout and sturdy, brown skin, ruggedly handsome, black bearded with a neat tiny fro. That was how he appeared in the photo he later showed me, the one of him and his son on his son's ninth birthday. The one in which his face and eyes beamed with pride and affection at being hugged by a child who was clearly his own.

At the time of our meeting his head was clipped near bald and his face vacant its beard. The handsome face appeared distraught with no light of joy or pride or affection to be found. He was wearing indigo blue bib overalls, a denim long sleeve work shirt, dark brown steel-toed work boots and a sweat stained baseball cap that had seen better days. Even from a distance I could tell the dark stains on his overalls and shirt were from blood. Besides a couple of minor cuts that had been attended to on his forehead, physically he looked fine. His state of mind was clearly in question.

He appeared to be in shock or well on his way. His body was heaped into the lime colored vinyl chair in the farthest corner of the near vacant waiting area. He hugged himself as if squeezing the life out of some distressed infant as he rocked forward and back staring down at the floor. I felt sorry for him. For me pity comes easy. Compassion is a big part of why I became a therapist, the stalwart emotion of my profession, my Achilles heel in life according to my father.

I approached the stranger with caution. It seemed to do otherwise would have literally frightened him to death. In my softest voice, I asked if he were okay. He stopped rocking and looked up at me. His puffy brown eyes were red and bleary with tears and darkened with misery. While his flow of tears had subsided, they had left salt trails through the prickly growth along his rugged jaw line that had met at his dimpled chin. His startled face suggested my voice had snapped him from whatever torment gripped him and bungeed him back to the present. If I were to venture a guess at his age at that moment, I would have said late forties. He was in fact thirty-eight. Whether he had aged so from what had recently transpired or suffered a hard luck life, I can't say. I do know his agony erupted from his soul.

He absent-mindedly nodded in response to my question as if in a daze. For some inexplicable reason, bearing witness to that tormented man made me accept the fact Daiyu would be all right. I'm certain it was that same acknowledgement, that equivalent awareness, which compelled me to ease down in the seat next to him. His look told me he didn't mind. In fact, a small light in his expression suggested he welcomed my company.

"I'm here about my daughter," I volunteered. "She broke her arm rollerblading . . . and you?"

He said after a moment, "My son," as if he needed time to recollect.

"Children can be a handful," I said. "My daughter's accident prone when it comes to rollerblading; we can't seem to keep her off 'em. She loves those wicked things."

He glanced at me with a slight smile as if he understood before pinning his eyes again to the floor.

"My daughter's ten," I said. "How old is your son?"

"Sixteen," he said with a burden. "He just turned sixteen last month."

"They grow up so fast, don't they?"

Once it became apparent, he wasn't going to respond I said, "I'll bet he can't wait to get his driver's license. My sons sure couldn't." I focused on gender in order to strike up a sense of male bonding. I, in retrospect, suppose, it worked.

"I wouldn't let him," he said as if the words cut his throat as he spoke.

He removed his tree trunk arms from about himself, and dropped his huge hands on his strong thighs like dead weights. He looked up, staring straight ahead at nothing in particular. His mammoth shoulders drooped. His barrel chest collapsed. I let the words drift in the breezes of our silence.

A doctor Davis was paged to go to the intensive care unit. The page was repeated, concluding the second time with the command "*stat.*" An adult male in his mid-thirties limped in. Whatever was wrong with his leg looked as though it hurt like hell. He hobbled his way up to the reception area before anyone else seemed to notice. A nurse summoned an orderly to bring him a wheelchair. The man was responding to the nurse's question about how it happened when the orderly returned posthaste. The orderly helped the injured man into the wheelchair. The agonized man thanked the orderly, who posted himself at the helm of the wheelchair. The nurse continued with her questions before either of us spoke again.

"My name's Huiliang," I said, offering him my hand. He shook it before telling me his name, which sadly I can't recall. I remember the effortless vice-like grip of his callused hand as it enveloped mine. The direct eye contact by someone accustomed to making eye contact.

"He couldn't have been happy about not being allowed to get his driver's license," I said in jest.

"He wasn't."

I waited a few beats to see if he had more to say. When he didn't, I asked, "How many children do you have?"

"One," he said. "He's my only child."

I felt like a fool at that moment. It didn't take a genius to figure out his only child was in the hospital for something very serious. He was doing what most of us do in those vulnerable times, waiting out the worst of it while praying for the best.

"I was driving him to school this morning," he said, almost as if he were talking to himself. "He missed his bus. He'd been making a habit of it since I told him I wasn't going to help him get his driver's license until he changed his attitude and brought up his grades. He's going through that teenage rebellion stage. I told him getting bad grades was unacceptable, especially since I knew he could do better. It's only been the last couple of semesters he went from an A, B student to failing almost every class."

"What changed?"

"He met this girl, bad news. She's not only a tramp she's a bad influence. She talks him into skipping class, blowing off homework, acting up in school, making him think he's a bad ass by doing all of that dumb shit."

"Let me guess," I said. "He thinks he's in love."

"Yeah," he said with a sad smile and shake of his head. "His first time and it's with a girl who has nothing on her mind but sex, drugs and getting into trouble."

"It's a phase," I said. "All teenagers go through it." I thought of my teenage boys whose rebellions had so far been small potatoes by comparison. Drugs and trouble had not been an issue. Sex was another matter, although I suppose you could have classified sex under the getting into trouble category. "I'm sure he'll grow out of it," I said.

"It hasn't been easy," he said. "It's just the two of us. I work a lot. I have to for us to live. I'm in construction. When he was little, work in the area was plentiful. Now I have to go where the work is. Sometimes that means leaving him home alone for days at a time, not good for a young person to be responsible for themselves. If I were able to spend more quality time with him, maybe this wouldn't have happened. He wouldn't be acting up."

Shale gray light drifted into the reception and waiting areas like weary travelers in need of comfort, creating a penumbra existence for those whole dwelled within. As a therapist, I knew we had reached a critical crossroads in how far this man in pain was willing to open up. The question was out there. The bigger question was should it be asked or should I wait to see if he would be forthcoming. He wasn't.

"If you don't mind my asking what happened?"

He let out an audible burst of air through his nose followed by a sigh. "I was driving him to school this morning because he was running late. We were arguing. We do that a lot these days."

"What were you arguing about?" I asked.

"The usual, school, the crowd he's been hanging with, his no good girlfriend and him getting a driver's license. Our arguments have gotten worse since he's turned sixteen, louder, more aggressive. My son's a big kid, almost my height, only leaner. I told him under no circumstance was he going to get his driver's license while I had a say in it until he got his act together. I looked at him when I said it to drive home my point, taking my eyes off the road."

He stopped. The grief was returning like a tidal wave. He started rocking again. His arms crushed the unfortunate infant. His breathing became shallow. A nurse entering the reception area looked our way exhibiting concern. I put one arm around his massive shoulders, quite a contrast to my less formidable physique. The other hand I rested on his hefty bicep using both points of human contact as stress gauges as I leaned in close.

"It's going to be okay," I said. "Everything's going to be alright."

"I didn't see the red light until it was too late," he said in a whimper. "I slammed on the brakes. If I'd kept going the car would've hit us but not where it did."

"What hit you?" I said.

"A Suburban plowed into the passenger side of my pick-up," he said. "He must have been timing the light to have been going that fast. If I'd kept going instead of hitting the brake—*if I'd just kept going*—it might have hit us in the truck bed instead. I walked away with barely a scratch. They carried my unconscious son away on a stretcher. There was blood everywhere. It should have been me, my *blood*, my *body* on that stretcher not *his*. I'm the one who should have gotten broadsided."

Guilt is the typical reaction when a loved one gets hurt and you're somehow involved. Placing blame wasn't going to make matters better. He was in no condition to digest that logic so I didn't try to feed it to him.

"Where's your son now?" I asked.

"In surgery," he managed to blurt out, warding off a sob. "That's my only child up there fighting for his life, and there's not a damn thing I can do to help him!"

"I'm sure the surgeons are doing everything they can." It was a cliché I happened to believe. He looked at me as if he believed it too.

"I love him so much," he said, dropping his chin to his chest.

I glanced away for a moment toward the reception area to gather my thoughts. Emotion begets emotion. That's not good for aiding someone in pain. The nurse who had been watching us mouthed the question, "Do you need help?" I gave her a quick shake of my head. She nodded and found someone else to assist. I returned my attention to the man in need.

"If he doesn't make it," he said, "the last thing he's going to remember is I hated his girlfriend and stood in the way of him getting his driver's license."

"He knows you love him," I said.

"I work in construction," he said. "Have since I was a teenager not much older than my son. It's a hard life when you have work and even tougher when you don't. I want better for him. I want him to make something of himself. He's got the brains; all I'm asking him to do is use them. Not waste them on this girl he thinks he loves and that loser crowd she's got him hanging out with."

The loving parent's mantra, we all want better for our children. It's amazing how rarely that desire is fulfilled.

"People argue all of the time," I said. "Say things they don't really mean, or wish they said differently. He knows that. I'll bet you'll get the chance to tell him how you feel sooner than you think."

"How do you know?" he asked, raising his chin but continuing to rock.

He looked at me expecting a plausible answer. I knew I'd gone out on a feeble limb with my last proclamation. It was something I'd been trained never to do. Say things that weren't credible or couldn't be substantiated. I didn't know. This father needed confidence for the moment his son would survive. Believe he would have an opportunity to make amends. It was in my estimation, the proverbial glue that would hold him together. That was more important than facts for the moment.

"I have faith," I said.

He stopped rocking. His shoulders crumpled. He dropped his hands back into his lap. I could feel the tension draining from his bicep.

"What are you, some sort of Jesus freak?" he asked.

"Close," I said. "I'm a therapist."

"A shrink," he said.

"We're not as well connected," I said, trying to lighten the mood. It didn't work.

"You work for the hospital?" he asked.

"No, it's like I said, I'm here with my daughter."

"Right," he said. "You did say that." He took a deep breath, and then another. "I'm sorry to drop this on you—should I call you Doc?"

"Huiliang will do just fine," I said.

"Thanks for listening." He took another deep breath before he spoke again. "My son has a fifty-fifty chance of making it. Anything that could tip the scales in his favor would be appreciated."

"If you mean prayers, to be honest, I'm not a religious man," I said. "Listening is my thing. If you want to talk go right ahead."

"Is it going to cost me," he said with a weak smile.

"This one's on the house," I said.

We shared digital photos from our touch phone collections along with warm hearted and at times amusing stories of our children to pass the time. We laughed and smiled between his bouts of melancholy and depression. The news was grim when I asked about his son's mother. She had abandoned them when he was three never to be seen or heard from again. Why was the question echoing through the crowded corridors of his memories without reply?

The world around us carried on with patients in varying degrees of injuries and illnesses checking in and out. We were spectators and participants in the caldron of human circumstances bred from chaos and ruin made orderly and mended by a system designed to correct physical plight or minimize the suffering.

Daiyu walked out, all smiles and excitement wearing her new cast as if it were a badge of honor. She was atwitter about the process and couldn't wait to share. The grandmotherly nurse who escorted my daughter boasted about Daiyu's bravery throughout the entire process. The nurse handed me a printed page of care instructions that she briefly summarized before she left.

The doctor and nurse had been the first to sign Daiyu's cast. I feigned disappointment. Daiyu saw through my act but played along. My daughter assured me my signature would be the most treasured of them all. I introduced Daiyu to the man whose son was locked in a battle for his life. He successfully managed a valiant face as he asked my daughter about her accident then attentively listened as she detailed her harrowing experience.

Daiyu asked if he would like to sign her cast. He told her he would be glad to. He snatched one of three silver ballpoint pens he had clipped to his bib chest pocket. He handed me the pen telling Daiyu with a wink he wouldn't want to be the third person today to make her father jealous. It made my daughter laugh.

His smile was genuine. His heart seemed full. I thanked him, signed my daughter's cast 'Dad loves you' and gave him back his pen. He signed his name and thanked Daiyu for granting him such an honor. I said goodbye and wished him all the best, with a firm handshake and gentle pat on the shoulder. My daughter gave him a warm hug. If I had learned to read him at all, my guess was at that moment, his appreciation for her affectionate gesture was infinite. Daiyu gleefully waved goodbye with her good arm as if it was a windsock caught in a gale as we walked away.

While I loaded Daiyu into the car and strapped her in, a privilege my daughter only allowed because of her injury and to empower my male ego, Daiyu told me how nice she thought our new acquaintance was. She asked why he was at the hospital when he didn't look sick. Whether my daughter had noticed his puffy red eyes and bloodstained clothes she didn't mention, and I didn't pursue. I told Daiyu a partial truth about her fourth autograph at the time. He was waiting on his son to come out of surgery. I left out the part that his son might not survive. I only shared that information with my wife.

Daiyu asked me about the man by name, a few years later, as I dropped her off for high school soccer practice. I had shared with Daiyu why he was there by that time. Even with my daughter's verbal prodding it took me a minute to recall who he was. It's both curious and poignant how life does that to people. Keeping us zipped up in the sleeping bags of our own worlds as all other matters float away downstream. Those you generally miss most when absent are your loved ones and dearest friends. From the moment Daiyu asked me about him in our family minivan, I found myself periodically haunted by the stranger, or perhaps I was more haunted by not being aware of his fate.

I couldn't tell my daughter what became of him. My hope was then, as it is now, that his son made a full recovery, and they had found a way to make peace with each other. Over the years, I've toyed with the idea of hiring a private investigator to track him down for my own peace of mind. The optimist in me is all for it. The pessimist is not. One part longs to confirm all was well because we had faith in the greater good prevailing. That's the belief I carried with me when we parted. Because we had faith, and as the saying goes, where there's faith, there's always hope. Or am I making that last part up? The other side warned my meddling might only result in learning the heartrending truth his only child had died on that gray day, and my prying would only serve to resurrect his sorrow. All other possible scenarios seemed to zigzag between my idealist and cynical self as to their potential outcomes.

To find him, I would probably need to recall more about him than our chance meeting in the emergency room of a hospital, although I do remember the date and approximate time, coupled with a description, place and circumstance. Perhaps tracking him down might not be as difficult as one might think. I already know what my wife will say when I pass this idea by her, "Let sleeping dogs lie." And she's probably right. Still it would be nice to discover things turned out well for him. That happily ever after isn't just for fairy tales and salvation can bloom from the worst of times. I'll bet Daiyu remembers him. My daughter has a great memory for names.

Another Side of Love

Lorenzo Crow stood alone on isolated grassy Daybreak Bluff in the Orion Peninsula staring out over Walden Sound. Rich cobalt skies stretched toward infinity. The deep turquoise waters of Lummi Channel, Chinook Strait, and Brinnon Canal carried its best wishes by way of Valerianos Strait to its blue Pacific grandmother. Corn yellow sunlight illuminated the scene, warmed the air, and graciously accepted grateful prayers from hungry vegetation. A cool satin breeze said hello, teased Lorenzo as did his first love, and left him yearning for more. This place subdued his tormented soul. It was heaven except she was an hour late.

"Hello, Lorenzo." Her voice made him weak. Dalia Cabral had a voice that flowed like baby oil over silken skin. The kind of voice that moved a man to erotic heights with her fingers of sound. He needed to be strong. Lorenzo closed his eyes, and took a slow deep breath to gather his strength. He turned his head slowly to face Dalia and greet her with a bashful smile and quick nod.

Dalia had approached Lorenzo with ease and a cool confidence, a confidence born from years of the most intimate ways of knowing this man. Dalia stood close enough to touch Lorenzo but refrained from giving him their customary hug and kiss. His chilly greeting meant something was amiss. Lorenzo turned back to the sound. A salty hint of the ocean was in the air. He drank it in as dreams into the subconscious. Dalia looked over the sound as well. Its magnificence not lost in her eyes.

"You wanted to see me?" Dalia asked in a near whisper as if not to disturb the tranquility god. Lorenzo remained silent. He peripherally watched Dalia. She was wearing a flowered sundress. Her dark brown velvet Brazilian curls caressed her smooth tan shoulders. Dalia had girlish dimples and big brown eyes that sparkled when she laughed, stormed when angry, and darkened when sad. Her cheeks were chubby as was her body, both of which Lorenzo loved. Dalia fit perfectly into his arms. Her soft flesh meshed perfectly with his body. Her head rested perfectly on his chest below his hairless chin. Lorenzo had once believed the sun bowed to Dalia and the stars kissed her feet. Her presence washed over him. Lorenzo took another deep breath, inhaling and exhaling Dalia to refocus on his purpose.

Dalia took in Lorenzo with the utmost subtlety out of the corners of her eyes. Lorenzo was wearing terracotta mai tai shorts and a rust colored short sleeve linen shirt. Perfect fits for his sinewy body and broad shoulders. His tar black dreadlocks reached his middle back. His copper skin glowed in the sun. All that was absent for Dalia was his crooked smile and gentle brown eyes hidden behind dark shades. Dalia longed for both. Out of respect for her dear friend, Dalia suppressed her curiosity, waiting for Lorenzo to air his thoughts. Their senses feasted on nature in the interim.

"What's wrong?" Dalia said, her patience at an end.

"More like what's right." Lorenzo's voice was sober and even.

"Why did you invite me here?" Dalia asked.

"Don't you remember?"

"Remember what?"

"Here is where we first kissed," Lorenzo said.

"I remember." A genial smile graced Dalia's lips. "I remember you tried to slip me tongue even after you said you wouldn't."

They shared a laugh. Dalia took in Lorenzo's smile but missed his eyes. Dalia had a fonder memory of a kiss they shared six months later. By then their mouths and tongues had learned to dance as one. Her recollection sent romantic shivers down her spine. Lorenzo did not notice. The memory faded into the serenity of the bluff leaving a solemn stillness in its wake.

"We could have come here together," Dalia said, her voice capturing the mood. Lorenzo did not speak. He did not move. Dalia waited.

"How's Al?" Lorenzo asked.

"Why would you ask me about that jerk?" Dalia rebuffed.

"He's your boyfriend."

"My ex-boyfriend," Dalia said. "I caught him cheating on me and dumped his sorry ass. You already know that."

"There'll be another," Lorenzo said matter-of-factly.

"Why can't you be my man?"

Lorenzo released a gentle sigh. "There was a time when if I saw you from a cliff of a thousand feet, I would leap from that precipice if only to gaze into your eyes once before I died."

"You can gaze into my eyes now if you want." Lorenzo did not look at Dalia.

"How frail a gift is sanity," he said.

"What are you talking about?"

"Nothing," Lorenzo said. Lorenzo was in one of his dark philosophical moods. Dalia knew not to push him or he would shut down. She reclaimed her patience and waited.

"Even a fool can become a wise man when given the right incentive," Lorenzo said.

"You've never been a fool," Dalia said. "Do you consider yourself a wise man?"

"Is anyone wise when it comes to love?" Lorenzo said.

"I suppose not."

After a moment's peace, "What do you want from me?" Lorenzo asked.

"Comfort and understanding after a bad breakup," Dalia said. "That's the least I would expect from my closest friend."

"You want comfort and understanding," Lorenzo said, "then go see one of your girlfriends. I'm not available to you in that capacity anymore."

"I thought you loved me," Dalia said, smarting from his comment.

"I did."

"You don't anymore?"

"Of course I do," Lorenzo said, "but it's redirected."

"What's that supposed to mean?"

Lorenzo removed his sunglasses. His eyes revealed his emotions, as was always the case. Dalia felt comfort in his gaze even in his agitated state.

"It stops now." Lorenzo spoke with firm commitment, an act that even surprised him.

"What stops now?" Dalia said trying to track Lorenzo's mood. He had never behaved in this way before and it made her uncomfortable.

"You and me," Lorenzo said.

"I don't understand."

"When you dropped me for that nit-witted asshole Al," Lorenzo said, "I fell flat on my face . . . again. I hurt to the very core of my being, again. Here I was a man who treated you like a queen. Loved you immensely, gave you freedom to be yourself, and always considered you in every facet of my life. And you discarded me for the first pathetic piece of muscle head handsome machismo that came along."

"I'm sorry, Lorenzo," Dalia said, meaning every syllable. "I didn't mean for it to happen."

"But it did, again," Lorenzo said. "And again, you're sorry."

"Please, I need you right now."

"No can do."

"Why?" Dalia said.

"I consider myself a good person."

"You are a good person," Dalia said.

"And we agree I'm not a fool," Lorenzo said.

"Of course you're not," Dalia said.

"Except when it comes to you," Lorenzo said.

"Isn't that part of being in love?"

"Is it?"

"Yes," Dalia said.

"Then why have you never been a fool for me?" Lorenzo asked. His words hit Dalia like a stampede over the horizon. Dalia remained silent. She looked out over the sound as if hoping to find the answer there. Dalia looked back at Lorenzo when the answer didn't materialize. It was his turn to be patient.

"I'm sorry," she said.

"Sorry didn't do it, you did."

"I don't know what else to say," Dalia said. "How can I make things right between us?"

Lorenzo had no answer. He ruminated. "By walking away and not looking back," was his eventual response.

"You mean that?" Dalia said, trying to mask her fear, a fright that had come upon her with the suddenness of a fever chill.

"Damn right I do," Lorenzo said with resolution, sounding as though he had just passed down her death sentence.

"You don't real-ly mean that," Dalia said hoping for a reprieve in Lorenzo's attitude.

"There's someone else," Lorenzo said, no change in his voice.

Dalia's heart sank. She eventually mustered the question, "Who?"

"You don't know her."

"Can I meet her . . . as a friend?"

"That would defeat the purpose of exorcising you from my life," Lorenzo said, "now wouldn't it?"

There was no other woman. Lorenzo needed Dalia to believe in his fictitious mate, a lie that would give him the strength to keep her charm at bay. Dalia paused as dismay swarmed. The hope of a loving reunion with Lorenzo had been dashed against the rocks. Dalia wanted to kiss Lorenzo and caress his face. She would do anything to recapture at minimum his friendship. His eyes said with fury, "*No.*"

"Can't we remain friends?" Dalia touched his chest. Her fingers were as light as mist, soft as down. Lorenzo felt his strength wane as water down a drain. The flashback happened as lighting striking a tree. He and Dalia were caught in the rain while having a picnic in a secluded meadow. They found shelter in a not long abandoned wooden shack. From its dry, dusty doorway, they watched the warm rainfall on the soft green. Lorenzo wrapped his arms around Dalia. Dalia encouraged his touch. Lorenzo kissed her neck. Dalia beckoned his passion by offering more of herself to Lorenzo. They made love. It was their third reunion as a couple. The memory made Lorenzo feel like fire fighting to burst from the darkness. Lorenzo needed a moment. He looked to the west to clear Dalia from his view. Gently removing her hand from his chest, he faced Dalia.

"I can't go on like this," Lorenzo said. Her eyes were the stuff for which men conquered nations. "I'm your friend and have at times been your lover. I'm obviously not the man for you. If I were, you wouldn't keep leaving me for someone else."

"I was wrong," Dalia said.

"No you weren't."

"I love you."

"You need me," Lorenzo said.

"It's the same."

"No it isn't. What you want from me is a shoulder to cry on, someone to comfort you when the waters get rough. After the crisis is over we'll be right back to friends."

"Can I borrow your strong shoulders now?" Dalia asked.

"As a friend," Lorenzo said.

"If that's all I can get, I'll take it," Dalia said.

"No," Lorenzo managed to say. His determination remained but emotion had weakened his stance.

"It was never my intention to hurt you," Dalia said.

"Your intentions were always to save yourself from the quicksand of self-pity," Lorenzo said. "I was the means by which you could accomplish your goal."

"You've always meant more to me than an endeavor," Dalia said with clear sincerity.

"We've been on and off six times in fourteen years," Lorenzo said. "Each time you've left me for another man."

"The seventh times a charm." Dalia's attempt at humor fell flat.

"I'm tired of being your safety net."

"I won't leave you again, Lorenzo."

"Promise," Lorenzo said, his resolve ready to buckle. Dalia couldn't speak. She wanted to say yes. Yes, I will love you from now to eternity. She had never felt that way about Lorenzo. Never believed him to be the man she wanted for a lifetime.

"Can we at least remain friends?" Dalia said.

His heart raced to the pit of his stomach. It had become an all too familiar feeling with Dalia. A full comprehensive knowledge of what it meant to be absent of hope. "There's no middle ground with us anymore," Lorenzo said. "It has to be all or nothing."

"I can't guarantee that," Dalia said. Her honesty surprised even her.

"If you did," Lorenzo said, "it would only be a lie."

Silence never cut so deep. "What are you thinking?" Dalia asked.

"Do I hate you more at this moment than I've loved you all of my life," Lorenzo said. The comment grabbed Dalia's emotions and squeezed. His eyes supported that truth. Dalia was surprised by how quickly tears welled in her eyes. "Every time one of your relationships sours you rubber band back to me. Well that ends here and now."

Dalia struggled to make sense of an important piece of her life suddenly being ripped away. Crippling grief that she had only known at funerals of loved ones gripped her chest. "This is the place you chose to tell me," Dalia said. "The place you chose to break my heart?"

"Can you think of a better place for us to say goodbye?"

Dalia could not. Her heart ached and her breathing became labored. Anguish was overwhelming her. Dalia had to leave for fear of collapse.

"Goodbye, Lorenzo," Dalia said. "I truly am sorry I disappointed you"

"Not half as sorry as I am," Lorenzo said as much to himself as Dalia. "Call me if you change your mind." Dalia reached for Lorenzo.

"Don't touch me!" Lorenzo yelled. Dalia was startled. She could only stare in shock at Lorenzo. "I simply wanted to hug you goodbye."

"Not necessary, just go away," Lorenzo snapped.

Lorenzo put on his sunglasses if only to hide his encroaching tears. He had to remain strong. No longer able to fight back her tears Dalia turned and scurried away. Lorenzo watched her for as long as he could bear it. If he did not break her hold now he would never be free. Lorenzo turned back to the wondrous scene moments before Dalia glanced back at him. Lorenzo said, "Goodbye, Dalia. I love you." Dalia could not hear him, of course, just as Lorenzo did not see Dalia wave goodbye.

Lorenzo felt empty but he had done it. He had stood firm. He had taken that first much needed step to purge his life of Dalia. He could move on without her. A feeble smile was a minor miracle. Lorenzo drew a deep cleansing breath from the cool ocean breeze that had come to play. His tears escaped his shades. He watched the sailboats in the distance wishing he were aboard one of the heartier crafts. He would set sail for Valerianos Strait out into the open waters of the Pacific. In that instant, he made a decision.

Dalia sobbed as she eased shut her car door like an eyelid closing upon a nightmare. She drove from rote, tears pouring from her eyes like northwest rain. Dalia did not look back. She never saw Lorenzo step off the cliff into oblivion.

The Virgin Bank Robber

The Lucretia Coffin Mott Women's Correctional Facility Conference Room C was half the size of the public defender's medium sized, paper-overrun office. The bright ceiling light burst forth from its cage to flood the conference room in white. Drab was the decorum from the pale gray walls and ceiling to the bare concrete floor. The big round black and white institutional clock perched on high was caged as if to prevent time from escaping. At the center of the room was a shiny metal table bolted to the floor by its shiny metal legs. Two straight back dull metal chairs with plump green vinyl cushions faced each other like stolid identical twins. The silence was oppressive as if it too had been imprisoned. Tomb-like to the extent the public defender could hear her warm breath and steady heartbeat.

There lingered the fragrance of disinfectant that reminded the veteran PD of a sanitized hospital room. The attorney of record rather liked the aroma. It reminded her of her teenage years. On occasion she would stop by after school to surprise her mother who worked as a floor nurse at a public hospital. The fiercely independent young woman began doing so more often after her mom and dad divorced as a show of support. Her mom was having a difficult time letting go of her chronically adulterous father whom her mother had loved with all of her being. Everyone at the hospital always treated her with such kindness and warmth. In distant reflection, the PD wondered if her cozy treatment sprang naturally from their hearts or from sympathetic souls seeking to comfort the victim of a broken home.

The public defender stood near the locked metal door with the shoebox sized, wire mesh peep window of the private visiting room awaiting the arrival of her client. She appeared relaxed and confident in her professional dark blue skirt suit, comfortable black leather pumps and crisp white long sleeve shirt. The public defender preferred her face to be the first thing her client saw when she entered. She had learned over the years that a confident smile and reassuring handshake at the onset did wonders in gaining client confidence. A confident client was more forthcoming and honest than not about the details of their alleged crime. Knowing the unembellished facts were a lawyer's best weapons in the clash for courtroom justice. The PD needed to wring every kernel of truth out of this particular client in order to establish due diligence.

When the same guard who had escorted the public defender to Conference Room C arrived with her charge the PD was pleasantly surprised. The prisoner was neither shackled nor handcuffed. The two entered smiling and joking rather than exhibiting the edgy, bellicose relationship that normally accompanied people on opposite sides of the law in this environment. If not for the guard uniform and fluorescent orange prison jumpsuit that earmarked their status, one would have mistaken them as girlfriends, on their way to an entertaining social event as opposed to the law and offender.

The public defender introduced herself to her client. The Virgin Bank Robber welcomed her with a tentative smile and gentle brown eyes. They shook hands. The Virgin Bank Robber had dry palms. That surprised the PD. Most of her incarcerated clients had sweaty palms for obvious reasons. Once the PD gave the prison guard the nod, the guard sincerely wished her client "good luck" before stepping outside and closing the door behind her.

"You're a bank robber?" The forty-something PD said with curious surprise as they sat.

"So they tell me," the young woman responded with neither shame nor arrogance.

Even though the public defender had seen pictures of her client splashed all over the news, newspapers and internet, she was still taken aback by her youth. The PD eyed the sweet chocolate baby-faced twenty-two year old seated across from her, erect, shoulders back, relaxed. There was no fear in this young woman's eyes, no sense of guilt or remorse. If anything, her client gave the PD the obdurate impression that whatever happened, this offender could handle it. For some reason that feeling gave the PD even more impetus to fight harder for this young woman than usual, which for her was like giving more than one-hundred-percent.

The prison guard kept a wandering eye on them through the wire mesh. It was a common scenario for the defense veteran. The guard's job was to assure the safety of the PD and to be watchful of anything illegal transpiring between lawyer and client. This prison guard was a good one. Others never took their eyes off the public defender and her client the entire time they were in conference as if they were voyeurs watching some peculiar peep show. Those prison guards gave the PD the creeps.

"You're a virgin?" The public defender asked, adjusting her carousel skirt after crossing her legs.

"That's right, although I got no idea how that information got out," The Virgin Bank Robber said in the airy tone of a young woman in the spring of her life.

"Probably someone involved with your routine physical said something to someone who leaked it to the press," the PD matter-of-factly stated.

"You'd think the press would have better things to do than worry 'bout my sex life."

"Obviously they don't," the PD said, followed after a moment's pause by the question, "how'd it happen?"

"You mean 'bout me bein' a bank robber or a virgin?" the young woman said in an amused tone that her expression reflected.

"I know how—or why—a woman's a virgin," the PD said in an amused tone of her own. "I'm simply curious how someone with such a strict moral code could show no inhibition about breaking the law."

"One ain't got nothin' to do with the other," The Virgin Bank Robber said with a smirk.

"You're a good looking woman if I do say so myself. Men must have been buzzing around you like bees to pollen."

"Thank you for the compliment." The young woman flashed a smile that belonged in the best picture section of a high school yearbook. The PD could not resist returning her smile.

"Don't mention it," the PD said as she removed her legal pad and stick pen from her battle worn brown leather classic brief bag resting next to her on the concrete floor. The PD placed the pad and pen delicately before her on the sternum high cold metal table. There was a moment the PD gazed at the tools of her trade in front of her as one might find an avid philosopher regarding a sacred text of uncharted wisdom before daring to venture inside.

It was an involuntary action on the public defender's part. The Virgin Bank Robber noticed the instance of reverence. Through her eyes, it was divine, as if her PD were offering a silent prayer on her behalf. It gave The Virgin Bank Robber a warm feeling to know that this public defender had been sent to represent her.

"Have you ever stolen anything before?" the PD asked matter-of-factly.

"I stole a pair of pretty pink earrings from the five-and-dime when I was nine." The young woman perked up as if giving the correct answer to a challenging classroom question. "Felt so bad 'bout it I took 'em back the next day with the money to pay for 'em."

"You took that action without any prompting from anyone like your parents or friends?"

"No one knew," she said, settling down. "If my parents would ah found out I stole somethin' my momma would've tanned my behind."

"Where did you get the money to pay for those earrings?"

"Out my piggy bank," the young woman answered with pride.

"Have you ever committed any type of crime before these bank robberies other than the five-and-dime incident?"

"No ma'am."

"That's good."

"What's good about it?"

"It shows you have strong character," the PD said. "Up until the bank robberies you were an upstanding citizen. We can use that in court."

The PD wrote something on her legal pad. Her handwriting was not legible to The Virgin Bank Robber. To her it looked more like shorthand than longhand. Jotting down things was a process the PD would repeat during the course of their interview. The Virgin Bank Robber resigned herself to remaining ignorant to what was written on the pad.

"I know I have strong character," her client said with indignation. "I don't need a story like that to prove it."

"You do in a court of law," the PD said, "and one other thing."

"Ma'am?"

"Stop calling me ma'am. It makes me nauseous."

"What should I call you?"

"Simply answer my questions."

"Can I ask you somethin'?" The Virgin Bank Robber said as if about to ask the PD what color nail polish she was wearing.

"Sure."

"Why do people get paid so little for good hard labor?"

"What do you mean?"

"Manual labor; people act like it's a sin to do manual labor. Most manual labor jobs pay next to nothin' and often times people gets treated worse than stray animals for doin' 'em."

Throughout history, manual workers had predominately been treated like a necessary scourge by elitists, commerce controllers and power brokers, the PD thought, with compensation for their labor to be kept at a bare minimum, a practice and attitude that was maintained today. It was an insight that would do her client no good in court.

"You got me," the PD said. "A shift in American values I suppose."

"Maybe you're right. Even with all the technology and computers and what not, it don't happen without the hard workin' folks that puts 'em together."

"I can't argue your point but we're getting off track."

"I'm sorry," her client sincerely said. "I do that sometimes. My mind has a tendency to wander."

"I know the feeling."

"You do?" the young woman said as if having discovered they shared the same tastes in clothes.

"I do, but this isn't one of those occasions," the PD said in her most professional tone. "Now back to your case."

"Exploitation," The Virgin Bank Robber said as if plucking the idea out of thin air.

"Excuse me?"

"Ain't that what they call it when you take advantage of somebody?"

"In general, yes, but what has that to do with anything?"

"Not payin' someone a decent livin' wage, ain't that exploitation?"

"It can be regarded as unfair compensation dependent upon the type of work and circumstances. Employers are free to pay whatever they choose as long as it's legal."

"Where I used to work was unionized. The unions made sure we got fair wages, health benefits and decent workin' conditions. Without 'em, who's goin' to look out for us?"

"The system has laws on the books to protect worker's rights."

The Virgin Book Robber let out a huff of a laugh. "How much it cost a person—an individual—to protect they's worker's rights in court, a thousand, ten thousand, a-hundert thousand maybe more? I'll bet big business likes those odds."

"It can get expensive," the PD expressed with more passion than she realized. "There are organizations and lawyers who do pro bono work on such cases. I'm one of them."

"And your efforts are appreciated," her client said with earnest. "If you don't mind my askin', how many workers' cases you won doin' pro bono work?"

"To be honest, none yet in a courtroom," the PD confessed with a hint of shame. "I have had some settled out of court in favor of clients."

"Good for you! But you have to admit goin' up 'gainst them business titans who can make a case drag on for years, it don't bode well for us workin' folks do it."

"To be perfectly frank the odds aren't in your favor."

"Our favor."

"Pardon me."

"You workin' class just like me."

"That's true."

"I know that's right. I hear tell Reagan and Bush did a good job stackin' the courts for the big boys. It sure looks that way to me all the way up to the Supreme Court."

"It can be daunting but it's not impossible."

"So an employer can pretty much do what they please." The young woman lightly nodded her head as she seemed to formulate her next statement. "Treat us fairly if they feel like it; treat us unfairly if they don't."

"That's how our free enterprise system works at the moment," the PD said.

"Ain't nothin' free from where I'm sittin'."

"I'm free."

"You get paid by the taxpayers. Someone I used to be."

The PD gave a quick nod in recognition of her client's assessment. Before she could speak, The Virgin Bank Robber continued.

"If a business can't afford to pay a livin' wage why should they be allowed to dilute the labor pool? Shouldn't they be forced to fold and let them who can pay the fare move in? Ain't that capitalization too?"

"It is capitalism, and it does work that way in theory."

"Well it sure don't seem to work that way in reality. It seems to me when a person's down these days people look to exploit 'em for everything they can get instead of helpin' 'em if they can. Some people even enjoy kickin' a person when they down."

"There's a lot of that going around."

"What makes people mean like that?"

"I'm not a psychologist. I'm a lawyer here to get information to prepare your case and ready you for trail."

"I'm sorry," her client said with that yearbook smile. "I have a tendency to do that sometimes. My mind will drift away."

"So you said," the PD said, smiling back.

"My Boo says I'm star trippin' when I do that 'cause my thoughts sound to him like they come from outer space."

"That's nice, now back to your case."

"I'm with you," The Virgin Bank Robber said, her smile morphing into a bashful grin. "What would you like to know?"

"I have to admit I'm baffled," the PD said, cocking her head slightly to one side.

"'Bout what?"

"How you managed to go so far astray of the law?"

"I never got married," her client flippantly said.

"So?"

"I mean we planned to and everything but things kept happenin' to not make it seem like such a good idea, omens if you will."

"Like what?"

"The Bible says one should not fornicate out of wedlock."

"The Bible also says one shall not steal."

"I told my fiancée that same thing, 'bout the stealin' part I mean."

"Your fiancée?" the PD said with raised eyebrows.

"Um-hmm," the Virgin Bank Robber said with a grin.

"Your fiancé was your partner in crime?"

"He was." The young woman leaned forward with a hearty laugh as if she had confessed a long held secret to a close girlfriend. "He planned the hold-ups. I planned the getaways. Why are we bein' tried separately?" she asked, leaning back. Her mood switching from playful to mystified.

"Because the prosecutor believes he has a better chance of getting a full conviction for both of you by doing so. Female defendants generally receive more sympathy from juries than men. If the prosecutor can set the stage by having your male partner sentenced to the maximum, a following jury will have difficulty justifying not giving you the same sentence for the same crimes."

"That's pretty sneaky."

"Shrewd is what it is but I agree," the PD said. "You sound religious."

"I'm a dutiful servant of the Lord," The Virgin Bank Robber said with pride.

"Then why would you allow anyone—even someone you love—to talk you into robbing banks?"

"It's like my fiancée said, the Bible says thou shalt not steal. The Bible also says God helps those who help themselves. We were merely applyin' one religious precept over another until we landed on our feet again."

"What happened to knock you off your feet?" the PD asked.

"The economy," The Virgin Bank Robber said with a frowning shake of her head. "We lost our jobs. My Boo when the factory shipped his job overseas. Mine disappeared as part of a union bustin' labor cut back. Our unemployment ran out. What little money we had put away got gobbled up pretty fast with bills and health care costs and so on."

"Health care costs? You look pretty healthy to me."

"It wasn't me or my fiancée we were concerned 'bout 'though you never know when it comes to your health. It was my daddy and his momma. My daddy got colon cancer, and his momma got breast cancer. Their insurance didn't cover most of their costs for treatments and care so they had to come up with it out of pocket. Of course, they lost their jobs 'cause of their illnesses and what not. What little insurance they had went down the drain when that happened. Our family pitched in to help with whatever we could. It wasn't near enough. That medical stuff is *crazy* expensive. It nearly cost our folks their homes. They worked too hard and too long to be put in that position when they needs a little help."

"I'm sorry to hear that," the PD said with a sympathetic nod. "Things are tough out here for a lot of people right now."

"My Boo and I moved in with our folks to help take care of 'em and try to save money. We helped as much as we could but then our money ran out. Me and my fiancée come from hard workin' class folks. We know how to get by on a little. When you got nothin' comin' in the door, I reckon most folks would agree that's askin' a bit much. We felt like we was becomin' more of a burden to our parents than a help. That's when my fiancée got the idea of us goin' where the money is."

"Were you and your fiancée living together before you moved back in with your parents?"

"Heaven's no!" the young woman said as if asked if she were from

Mars. "That would be livin' in sin. We had our own places."

"So it was your fiancée's idea for the two of you to rob banks?"

"They've got way more money than they need and poor folks like us only needs a little to get by. Why not help ourselves?"

"Because it's against the law," the PD said.

"Why's it 'gainst the law for somebody to rob a bank but there's no laws 'gainst somebody bein' homeless or not gettin' the medical attention they need to get better?"

"The law's the law."

"What kinds of laws is it that put money before people?"

"What about the people's money you stole. What about what could happen to them if they lost the money they need to pay for things?"

"We're sorry if we harmed any needy or hard workin' folks out there. We only tryin' to survive. Seems to me that's the real crime being committed all across this country, people bein' denied the simple right to survive." As if struck by an epiphany The Virgin Bank Robber asked, "Why do so many people accept their fate instead of fightin' for the right to survive?"

The PD raised an eyebrow to the question. "Suffering in silence is part of an American tradition." She thought for a moment before deciding to continue. "One thing that organized religion teaches us is to remain docile in the face of adversity so that we may receive our rewards in the afterlife from the suffering we endure in this one."

"You sayin' religion teaches us to be passive lambs even when we bein' led to slaughter."

"Pretty much," the PD said.

"Religion can be a source of strength, too," The Virgin Bank Robber said with quiet conviction.

"If directed to, yes, it can be a tremendous source of strength. We don't have much of that kind of positive energy in the world right now that I'm aware. Most of our organized religions are self-serving or serve the wealthy and powerful in their own way whether it's their intention or not."

"Even a high school dropout like me knows our modern democracy is run by the rich, and few of them care little 'bout anybody but themselves."

"I can't disagree. Corporations are sociopathic by nature."

"What does 'sociopathic' mean?"

"In this case, I mean, they don't care about anything but their bottom line. Multinational corporations, banks and their lobbyists call the shots in our economy. Their main objective is to protect the wealthy no matter the cost."

"The Bottom Line is the insatiable whore of capitalism," the young woman said with a knowing nod.

"Where'd you hear that?" the PD said.

"My fiancée," her client said with a proud grin. "He's always saying stuff like that. It's one of the reasons I love him."

"I can't say he's wrong."

"No one in their right mind would."

I feel sorry for the youth of today, the PD thought. *They have a lot of great ideas on how to make this world a better place, but they're being suffocated by an ancient generation that are mired in the pit of some deluded culture sprouting distorted or false memories from a romantic rather than factual view of history.* For a moment, the attorney considered sharing her insight with a woman she had come to see as more than a client, but almost a kindred spirit. She decided against it. There was no advantage adding fuel to a fire that would not be useful in a court of law.

The Virgin Bank Robber looked away from her PD for a moment as if referencing some phantom book only she could see. Her face calm, her body relaxed. "You may be right 'bout what you said 'bout religion if people let it be that way," her client said, seemingly as much to herself as to her PD. "I'm a Christian so I can't vouch for no other faith. My faith has taught me to stand up and fight for what is right and just in this world, no matter the odds, no matter the cost. I believe in my Lord and Savior Jesus Christ. He'll help me through these hard times now as he has in the past."

"I hope you're right," the PD said with heartfelt sincerity.

"I know I am. And that's why I'll go on fightin' this fight."

"I don't follow you."

"Don't people have the right to survive? The majority of us don't ask for much, food, clothin', shelter, health care, dignity and respect. Ain't that every human bein's' basic rights?"

The PD happened to glance at the peep window as she gave what her client had said a moment's thought. She knew the guard could overhear them despite its fortress like structure. She noticed the guard nodding in what the PD believed was in the affirmative of what she had overheard her client say.

"I happen to agree with you," the PD said. "That doesn't give you the *right* to break the law."

"Then why is it that the haves are the only ones who *have* access to these things and them that *don't have* needs to go without? That seem fair to you?"

"No it doesn't, but the *haves* are not on trial here. As your attorney, I need to stick to the letter of the law."

"Sounds to me like those letters need rearranging to make it easier for most people to stick to 'em," The Virgin Bank Robber said.

"We're going to need to work on your defense," the PD said, eyeing the caged clock. She noticed they only had thirty minutes left of their hour.

"I did it and I won't lie and say I didn't," the young woman proclaimed with calm conviction.

"What about your fiancée? Did he coerce you into those robberies?"

"First of all, my fiancé is the sweetest, most lovin' and carin' man on the planet. He loves me like the mornin' glory loves the sun. The next thing you need to know is that I don't let *nobody* talk or bully me into doin' nothin' I don't wanna do."

"Is that why you're still a virgin?" the PD asked with a grin. The Virgin Bank Robber smiled back.

"No marriage, no whoopee, that's the way it is with me. I mean what's the big deal anyway. Nobody got hurt in what we did."

"Robbing a bank is a federal offense."

"What's that mean?"

"It means you committed a crime against the federal government, and they are obligated to do everything within their power to make certain that you and your fiancée are punished to the fullest extent of the law."

"Can we charge big business and government?"

"With what?"

"Crimes against humanity; there's millions of people hurtin' in this country—all over the world for that matter—through no fault of their own. Hard workin', tax payin', decent folks who been cast out like garbage because in their opinion we don't add value to someone's bottom line or are suddenly unworthy because we're unable to pay taxes due to a string of bad luck. We paid our taxes when we had the chance. Don't we deserve the same support from our government in our darkest hour that they gave Wall Street and the banks?"

"You make some valid points from a moral and ethical position. There is little within the law that is applicable in this case. And may I make a suggestion?"

"I'm all ears."

"Don't say those kinds of things when I put you on the stand. In fact, don't talk that way anymore. If you feel a need to vent then use me—and only me—as your sounding board."

"Why should I remain silent?"

"The judge may dislike it and in all likelihood the jury won't agree with your position. And the prosecution will use your views to demonize you."

"They got somethin' 'gainst the truth?"

"The truth is they'll probably view you as anti-American for saying such things."

"But I am American! I was born and raised here. I would die for this country if need be. All people like me want is to be treated fairly as *Americans.* Don't we deserve that much?"

"If you speak out against capitalism or condone government intervention it could be misconstrued as anti-American in certain sectors. That will work against us trying to create sympathy for your case."

"What's wrong with pointin' out the shortcomin's of capitalism?"

"Too many people are convinced that capitalism works for all. To them it's sacrosanct."

"By sacrosanct I take it you mean sacred like the Bible," The Virgin Bank Robber said.

"I do," the PD responded.

"It didn't work for me or my fiancée or our folks or our relatives or our friends and neighbors for that matter. Capitalism has failed more people in this world than it's helped if you ask me."

"I can't argue that point in court."

"Why not?"

"Because it's irrelevant to your case for starters; and because it may paint you as anti-American, a Socialist or maybe even a pinko Communist."

"People still buy into that pinko Communist nonsense?"

"Like it was yesterday's news," the PD said with a touch of exasperation.

The Virgin Bank Robber considered her PD's advice. Her fiery eyes cooled and her baby face settled into conciliation along with her decision. "What do you need for me to do?" she asked with resignation.

The PD began to instruct her client on how they would approach her defense in order to lessen the burden of guilt for her crimes.

"Do you really think I got a chance to beat this?" The Virgin Bank Robber asked.

"You'll do some time, but if we're lucky it'll be the minimum. With good behavior you could be out in no time."

"What about my fiancée?"

"What about him?"

"Will I ever get to see him again?"

"I don't know."

"We can still get married can't we?"

"I don't see why not; unless the prosecutor decides to play hardball."

"Then we could have conjugal visits?"

"That's usually how it works," the PD said with a smile.

The Virgin Bank Robber leaned forward. The PD did the same. "If I let you in on a little secret you promise not to tell anyone?" The Virgin Bank Robber whispered.

"We have attorney, client confidentiality going here," the PD whispered back. "That's usually how it works."

"Is that a promise or what?"

"I promise," the PD said with a reassuring grin.

"I'm not the only one who's a virgin in this relationship."

The PD stared sideways at her client. "Are you telling me that your fiancée is a virgin, too?" her voice rising near the end of her sentence.

"Shhhhh!" The Virgin Bank Robber glanced toward the door. The guard wasn't peering in at them. "He tries to pretend he's not but I can tell he ain't ever been with a woman in that way before."

"Are you sure?"

"I haven't flat come out and ask him if that's what you askin'."

"How old is he?"

"Twenty-four," The Virgin Bank Robber said.

"What makes you so certain your fiancée is a virgin?"

"On account of how shy he is when we make out. Sometimes he shudders when we embrace. His hands tremble so much when he touches me that I'm afraid the poor dear is goin' pass out. He's a good kisser now, but when we first started out, he was awful. I had to teach him how to French kiss and everything."

"How do you know so much about kissing being a virgin?"

"Just because I never went all the way don't mean I ain't had my fair share of make out sessions with boys."

The PD gave a slight headshake. "I find it difficult to believe a man twenty-four years old would be a virgin, especially these days."

"Any harder to believe than finding a twenty-two year old virgin woman these days," The Virgin Bank Robber said with a knowing smile.

The PD quietly considered the odds in her head. The Virgin Bank Robber had an infectious smile. The PD again smiled at her client. The PD liked this woman. That could be dangerous. Emotion, even an affirmative one, could only get in the way. Prepared professionalism always trumped sentiment when it came to getting her clients off or the best deal possible in a court of law. The PD had to reel in her sentiments. Her client didn't need a friend. She needed a skilled and organized legal advocate who was focused on her defense. She needed a shark. The PD dumped her smile. The Virgin Bank Robber picked up on her PD's mood swing and did the same.

"I understand," the PD said. Her voice returned to normal. "I'll do everything I can to aide in your marriage. For now we need to concentrate on your defense."

"I miss him," The Virgin Bank Robber said at her normal speaking volume.

"Your fiancé"

The Virgin Bank Robber nodded. She ran her eyes over the PD's wedding band. "I see you're married."

"Almost fourteen years."

"Got any kids?"

"A boy and a girl," the PD said with pride.

"You look happy."

"I am."

"I want that kind of happiness with my man."

"I understand."

"Wonder what he's doin' right 'bout now?"

"He's probably helping his attorney with his defense."

"I suppose you're right." The Virgin Bank Robber sighed. She gazed past her lawyer at the gray wall behind her as if staring at a melancholy movie. When she looked back into the eyes of her attorney there was a firm resolve and wisdom in her eyes that gave her attorney quiet pause.

"Are you alright?" the PD asked.

"I'm fine," The Virgin Bank Robber pensively answered. "We gave a fair amount of the money we stole to other people in need. It wasn't much but it helped 'em a little. And don't ask me who they were 'cause I ain't naming no names, and neither will my fiancé"

"That's good," the PD said. "We can use the Robin Hood defense, robbed from the rich to give to the poor."

"There doesn't seem to be any other way to get out of poverty in America anymore; everything costs more and jobs pay less."

"I'll make you a deal," the PD said.

"What kind of a deal?"

"You cooperate with me now, and I'll do everything in my power to get you and your fiancé married as soon as possible."

"Do you mean it?"

"I swear on everything I hold dear and holy."

Her client's smile was beyond comprehension, shimmering with natural pure light. Her face and eyes echoed their joy. "Where do we start?" The Virgin Bank Robber asked, barely able to contain herself.

The PD took it from the top. The Virgin Bank Robber offered her full cooperation, even accepting advice that went against her ideological grain. By the end of their first session, the PD became more convinced that she could get her client the minimum.

To the PD's surprise, no one involved in the bank robbing cases had the slightest objection to the modern day Robin Hoods getting married. During the course of their separate trials, The Virgin Bank Robbers were no more.

Anniversary

My father sat on the edge of his rumpled bed wearing woolen plaid pajamas, tracing his burnished lifeline with an arthritic index finger. His shoulders slumped forward. His back was as crooked as his finger. Across his callused palm, he examined his life as if willing a miracle to happen. I watched in silence from the bedroom doorway.

I'm here to escort my father to my mother's grave where we will place flowers and pray for as long as he wishes. My father found her in this room on that bed five years ago today. He telephoned me at work. His surly voice was somber, soft as yarn. "Son, your mother's passed away," he said. "I need your help." Then the line went dead.

In the rustic home of my childhood, I found him kneeling beside their bed clutching mom's hand to his heart. His puffy eyes red. Face swollen and wet with tears. I collapsed, sobbing in the doorway. He glanced my way, unashamed of his grief or mine. He laid her hand to rest by her side. Her death had come as sudden as the gentle rain that late afternoon. Daylight had made my mother's face shine, my father's tears glisten. A parting kiss he placed on her lips before he staggered to me. Together we began the arduous process of emptying ourselves of sorrow.

I felt like an intruder violating his sacred ritual tiptoeing across the room. I said standing over him, "Dad." His concentration never wavered from his crooked wandering finger. He smelled of Ben Gay. I touched his arm. He stared up at me. His puffy eyes red. Face damp and swollen. I sat beside him. I hugged him. His bald head rested on my chest. I leaned into his good ear and whispered, "Father . . . it's time to go."

Dr. Feel Good

A blind man sat alone at a table outside upscale Maconha Cafe eating a Cobb salad on a clear and sunny afternoon. A man asked if he could join him because all other tables were full.

"No problem," the blind man said with a smile. "I'd enjoy the company."

The man sat with a heavy sigh.

"Having a rough day?" the blind man asked.

"More like a rough year," the man said with a smirk.

"I hear yah." The blind man shoveled a forkful of salad into his mouth. The man could see his reflection in the opaque blackness of the blind man's wraparound sunglasses. He looked fine. He felt tired. Beat down to the bone kind of tired. *Must be the job, he thought. I need a vacation.*

His dining companion ate with gusto. The man placed his food order. The blind man took a long drink of lemon water. The man made himself comfortable. The blind man dabbed his mouth with his cloth napkin and then sniffed the air a couple of times before he spoke.

"Listen, I consider myself a good judge of character and you seem like a nice fellah. That's why I'm going to turn you on to something that's going to make your life better."

"You're going to give me the winning lottery numbers?"

The blind man chuckled. "Not quite but something almost as good." The blind man turned his head right, pausing for a moment as if listening to the wind. Then he turned his head left, and did the same. "Lean in close so nobody can hear us."

The man did as instructed.

"I've got some of the baddest weed ever grown," the blind man said in a clear whisper.

"Really," the man whispered back.

"No doubt; you won't find any better; no way, no how."

"And?"

"I'm going to let you have some of this amazing bud for a rock bottom price. 'Cause I like you."

"Let me check it out?"

They straightened. Under the table, the blind man slipped the man a Beech Nut chewing tobacco bag. The man peeked inside and took a whiff. It was definitely marijuana. He pocketed the evidence.

"How much?"

"Normally that bag goes for a grand, but I'll let you have it for eight hundred because I like you so much."

"Price seems a bit steep to me."

"Not for this ganja. It's golden. That's four ounces of premium smoke you're holding."

"What's your name?" the man asked.

"Doctor Feel Good at your service," the blind man said with a salesperson's grin.

"Well, Doctor Feel Good, my name's Officer Darvell."

"You've got to be kidding."

"And you're under arrest."

"Something must be wrong with my nose."

"Why's that?"

"I can usually smell a pig a mile away."

The Poet's Touch

There are no lawns in my neighborhood. Trees and sidewalks and disconnected houses don't exist. No butterflies flutter over the gravel lots flourishing with weeds fertilized by fractured bricks and shattered glass. The grasshoppers are a sick green coexisting with an omnivorous insect kingdom. Pigeons are abundant, along with rats, roaches and houseflies. Step through our narrow front doorway and your foot lands on a concrete step, a step that doubles as a stoop on hot summer days. Take another step and you're on Title Street, a road barely roomy enough for one lane of traffic. I live here along with my younger sisters, Twanee and Preea and Moms. My name is Malik.

School starts next week. I'll be a senior. Next January, before I graduate, I'll be eighteen. My body's gotten too long for the narrow single bed I'm sitting on in my cramped room. I have to bend my knees to get all of me on it. This is my sanctuary. For the last three days, it's been my prison. No visitors or telephone calls allowed only meals and bathroom privileges, moms' orders. I'm getting stir crazy. Moms' sentence is up tomorrow. When I'm free, first thing I'm doing is taking a long walk to *nowhere*.

I'm confined because Tate and I stole a car. Tate's the one who actually *stole* it. I went along for the ride. Tate's in Juvee, it's his third time caught stealing cars. I was placed on probation being a first-timer.

I love Tate, but he can be a fool sometimes. He's impulsive, hardheaded, fickle and silly. I'm pretty much the opposite, except I'm hardheaded, too.

When Tate and I roam, running our mouths, we sometimes wind up walking as far away as downtown. There are tasty vehicles everywhere downtown. Tate gets a fever when he's 'round great looking cars. He *has* to have one. If I'm lucky, I can talk him out of stealing one. When I'm not, I let him be. Occasionally I catch his fever. That's what happened last week. Moms says, "Knowing somebody's a fool is one thing. Following a fool being a fool makes you a bigger fool than he is. "That's how I felt when five-o rolled up on us.

He sits in the sharp corner
bare knees drawn tight
to hairless chest
strapped in place
by angular arms . . .

Dawn is near. Everyone in the house is asleep. A film of moisture coats my window. My neighborhood's quiet. Nobody's kicking nobody's ass. There are no gunshots or suckers arguing or screaming sirens or Gangsta Rap heckling my muse. It's quiet as snowfall.

Amused eyes watch
soothing raindrops
drip
drip
from the jagged tip
of a single
remaining
sliver of glass,
lodged stubbornly
in the saturated
wooden cross . . .

In my sanctuary, I harbor a secret life, one that began in Fourth grade. We were asked to choose a poem from a photocopied collection of poetry that our English teacher Mrs. Browning had put together. She had made enough copies for each of us. We had until Friday of that week to pick five poems, only one of which she would assign for us to memorize and recite in front of the entire class. And no one was allowed to recite the same poem.

Most of the kids thought as I did. They wanted the shortest, easiest poems in the collection. Some of the words were hard for me then. Moms helped me learn them, and explained what each poem meant, even though her explanations were sometimes more perplexing than the poem she was trying to clarify. But there was a way she read each poem, made me feel connected to words for the first time in my life. Without intending, you might say, Moms was responsible for my first interlude with creative passion.

> *The sound of crying*
> *must resemble that shape,*
> *he thinks;*
> *the touch of loneliness*
> *the kiss of war . . .*

Incident was actually last on my list. *Life, Rhapsody, The Poet Speaks* and *Tableau* were already taken by children fortunate enough for their last names not to start with "W" for Wingate. It could've been worse. If none of your five poems were available when it came time to choose, Mrs. Browning made your choice for you. Typically, Tate forgot to do his assignment. Mrs. Browning assigned him *Frederick Douglass*, a poem five stanzas long. Tate choked on it like a broke-neck chicken.

I practiced *Incident* so many times I could actually recite it last line first to first line last. But when I stood in front of the class, I almost pissed my pants. My knees shook, throat went dry, palms sweated and I drew a blank. 'Til this day I believe Mrs. Browning knew something in that mystical way some adults instinctively recognize a trait or ability in children. First she smiled—and Mrs. Browning don't smile. Then she winked at me over the flat of her half-mooned eyeglasses. My thoughts honed in on my mother's voice. Moms had explained how that boy must've felt on that day in Boston. A child no older than I was then, in a strange place, wanting only to be accepted for who he was. Something simmered in me, similar to anger but more focused and less destructive. I took a deep breath and it came out. While I remember hearing my voice, feeling my vocal chords inflect each syllable, I don't remember reciting *Incident*.

Dank air shifts

sweeping bemused dust
toward a pale sky.
Dust,
destined to cultivate
his isolated sanctuary . . .

Teacher's pet I've never been. But when I finished, Mrs. Browning applauded. She rushed to me from the back of the room, where she judged each reading, and enthusiastically shook my hand between her own. With her fleshy arm around my shoulder she went on to explain to the rest of the class what I had just exhibited, and exhorted them to tap that fire which she claimed, burned in all of us. Some tried. There were four kids I thought were very good. Mrs. Browning only seemed mildly impressed. After class, she thanked me again for such an inspirational reading. I remember feeling awkward and wishing she wouldn't make such a fuss.

What stuck most in my mind was how my friends treated me afterwards. You would have thought I'd grown a huge mole in the center of my forehead. Some told me, in their own fourth graders' fashion, how they felt about my recitation skill. Lana and Aaliyah were the only ones who congratulated me. Their being girls only made the ribbing from my male friends worse. Tate asked if I really liked that stuff—in reference to poetry. I shot back, "Are you kidding," balling up *Incident* with the big blue A+ I had intended to show Moms and tossing it in the nearest trash can. Every time I think of sharing my passion with anyone, I remember that day and freeze that thought to thaw at a more auspicious time.

Light,
dull as used dishwater
shades outside
inside
and darkness;
harboring culprits
disguising villains
who often delight his eye . . .

My sisters know I read poetry. So does Moms. Twanee hasn't told anyone because she doesn't care. Preea considers it stupid and fears the embarrassment she'll suffer if any of her friends find out. Moms thinks it's sweet but keeps quiet about it because I asked her to. What none of them knows is that I also write poetic prose.

Hovering in the distance
behind the lonesome glass
a willing willow
blows wet
friendly kisses
toward his crystalline flesh . . .

I started writing poetry last year. A day doesn't go by when I don't find time to work on one.

His narrow head
slowly falls back
synchronized with the blinding
of melancholy eyes.
Sinful must dampens his palate
tickles pitch eyebrows
and dimples ends of an operculate
crescent moon smile.
They'll never find me here,
he thinks,
in this toy box room
hiding inside myself . . .

The soft luminance of dawn touches my window, backlighting my pallid curtains through misted glass. I lay my spiral notebook of poems upon my ratty shag carpet with reverence. "Solitaire," a revelation in progress, bares its thoughts to the stucco ceiling. Ten thousand plastered tears point in wonder. As quietly as possible, I part my curtains and open the window. Wood stubbornly scratches against wood in an abrasive yawn. Its sound stirs not a soul. Dew drips from its paint chipped frame. Air fondles me with cool, delicate fingers. I manage to position myself so my chin rests in the valley of my folded arms; my feet settled flat on the floor; my eyes witness to a virgin sunrise. This compassionate morning light declares my day of emancipation. I sense oneness. There is no separation between the light and myself. My neighborhood is quiet, and I am saddened by the thought that this moment will soon pass.

Job Search

My name is Jerome Green. Most people call me Jay. Family and close friends call me Jerome. I don't have a girlfriend and am not in the market right now. I'm hardworking and open to exploring my options. At five-ten, I'm in good shape, with brown skin, brown eyes, tight dreads, and a devilish smile. I enjoy movies, music, reading, texting, video games and chatting, prime time television and sports. I have no love for reality TV, social media, TV talk shows, talk radio or negative folks. If I were to fill out an online profile that's cursory me in a nutshell.

I just turned twenty-two and celebrated small and big time. Big time on my birthday at my parents' house with a home cooked birthday meal. Topped off with plenty of gifts and my favorite homemade chocolate birthday cake. Big bro, Eli and big sis, Madison were there along with sis-in-law, Alexis and Madison's fiancé, Gregg. It was big fun. But then I love my family and they love me back so what else would it be.

Small time the next night with friends at Club Diva in an all-night epic blow out. At least what I remember about it was. I can't believe how little I'm feeling the effects from a club night drink fest. I guess drinking as much water as I could stomach and taking a couple of multi-vitamins along with four aspirin before going to sleep actually worked. After my involuntary morning purge, besides being a bit sluggish, I feel fine. Not much of an appetite though.

I want to call Monica. She's a woman I met at Club Diva. One reason

I haven't called or texted Monica yet is my phone died. I'm waiting for it to recharge. The other reason is kind of strange.

Turning twenty-two is not a big deal. I don't feel any different. Nothing changes as far as the law and society are concerned. That nothing includes for me a single lingering question that has been plaguing me since I graduated high school. What am I going to do with my life?

No one's sweating me. I mean, I'm holding my own. Taking care of myself across the board, physically, financially, and spirituality to some degree. Right now, I'm exploring my options in the spiritual department. Nothing new about that. I've been searching for enlightenment since the eighth grade. While the three major world religions are still on the table there are a few less notables out there that make a great deal of sense. So far, nothing's grabbed me by the ecclesiastical shoulders and pinned me down.

I started learning about Drafting and Design in high school. Earned my associate degrees in Drafting and Design, and Information Technology from a high prestige technical college. I enjoyed the educational process. I was learning new things in a hands-on environment and I embraced the challenge of being a double major. Once I earned my degrees and quickly found gainful employment with a multi-discipline design-engineering firm the fun stopped. I'm bored. Cranking out product as quickly as you can get it out of the door isn't rocking my world. It's not even raising the roof. I'm good at it. It would be easy to turn it into a successful career. The major problem is I don't want to.

Switching over to IT would be like jumping out of a lifeboat to swim ashore. The people who work in IT always appear stressed. Not to mention under appreciated. The only time they're noticed is when something goes wrong. Even the thanks they receive for resolving a technical issue seems derisive as if they were personally responsible for the glitch in the first place. My dad would call it going from the frying pan into the fire. I'll stay put for now.

My mom has this great upbeat expression she graced the family with on many a morning, "Today is the best day of the rest of your life. Make the most of it." Sometimes mom was right. Other times mom was wrong. Most of my days have been fair to middling. In any case, her intention is clear. Have a positive mindset for the day. Like seeing the glass as full rather than half empty. I know the expression. Is the glass half-empty or half full? Pessimism versus optimism. With the major optimistic spin my mom puts out there half full doesn't cut it. That mindset works pretty well for Eli and

Madison. Me, I'm working on maintaining a half full prospective.

Eli knew what he wanted to be by the time he entered eleventh grade. International finance was his calling. Eli wanted to help underdeveloped nations get on their economic feet. Eli just turned thirty this year. He's already a success in the international banking community. Respected and appreciated by his so-called "third world" clients as well. My big bro is living his professional dream.

Madison realized she wanted to be a microbiologist by the time she was in the tenth grade. At twenty-six, big sis is already working for the CDC. A dream job for Madison. I've talked to them about how they made their career choices and it all came down to one word, passion. They love what they do. That's what I've been searching for, that passion, that love of something to emerge and jumpstart me on the path of my future. So far, everywhere I've looked, nothing. Not a spark, not a trickle, not a light bulb moment pointing to my purpose in life, and I don't know what to do about it.

Jarmal and Khyree are adrenaline junkies who are buenos amigos of mine. The higher the risks. The greater the rewards in their mind. They will go to extremes to feed their habit even if it means breaking the law. Their motto is they would rather die living than live to survive. That's too extreme for me but I get where they're coming from. Life requires purpose in order to have meaning. That's what gives life its intensity, its strut, its focus, its manna if you will. It's what Jarmal and Khyree call a rush. Without it, you're little more than a zombie going through the motions.

Last week, I went through online post-graduate curriculums for a number of colleges and universities around the country. History, music, skilled trades, philosophy, agriculture, language, astronomy, religion, fitness, law, physics, literature, the environment, business, mathematics, engineering, social services, education, psychology, liberal arts, sociology, computer sciences, biology, communication and health care. All of these studies interest me but more as hobbies rather than lifelong professions. Not even the do-it-yourself degrees enlivened my curiosity. I'm seeking that perfect balance of creative, physical and mental. Something to connect with my soul.

My family and friends keep telling me to be patient. Sooner or later something will give. It's the later rather sooner part that concerns me. I expect to marry and raise a family. I don't want to be middle-aged stuck in some survival job for the sake of a paycheck and marginal benefits. Doing what is required to get by sounds like hell to me, or at least prison. I want to tackle this issue while there is still time to get out in front of it. I want to know there is work out there for me that makes me glad to be alive. A mission in life that gives me purpose. Something that makes me dismiss any-and-all bullshit that might accompany the profession because the gratification outweighs the grief.

I expected by now a career would have revealed itself to me. My aim in life. My calling. So far, everywhere I've looked, everywhere I've turned, nothing. Do I settle? Do I keep hope and expectation alive? Meditation, creative visualization, prayer and the like teach us that ultimately these answers come from within. I believe a light must burst through the darkness to draw out your fate. My star has not yet arrived. I've always expected my passion to find me, not the other way around. I'm already losing patience at twenty-two.

I've shared my search for purpose dilemma with a number of people, including Monica. To be perfectly honest, had I not had too much to drink I wouldn't have been that open to someone I just met. Even if I was strongly attracted to her. Monica seemed to think my quest for a meaningful career might be a symptom of a much larger question. That question being "What is the meaning of life?"

I can't say Monica is mistaken although I've never phrased it quite that way. Now that she's introduced that enormous enquiry into the mix, what *is* the meaning of life? Is there meaning to life or is life simply counterpole to death. Is life a mere biological existence we experience no more or less than that of an animal or insect or plant? Along the way achieving momentary victories only to lose the war in the end. Do we actually exist to serve a purpose, have a fate, or do we exercise arrogance believing we possess immortality and that some omnipotent powers have granted us ownership of our planet and supposed moral authority dictating the fate of our eternal souls. Are we living the most elaborate fairy tale ever devised by humankind or is there truth to our fiction?

Religion is basically a foundation, code, or structure of tenets held to with devotion and conviction most often used to form a philosophy on how to conduct one's life. Your religion can be spiritual, moral, cosmic, natural, physical, material, or based upon any combination thereof. Even atheists practice a religion of sorts in choosing not to believe in God. Albeit the opposite of what is considered the norm of faith. Agnostics are more within a gray empirical area. Believing God to be an unprovable unknown thereby choosing not to commit to either the nonexistence or existence of any god. Bringing us back to the age-old question, did man create God or did God create man?

Is the major sum of our lives random coincidences in which our philosophy or religion plays a role in how we proceed, permitting us a false sense of control within the chaos? Who are we? What are we? Why are we here? Those broad esoteric queries lead me right back to what is my purpose in life. A mystery that is daunting but fascinating and kinda cool.

Do I believe? Yes. Why? Because I believe. Not because of the religious viewpoints, I've explored. Although most have powerful and positive moral and life lessons worth abiding by. For me it's a potent energy at my core. A chakra connection if you will to the universe that leaves me with no doubt. Immortality does exist. God mediates but does not dictate lives. How will I exercise my faith? Unknown at this time. I'm still exploring the possibilities. For the time being, I'm focused on the here and now rather than the hereafter.

Is it actually belief or acceptance? For those not wishing to look beyond the surface and explore the depths of the unknown uncording myriad questions leading to a maze of dead end answers. Acceptance is the key. In order to find peace one must accept certain aspects of their lives for what they are. Settle, I suppose, in most cases. One day, I will accept my fate and settle into the life I've made whatever it may be. That day is not today. That day is not in the foreseeable future.

I'm lucky and I know it. Many people are out there struggling to survive and here I am whining about not being able to find direction. Guilt tripping don't make my dilemma any less real to me. Some people think I'm too young to worry about this stuff. I disagree. Now is the time to choose a firm direction and fully apply myself to the voyage. Now, not later, when the die is cast. When asked where I see myself in five, ten, twenty years from now I don't have a clue. What I do know is I don't see myself cranking out product like some automaton.

Maybe my spiritual exploration and job fulfillment quest do go hand-in-hand. If I discover a belief system in league with my soul then maybe all other matters in my life will align. Maybe, maybe, maybe, who knows? I certainly don't at the moment.

Monica had come to my place sharing an Uber car. I asked Monica if she wanted to spend the night. She declined. Her reason was she needed to look in on Pebbles and Barney, her Burmese cats. I sensed Monica was embarrassed. Like me, one-night stands obviously weren't her thing. Monica and I made this weird pact in parting. We agreed not to contact each other for three days. Why three days? I don't know. Somehow, we reasoned that three days would be an appropriate cooling off period. That would be sufficient time for the one-night stand buzz to wear off and clear our heads. Help us determine if what we had was one night of fever sex or something more. I blame our rationale on the booze.

The fact I'm still thinking about Monica answers it for me. I'm itching to call her. Set up a face-to-face date. I'm not a player or a dog but I do occasion a one-night stand. Monica and I were having a great time even before we hit the sheets. It would be cool to discover our sleeping together wasn't only about too much liquor and mutual horniness. If my hunch is right, then meeting Monica would make my small time night huge.

I sent Monica home in a taxi. Why? I trust taxi service more than Uber when it comes to precious cargo. I don't know why, I just do.

I walked Monica out to the taxi. Made a mental note of the cab driver's description, got his name from his ID, Andres Gallegos, and the make, model, color, license plate of his car. I already knew the name of the cab company since I called them. I even made sure he had a seat belt in the back seat, buckling Monica in with a kiss. I had Andres give me an estimate on how much the trip would cost. I gave Monica double that amount in cash despite her objections. Made her promise to call—not text—me once she was safely inside. Monica ribbed me for being old-fashioned. Guilty as charged. I'm unabashedly old-fashioned in some matters. I get the chivalry gene from dad.

Once Monica called then I could sleep. Strange way to behave for a woman I just met. As far as I'm concerned, my head is clear and I'm ready for contact. I'm hoping Monica feels the same.

My digital pipeline is charged and ready to go. Time to plug in.

Whoa! My phone has been blowing up. I'll check my text messages first. Let's see mom, dad, bro, sis, Abia, Alex, Beers, Ben, Big O, Double Shot, Ella, Gab, G-man, Hunter, Jarmal, JM, Khyree, Lisa, Little B, Maisie—Monica, cool! For those of you not familiar with texting lingo, I'll translate:

"I know we're supposed to wait three days before contacting each other. I'm squashing that idea. I had a great time last night. Just wanted to let you know. Thanks for the tips about vitamins, water, and aspirin. They helped a lot. Besides being a little sluggish, I'm feeling fine. Not much of an appetite, though. How are you feeling, Jerome? Call me when you have a chance."

Damn right, I'll call. I've gotta jet. I guess making money will be my goal for now. My career inspiration. I hope I didn't bore you too much with my quest for purpose drama. About finding my life's passion. Got any ideas?

Love

My father died three months ago. It had taken me that long to collect my share of his inheritance from what was now my mother's house. I opened the last box willed to me by my father. Eleven white cardboard storage boxes spread out over the living room all filled to capacity with 8x9 burgundy leather, double page, picture pocket, photo albums. Each album had been stored on edge, wrapped in thick white cotton and separated by thin pieces of polished hickory. The twelfth and final box was filled halfway with the same items. The photographs and photography equipment were all my dad had left his favorite child. I looked around the room at the sum worth of my father's life. I hadn't expected much. I hoped to leave my children more.

My father was a man of simple needs, and plain desires, with bronze colored skin, a clean-shaven face and close-cropped hair. He was a sinewy man in his youth that became more and more robust through his middle and twilight years. His taut features were menacing when he scowled, joyful when he smiled. Most times, he seemed pensive, as if being secretly amused by mischievous characters. Time taught us how to read beneath the skin.

Dad felt most comfortable in Bib overalls, a cotton work shirt, and leatherwork boots. His hands were thickly callused from as far back as I could remember, but his face remained youthful right up until the end.

My father had great hands and an ability to learn quickly. Gifts that steered him toward being a lifelong laborer who did whatever work came his way. His excellent reputation of doing high quality, timely work and his variety of labor skills kept him in high demand. I learned about hard work, focus, determination and doing things to the best of my ability from my father. I was also blessed with his gifts.

As I said before, my father was a man of simple needs, and plain desires. That was why it took our family by surprise when he developed an interest in photography. At every opportunity, my father had told his tale of how it began. Even my children had come to know the story by heart. It had become an annoyance to me over the years. *Who cares?* I had thought but never said. I wished he were here to tell his story now.

Photography became his passion by accident. While doing yard work for a wealthy family he discovered a camera in the trash. Dad rescued the 35 mm Nikon S3M with a NIKKOR-O 2.1 cm f / 4 wide-angle lens and several unopened rolls of 35mm 400 color film. The camera had a few nicks and scratches but dad believed he could clean it up and sell it.

Turned out, the camera was broken. Somehow, dad fixed it even though he knew nothing about cameras at the time. In his version mom, my older sister and brother, and me, were tripping over each other to pose for him while he made certain the camera worked properly. The truth was he made us pose for him, and then took forever to snap the picture. Only after he had taken the two rolls of pictures did dad realize he knew nothing about developing film.

That didn't stop my father. Uncle David knew a liberal arts professor at Lincoln University who was glad to develop the pictures for him. The professor was pleased with the results. He believed my father had a natural gift and was willing to teach him free of charge. My father declined. Taking pictures did not feed his family. The professor insisted on showing dad how to develop photos. My father agreed, if the professor would allow him to repay him with labor. A deal was struck. Less than six months after his discovery, my brother and I helped my father build a darkroom in the farthest corner of our country backyard. (That meant we built it in the farthest cleared area in the back of our house.) We also helped install all of the darkroom equipment supplied to my father by the professor as part of an amendment to their original deal.

Photography was an extravagance we could not afford. The professor found all sorts of creative ways to exchange photography supplies for labor so that my father could continue his passion while preserving his dignity. That may have explained why dad remained frugal throughout his life with his picture taking. He behaved as if he was still exchanging labor for it. Every photo I'd see him take, he would wait for just the right moment to snap the picture.

Between work and chores, my dad had little free time. What there was of it, he usually spent with us. Photography began to consume most of our quality time. My brother, sister and I didn't mind—when we had free time— we mostly hung out with our friends. Mom took it personally. She'd sometimes hide his camera from him, forcing dad to spend quality time with her before she would tell him where it was, although she never came out and stated her motives. Once dad caught on to her reasoning, he stopped getting angry and enjoyed the game. In no time, dad started putting mom first again.

Dad was always anxious to share his latest forays into photography with anyone in the family who would listen. Mom, my sister and my brother let him know they were not interested. I wasn't interested either but I didn't have the heart to tell him. Every time dad had a breakthrough, I was the first—and often the last—to hear about it. At first, I listened with a vacant ear as dad went on and on about aperture, shutter speeds, perspective, lenses, lighting, film selection, flashes, viewfinders, frames per second, and other photographer speak that I would give a sporadic smile or nod to as if I understood. On occasion, dad would drive home his point by letting me take a picture, something no one else in the family was allowed to do with his equipment.

Along the way, osmosis must have kicked in because I actually comprehended what my father was saying. My brother still kids me about that being the deciding factor behind dad declaring me his favorite.

I am my father's son. I look like him, and in many ways, behave as he did. My mother knows it. My sister and brother know it, and so does my wife. All-in-all, I had to go along with big brother's deduction on why dad called me his favorite.

For his 48th birthday, my brother and sister were stumped about what to get our father. I knew what I was getting him and was happy to influence their gift choices. I gave my father a brand new Nikon F3 Titan finished in champagne chrome, and a Nikon Zoom 70-210mm f / 4.0 Series E lens. I persuaded my brother to give him a Zoom-Nikkor 360-1200mm f / 11 ED-IF1.4 lens and a Nikon Speedlight SB-14 external electronic flash with the SD-7 battery pack. Big sister added the final touches with a large black leather gadget bag, a mini tripod, lens care kit, extra batteries, forty rolls of

35 mm color and eight rolls of 35 mm black-and-white film. Our mother was proud. Our father was overwhelmed. With tears of joy, he hugged each of his children so hard he nearly cracked our ribs.

The rest of the day dad kept us abreast of each newly discovered feature as he poured through the manuals. The only time he talked about anything else was during his birthday dinner. That was because mom teased that she would toss his "new toys" in the trash if he kept going on about "that stuff" during his dinner celebration. From desert on, dad was back on par.

As excited as my dad was about his new camera, he used his old camera to take pictures with that day. Dad said he needed time to digest his new camera before using it. I remember being disappointed, but I didn't show it. A couple of months later, dad and mom paid me a surprise visit. Dad was snapping photos with his new Nikon as if he'd had it for years.

Dad never lost the zeal to develop his own film. Taking his negatives to a place for someone else to bring to life what he had captured made no sense to him. He appreciated the process as much as he did taking the photos. With childlike giddiness, dad told me, "Developing my own pictures, is like being handed wrapped unexpected gifts. Even when you think you know what's inside, there are always surprises."

My father died as he lived, working with his hands. At age 76, he was helping a friend patch his roof when he fell. His neck was broken. The coroner said he died instantly. It wasn't until after I viewed the body that I could accept he was gone.

I surveyed the room. My wife would not stand for the clutter I saw, even if it represented the majority of the estate my father willed to me. I had left the lids off the boxes, which made it look worse. I needed to clear them out before Deniece returned from back-to-school shopping with our teenagers. I decided to move the boxes to the basement for the time being.

Our basement was dry and clean, with plenty of storage space. On the south side of the basement was my workshop. Nearest that were my kid's bikes and a few miscellaneous items we needed on occasion. I placed my dad's photography equipment on the north side. He had never gotten rid of his original camera and lens. Mom said dad cleaned and used them once every year "to keep them in working order," as he put it. I stacked the boxes in threes near his equipment. That was where my father's inheritance would stay until Deniece and I could find a better place for them in our lives.

The naked bulb on the north side of the basement glowed like a dying sun in a cavernous darkness. Sunlight halted at the narrow basement windows. There was a hint of dust in the air. None of the boxes or albums had been dated or cataloged. That was unlike my father who was an organized and precise man. I presumed dad knew his photo collection like a carpenter knows his tools, by heart.

I carefully removed and unclothed a photo album at random. It fell open to one of the clear plastic sheets with photographs of Deniece and me when we were in high school. The one on the sofa at my parents' house made me laugh out loud. Deniece sat upright and very lady like. She was smiling and the light in her brown eyes could have ignited a universe. I was slouched on the couch trying to look cool. Not gangsta like so many of the youth today, but a laid back, nonchalant kind of cool. I would have been better off just being my silly self. Come to think of it, that's exactly what I was doing. I was imitating Brian Worlds, the man who stole Michele Miller from me. At least that was the way it was in my version of the story. The truth be told, I never had a prayer with Michele.

I could not take my eyes off Deniece in that sofa picture. I couldn't believe how young we looked. It didn't happen overnight. I mean, I cared about Deniece, and we got along well on a personality and intellectual level and all that, but I didn't love her. Not in the way a man loves a woman he wants to marry. As a matter-of-fact, I didn't expect to love her. So why did I marry her before I fell in love with her?

In the beginning, we were passing acquaintances. We attended the same high school and the same church. A summer party at a mutual high school friend's house changed all of that. Deniece had her eye on Tyrone Davis. I had my eye on Michele Miller. Both of us struck out to the more popular high school jock and cheerleader. While Deniece and I did well in our social circles, we could not compete with the high school elite. Since Michelle was a cheerleader and Tyrone was our star running back, our failures to make love connections should have come as no surprise. What is surprising in retrospect is that neither of us seemed broken up about it. After dancing with a variety of other people at the party Deniece and I found our way to each other.

Deniece was thin then, not anorexic, but more like lean. She had caramel skin and deep brown eyes. Things I hadn't noticed at first because I was so fixated on Michelle Miller. Her face was very expressive, so were her eyes. Her smile was wide and crooked, sometimes resembling a sneer. She had a pinched flat nose that went well with her crooked smile and round face. The two things that immediately drew me closer to Deniece were she laughed at all of my jokes that so few others got, and she had a great hearty laugh, which surprised me since her voice was a bit reedy. Our friendship was instant.

All during high school, Deniece and I dated other people. We talked openly about our relationships before, during and after the breakups. We went out on several dates as friends during high school. There wasn't a time in high school I didn't consider Deniece more than a friend except on graduation night. We were at our high school graduation party when it dawned on me that I might never see her again. I became dismayed by the prospect. I didn't tell Deniece how I felt. Instead, I monopolized as much of her time as I could that night. She didn't seem to mind. Maybe she felt as I did.

Separate colleges led to separate lives. We did much of our catching up during holidays and summer vacations when we would resume our friendship full bore. Deniece changed during her college years. Her figure blossomed in a complimentary way. Her mind was always sharp but now she had a broader range of topics she liked to discuss. Our light-hearted high school banter evolved into serious philosophical, political, social and scientific discussions. I found myself in a daze sometimes when she talked. I knew Deniece was brilliant but she had also become beautiful. My physical attraction to her became a constant disturbance to me. We started holding hands a lot. We would put our arms around each other as we walked and talked, and we would talk for hours. While we kept referring to ourselves as good friends, both of us knew there was something stronger brewing underneath. Fall arrived too soon and we were forced to return to our separate lives.

College wasn't hard, just boring. I dropped out after my sophomore year. A paper pushing future wasn't for me. I missed working with my hands. I wanted to be a carpenter. My family was disappointed. Dad could relate to my choice even though he emphasized he had wanted better for me. Mom conceded when she saw carpentry would make me happy. My brother thought I was wasting my potential. He always believed I would make a hell of an engineer. My sister argued that a professional career would be more stable and lucrative in the long run. I didn't know about that logic. In the end, they gave me their support. I went to trade school.

It was that summer following my dropping out when it happened. Deniece and I were talking about the movie I had just taken her to see. I don't remember the name of it, but it was a romantic comedy of her choosing. We were being silly re-enacting one of the scenes that concluded with a kiss. We kissed. The moment stilled, we both looked scared as if we had just stumbled onto a dead body. We were able to babble our way onto another topic until our comfort zone was restored. Then life went on, as we knew it, or so I thought.

I could not stop thinking about that kiss. Deniece confessed it had aroused feelings in her she had not realized existed until that moment. That summer changed our lives forever. That summer, we became lovers.

I thought about Deniece a lot when she returned to school. We talked twice a week on the phone, and wrote each other almost every day telling of the day's events. I visited her on weekends at Fisk whenever time and circumstances permitted. Besides taking a full class load, I worked part-time doing whatever manual labor I could find of which there was plenty. Deniece had a part-time job tutoring other college students. My old pick-up wasn't good for long distance trips. I was too proud to ask my parents to borrow their car, so I usually took the train. Most times my visit lasted only a day. They were always worth it. Her smile alone was worth the trip. In many ways, our relationship remained on a best friend's level. While we professed how much we missed each other, neither of us ever used the word love.

I was able to visit Deniece once every two weeks until I landed a carpenter apprentice position with a local housing construction firm. That forced me into night school. Deniece suggested she could come home every other weekend instead of me having to be the one to always make the effort. I insisted on paying for her trips. She agreed. Everyone won. Her family was as happy to see her every other week, as was I.

The year of graduations was hectic. Deniece and I graduated at the same time. We saw little of each other. Deniece was interviewing for teaching internships all over the country. To my surprise, my carpentry skills had been touted over the construction grapevine. The buzz was leading to job offers all over the country. Whether it was coincidence, fate, providence or karma, we both accepted positions in Detroit before we knew the other's plans.

Deniece first told me she loved me during our wedding dance. I told her I loved her. I didn't feel it, but I meant it. Our lives went on that way for years. Through the good and bad, sickness and in health, we endured, prospered, grew closer and . . . .

I closed the photo album from which one picture had generated a swell of memories. Just as my father had done, I wrapped it lovingly in its thick white cotton blanket and placed it gently on edge between two thin pieces of polished hickory. I could not guess at my father's intentions for taking so many photographs. Was it mere passion, or was this his way of chronicling the history of his life, and in the process, capturing the people he cared for?

Guilt swept over me as I placed the lid on the box. Twelve boxes representing a lifetime stacked before me. I felt ashamed for having thought that I needed to will more to my children than my father had left me. I would be fortunate to do as well.

The Nikon F3 Titan felt foreign in my hands, even though my father had allowed me to take a few photos with it along the way. I attached the lens and turned it on. It powered up immediately. The battery was fully charged and there were eight shots left on a twenty-four 35 mm 400 color roll. I removed the lens cap and took aim at the twelve boxes.

"Wait. Is that the photograph you want?" It was my father's voice. I searched for him in the cool basement light. I was alone. A warm light ran up my spine. I took a deep breath, thought for a moment. "No," I heard myself say. I stepped to the right twice and took aim again. It still was not quite right. I bent at the knees with the subject still in focus, seeking just the right lighting and perspective. The dull yellow light in the basement surrounded the white boxes like a quiet aura. "Almost," my dad whispered into my ear. I took one small step backward. The limestone wall gave the still more depth and texture. "What do you think?" he asked. "What do you think?" I asked him. "This is your photograph, son. You're calling the shots from here on out." I took one small step to my right and back. "Perfect," I thought the moment I took the picture. "How was that?" I asked. I felt the firm weight of my dad's hand my shoulder. "You'll know when the gift is unwrapped," he said.

I took the same approach with each photo I took in the basement. Positioning and re-positioning myself, waiting for just the right instant before capturing the still. By the time Deniece and the kids got home, I had attached the electronic flash, finished the roll left in the camera and had started another. I felt an enthusiasm about taking pictures I had never felt before. I found the camera strap in my father's camera bag and hooked it onto the camera. I slipped the camera around my neck, grabbed my dad's gadget bag and headed upstairs. Even though his photography equipment and photographs were legally mine, I still saw them as my father's. Perhaps in time that would change. Just as in time my wife and children may become patient with my new shutterbug hobby.

The next morning, I managed to sneak up on my wife. If her high school students had seen her then they would have run for cover. Her hair was a crown of pink hair rollers. She was wearing her fuzzy bunny slippers, her grandma robe, no makeup, enjoying her Wheaties, chamomile tea with honey, toast with strawberry jam and orange juice while reading the Sunday paper. Her body had burgeoned from age and the birth of two children. The children were still asleep. It was her quiet time.

Her uneven skin tones were more prevalent without makeup. She chewed on one side of her mouth making it look more crooked. There was intensity in her brown eyes as she read the Sunday newspaper. A fire raging back to her youth, I felt it in my stomach, throughout my chest and abdomen, emanating from my heart. For the first time I knew I loved Deniece. Somehow, I managed to sneak up on her and take a photo. She protested. I slipped in behind her to give her a hug and peck on the cheek, after setting the camera down out of her reach. I smelled apricot on her skin. She let out that warm sigh I liked so much before asking me why I was up so early.

Sunday was my only late sleep in day. I usually milked it until a messenger—usually in the form of my son—came to me with his mother's dire warning that if I didn't get up now we were going to be late for church.

"I love you," I said. Her crooked smile made my love grow stronger.

"I know," she said. "I love you, too."

I joined my love for breakfast after promising not to take any more pictures of her "looking like such a mess."

Writer in the Attic

On a humid Friday late summer evening, gnats dance around flaming streetlights. The air is as still as silent wind chimes. Come the weekend lawns will be mowed, trees and bushes pruned, gardens tended and hedges trimmed. Home and vehicle maintenance projects will be tackled by the do-it-yourselfers. Honey-do lists will be addressed by some, procrastinated on by others. Phalanxes of curb aligned parked vehicles lacquered in metallic colors mainly borrowed from nature are settled in on both sides of the landscaped median strip, electro-mechanical troops awaiting their orders. A determined teenage bicyclist with blond tipped dreads almost to his waist pedals by in allegro legato rhythm wearing blood red basketball shorts, expensive sneakers, an orchid T-shirt exclaiming "GRATEFUL LIFE!" and no safety helmet; the lingering buzz of his bike dissolving in the moist air in his wake. Vehicles roll to with their white headlights proceeding and red brake lights glowing as they recede. When vehicles are not passing through, the sounds of music, voices and televisions are low keyed, floating from open screened windows and doors. Without the intermittence of sound, a silence hovers over Lambert Boulevard, the sort of hush that can be ripped open by a telephone ringing from across the street.

It's difficult to believe that Lambert Boulevard exists within the city limits. Aside from the intimate proximity of homes, there are times when Lambert Boulevard could easily be mistaken for an out of the way suburb, not in populace but in the serenity of its atmosphere. A parked car stereo drowns out all other noises with a familiar song of the time blaring from its radio. The lemon yellow VW Beetle takes off screaming down the street with Noah the head bobbing adolescent rapping along.

The baritone voice of Mr. Grimes finds its way into the mix when his beckoning for Mrs. Grimes—who is somewhere inside their home—to help carry Wal-Mart bags goes unheeded. Mr. Grimes emphatically states for his wife not to say "a goddamn thing" if he loses that "gossip rag" she calls a newspaper. Mrs. Grimes still does not reply or lend a hand.

From the Barkov's house, one could hear an argument brewing. Valentin and Darya's voices carry out into the street. Their voices go from howls of laughter to bitter anger. Sharp verbal barbs prick each other's feelings by flinging insults and foolish events to the surface. With Valentin marching out onto their front porch to have a cigarette, the argument withers away to make its bid to blend into the silence Lambert seems to induce.

Like everyone in this neighborhood, we have at least two vehicles. I prefer to take the bus whenever possible. I enjoy writing on the bus. People will peek at what I'm jotting down on my laptop or notebook sometimes but most are discreet about it. That doesn't bother me. Interrupting my process does.

There's a sign posted on some buses that reads "Please Help Us Feed And Shelter The Homeless, Call 235-HELP, United Baptist Ministries, Take One." The ones to be taken are flyers telling people more about their shelter and ministry. There's a black-and-white photograph of a man seated at what I assume is a shelter table eating something off to the left of those words. He reminds me of a picture I had seen of Walt Whitman. White disheveled hair, albeit shorter than Whitman's, heavy mustache and a mischievousness glint in his eyes. As if immediately after the photograph was taken, this man went to his modern car and drove to his comfortable home to tell his family about the great joke he'd played on unsuspecting succors.

A destitute person clandestinely rustles through the trashcan on the side of Grange's home. The phrase "nothing more than ill winds traveled their way," comes to mind. How a person appearing as beaten down as that man made his way into this neighborhood undetected is beyond me. One can see his clothes and shoes are too big. Whether his wardrobe is ill fitting or malnutrition is the culprit is impossible to say. Even from a distance, I can tell he is in dire need of a shower and a Laundromat. Had I known he was coming I would have prepared a care package to give him.

I was about to go downstairs and try to get his attention when Jerry Grange caught him and ran him off. The poor dude snatched up his gunnysack half filled with whatever and took flight faster than I would have ever expected. Appearing hobbled, his getaway looked more like a hurried duck waddle than a run. Jerry's in good physical shape. If he wanted to apprehend him, he wouldn't have had any problem overtaking the man. From the looks of things, Jerry had simply wanted to scare him off.

While my city abounds in hills, Lambert Boulevard could be regarded as the city's version of The Plains, flat from one end to the other. An elderly, slightly hunchback, fearless woman marching straight ahead like an arrow shot from a bow, wearing green plaid pants and an ivory colored blouse, is out for her evening walk. That's Mrs. Marcella Davis, known as Marcie to her friends. Marcie takes her after dinner walk almost every day at about this time, winter, summer, spring or fall. Sometimes her husband, Joe, joins her but not tonight. Joe was probably plopped down in front of the TV on the leather recliner sofa of which he is so proud.

Marcie's fine white hair, meticulously harbored and groomed, diminishes her regal scowl, acerbic wit and damning disapproving glare granting her a false demeanor of high etiquette and culture. Anyone who knows Marcie knew she swore like a drunken sailor and at times drank like a fish. A well-groomed, conservatively dressed, Mormon couple could attest to those facts. They had the misfortune of disturbing her one afternoon during drinks and soap opera stories and Marcie let them have it with both barrels. Those poor people vamoosed as if they'd stumbled upon Satan and she'd invited them in for sin and damnation.

Evening is one of those times one can appreciate the wealth of trees in our area. They seem as bountiful as clouds on a rainy day. Elm trees loom over Lambert Boulevard like sheltering hands protecting it from harm. Pink and White Dogwoods extol their summer splendor as contestants in a beauty pageant. The Arbor Day newbie saplings of Bush Clovers, Hydrangeas, St. John's wort, Bluebeards and Seven-Sons meekly exist, their presence as noticeable as bashful children desiring attention. Attention they receive aplenty from an insect kingdom in search of food and shelter.

A few people come and go during the evening. A sky already sprinkled with stars and a hairline quarter-moon destined to peek out from the blue ink heavens of night. My grandmother once told me when I was very young that God used the tip of his thumbnail to slit the sky so he could pour a little of his golden light upon his children on special nights like these. This amounts to a rather typical mid-summer evening on Lambert Boulevard. A place I call home.

There are no mirrors in our home, not even in the bathroom, for vanity is not a characteristic of my beautiful wife, Olivia, who did the interior decorating of our love nest. The theory behind being a mirror-less household was "the only reflection one sees originates from one's mind, heart or soul," as Olivia so idealistically put it. When we need confirmation on our physical appearances we ask each other or literally use each other's eyes as mirrors. Of course, it's easy to cheat. There are enough glass and shiny surfaces in our home to usurp that modesty commitment.

Olivia works. I write and am a househusband, gardener and handy man. At least until I find a real job, according to my in-laws. Olivia makes great money as chairperson of Phillips Pharmaceuticals. A Fortune 500 company she founded, quite an accomplishment for someone just shy of thirty. I'm certified to teach primary and secondary English and do so on occasion as a substitute. Teaching only reminds me I'm a much better writer than teacher. A fact I'm not of the least bit ashamed.

There is the swell of creative promise in the warm nest of our home, a moment's opportunity for me to filter the world through my senses and reason, bringing life to a crawl, marinating its moments. Perched in my writing loft, also known as the attic of our three-story home, I lean back comfortably in my writing chair with an unobstructed view of the world I inhabit. A veil of gray provided by the roof overhang shades. My attic window enough to blind me from casual observers. Moving back just a bit from the window alters my shadow to a shroud of darkness making me virtually invisible. I survey in evening twilight the world in which I live.

Having grown-up black urban ghetto and now living what amounts to a rather quiet suburban existence has posed some writing challenges for me. Not being one who holds any sort of fascination or romanticized vision of my hard-luck life childhood, I have a tendency to create stories that encompass a more commonplace ghetto existence. I don't glorify gangstas, pimps, playas, niggahs, bitches, prostitutes or hoes like the entertainment media, but I do place their characters in the proper negative positions they often hold within run-down overpopulated communities. Much like a good deal of mainstream American entertainment, I do toss in characters that are loud, obnoxious, ignorant and proud of it. In short, the accepted current black American mainstream stereotypes of whom we are supposed to be as a people. They often provide comic relief in my stories, much like conventional entertainment.

Many of the black female characters that I incorporate into my stories—like those in my real life—can hold a conversation and debate without being domineering or losing their tempers or going ghetto on a brother. Juxtaposing my youth life with my adult life has been healthy and somewhat cathartic, which leaves me in a peaceful place. The same circumstances also manufacture a quandary. A quiet existence suits me perfectly. Peace is not the friend of a literary writer. Drama and conflict are. For that reason, I find myself jettisoning back to my impoverished days for inspirational grist as well as heeding those persistent injustices throughout the world.

A gold 1978 Lincoln Continental Mark V Diamond Jubilee edition rolls by with a dark green trash bag replacement for the rear driver's side window, giving the vehicle the equivalent of a black eye. I recognize the car because at one time I used to be what some would call a car fanatic but I preferred the term automobile historian. The limited classic edition pimp mobile reminded me of my ghetto life but the vagrant didn't. Perhaps it's because in poverty the homeless go unnoticed. Perhaps it's because there are fewer destitute rummaging in ghettoes because poor people have nothing to give, salvage, or maybe they just blend in.

A few doors down and across the street from us in the largest house on the block lives a highly successful surgeon by the name of William Ono. William insists everyone call him Billy. Billy is a fun loving, outgoing soul that loves to let the world in on who he is and what he does. His wife, Margaret, who Billy insists everyone but their children call Marge, is much more the introvert, although Marge is enamored with her husband's gregarious personality and playful ways.

Their oldest child, Conner, follows mostly in his mom's personality footsteps while their daughter, Serenity, is a chip off the dad block. It's difficult not to get caught up in the vibrant personality of Hurricane Billy. You find yourself belly laughing at things he says that if coming from the mouths of most people would barely generate a courtesy smile. Olivia says Billy could sell dirt to farmers if he had a mind to because people like him so much. The dirt to farmers statement goes a little far for my taste but it does characterize Billy's effect on people.

The Ono family has been away on a cruise vacation for almost two weeks. Everyone knows about their vacation plans because Billy and Serenity bragged about it to anyone who would listen. Fortunately, for them, we keep sharp eyes out for each other in this neighborhood so the chances of burglars taking advantage of their absence are close to nil. They're due back in a couple of days. The house still appears locked up tight from what I can see with no signs of forced entry. For their sake, I hope it will stay that way.

In the ghetto community of my youth there was a drug dealer known as The Medicine Man, his motto, "drugs for less." He has since been retired to a maximum-security prison for life on multiple counts of murder. A modern entertainment spin on this criminal entrepreneur would be to make him charismatic, even noble and enigmatic, endearing him to our youth and thereby—intentioned or not—as an example to follow. A tough as nails streetwise character who's doing what he needs to do to get by in those mean ghetto streets, and lending a helping hand in the community when he could. In short, he would be glamorized. Ignoring the truth that The Medicine Man was nothing more than a brutal, sadistic, exploitative, greedy leech who fed off everyone in his community to satisfy his own distorted desires. That was who that man really was, nothing more, nothing less. To depict him as a victim instead of persecutor does an injustice to all of the honest citizens within the community who struggle to get by with integrity and hard work. They are the real heroes, the stories worth telling. Theirs are the stories that I write; stories of ghetto strength of character and fortitude of soul. Now you may ask how I know The Medicine Man so well. In the best way human beings can get to know each other. He's family. The Medicine Man is my uncle.

Dog wanders into my loft like a prowler in search of loot. Our tan and chocolate Siamese came to keep me company. Something he did at times during prolonged writing stretches. Dog leaped into my lap uninvited as he often does when he wants attention, landing as if he were made of feathers. A familiar sweet, heady scent clings to him suggesting he had spent some time amongst our lilac trees.

Dog owns us, and he knows it. We've had him since he was a kitten. I pet him. He purrs as he makes himself comfortable. Dog can go in and out, as he wishes through his pet door. Whatever Dog had been doing made him ready for a nap. I ask my feline buddy how he's doing without taking my eyes off the world outside my window gently stroking his fine short fur. He purrs that life is good. At least that's my interpretation of his response. I've been wrong before. I continue petting Dog. His sinewy body goes limp as he dozes. Why name a cat Dog? Because I wanted a dog and Olivia wanted a cat.

My black ghetto father is a brilliant man who managed to feed, clothe and shelter my sister and me even after his wife, our mother, unexpectedly passed away from a cerebral hemorrhage when I was six. We lived in a ghetto up until my early teens. My dad taught my older sister and me just because we were growing up in poverty didn't mean we had to starve our minds, hearts and spirits. By the time my dad could afford to lift us out of the ghetto and into a blue collar middle-class community, my sister and I had made his teachings paramount in our lives.

My sister followed her passion and became a pediatrician, and a very successful one at that. Financial independence as a creative writer has managed to shirk me thus far. While I have a respectable list of compliments on the quality of my writing, and am pleased with much of what I've written up until this point, not commercially viable is the most constant refrain I here from solicited publishers, agents and editors. Discouraging but not surprising. I'm sure content wouldn't be a problem if I could get a celebrity to byline one of my novels. The question now is becoming do I sell out and go for, what amounts to in my mind as fool's gold. My current life headline reads Success Eludes Him like Justice for the Poor.

Olivia comes from money as the saying goes. Her father made millions during the internet boom and was wise enough to know when to marginalize his investments. Her mother was part owner of a nationwide fast food franchise that was unloaded at its peak. Olivia had wanted to clear her own path, so while she accepted the amenities of wealth up through college, it wasn't long after graduating with her MBA from Harvard and her MS in Pharmacology from Georgetown that she make her move. After working a couple of years in the Johnson and Johnson labs, Olivia decided to become her own boss. With financial backing from her parents, Olivia started Phillips Pharmaceuticals, taken from her middle name. Brilliant, aggressive, resourceful and educated, Olivia is made for business success. Believe it or not, being wealthy and business driven were primary reasons I never wanted to date my wife.

What changed my mind was seeing how Olivia interacted with people, especially those far less fortunate. How well she listened and advised. Olivia has a gift of compassion, and a dynamic willingness to make a positive difference. While that aspect of my wife won me over, it also helped me understand her business self.

Olivia and I are very much alike in one respect. We are chameleons.

We have the ability to adapt to different situations. Mine came about from growing up ghetto black but attending predominately-white private schools. I developed a motto of either adapt or perish. I chose to adapt. Olivia's development was similar. Being black and wealthy did not stop some from attempting to diminish her family along the lines of skin color. Olivia never shied away or apologized for her race or her wealth, and she didn't allow others to marginalize her either. Being articulate and even-tempered, she used her words to defend herself instead of her fists.

Olivia is at my in-laws, probably defending my career destiny over dessert to her parents. I begged out of going in order to continue working on my latest novel, which was true up until a little while ago. I had hit a creative exhaust for the day and the call of the world outside my window beckoned me. My in-laws are very practical people. In many ways so is Olivia which, is one of the things I love about her. Her generally grounded view balances out my sporadic impulsiveness. Most times we meet somewhere in the middle.

Next door to Billy Ono resides Jayden—"not Jay asshole"—Miller. Our sources told us Jayden and his wife adored each other. They were in the honeymoon years of their marriage when Jayden's wife died tragically from SARS. This happened about two years prior to our moving onto Lambert Boulevard. Apparently, his wife was the picture of health before her illness. Her death came as a shock to everyone who knew her.

We've been to Jayden's house for dinners and barbeques. They were actually business affairs masquerading as social events. Much of his home's decor was feminine in my opinion, not that I'm one to talk considering the same can probably be said about ours. It was presumed by us and confirmed by those who knew Jayden best that his fiancé had done the interior decorating, only allowing Jayden enough input to soothe his ego. While I had more leeway in the decorating decisions for our home, in truth, the only areas I had any real interest in were my writing loft and workshop. Olivia could—and did—whatever she wanted with the rest of the house.

Jayden included some of his neighbors in order to impress upon his colleagues and bosses of his good standing in the community. A rather common practice I'm told by my wife amongst ambitious company and corporate management anxious to move up the executive ladder. The most disturbing part about those experiences for me, Olivia, invited neighbors, and just about everyone we talked to was that Jayden still has pictures of his deceased wife all over the place, some with the two of them together in romantic bliss. I would have thought Jayden would have packed them away, only to be resurrected during his most distressed times. I have to confess my overactive imagination found there being on display a bit creepy. Like the ghost of his dead wife was watching over us. Their were times when I noticed Jayden longingly staring at her picture and smiling as if it had spoken to him. Olivia noticed it too.

As far as his catered affairs were concerned, Olivia and I actually enjoyed ourselves at his mock social functions. The food was always good and the DJs he hired kept the festivities light. From my prospective, it was primarily because my wife and I spent the majority of our time socializing with neighbors, his bosses and colleagues rather than Jayden, who was in an all out ingratiating schmooze mode. It was interesting to watch him work. He seemed to know exactly what to say at precisely the right time to whomever he was attempting to win over, like a professional spy working the room from personal portfolios he had memorized. Quite the contrast to his often curt, sometimes nasty, behavior he leveled at his neighbors.

Jayden Miller's love for his deceased wife was undeniable. Everyone within earshot of his home became reacquainted of how deep his affections for her ran on the anniversary of her death. Jayden literally drowned his sorrows by becoming falling down drunk and repeatedly blasting his dead wife's favorite song, Sarah McLachlan's "Angel" well into the night. From those who knew Jayden before the passing of his beloved, her death had turned him into a hardened man. I found the word hardened generous. I would go as far as to call him misanthrope. It's how some handle the acid injection of misfortune into their lives.

A successful iron horse businessperson, Jayden sees people as things to be manipulated, overrun and disrespected. While I have compassion for his situation, I will only allow his heartbreak so much leeway. Olivia is much more tolerant. My wife prays for him, believes time will heal his heart and soul. In the meantime, I tell Olivia, we have to deal with his person. As far as I'm concerned, Jayden needs to find other ways to vent his grief rather than using it as an excuse to abuse people.

Jayden isn't home yet. Late nights at the office are staples for him. It probably helps minimize his feelings of loneliness and depression, feelings that probably surface most when he enters alone the beautiful house they once shared. Carrying that kind of emotional baggage it's a wonder Jayden didn't awaken each day with the leaden thought throbbing in his head, "another day to survive." To be perfectly honest, if Olivia died—God forbid—there's absolutely no way I could live in this house. Everything about our home from the furniture she picked out to our flower and vegetable gardens to the loose basement step that I still haven't gotten around to fixing would remind me of her and I would lose it. I don't know why Jayden tortures himself by staying on.

My curtains flutter from humid summer breezes. A floral potpourri of summer fragrances brush my skin and tickle my nose. I see plants; shrubs, trees and grass sway to its undulating waves. I hear a mosquito pay me a visit. Wearing only shorts, a T-shirt, and a slick sheen of sweat leaves available many appetizing places for it to feast. I feel it land on my bare left forearm before I spot it. I give it a moment to have a last meal before I swat it dead with my right hand, wiping away its remains on a tissue that I toss into my wire frame waste paper basket.

Dog perks up to see what is going on. Once satisfied, Dog returns to his nap. A young child shrieks for his mom. He screams at his mother the question of why he can't have a smart phone. I cannot hear his mother's reply but I imagine she tells him he is too young.

The child is Wyatt and he is only seven. I know the family. I know their home. They are neighborhood acquaintances who regard themselves friends. We allow each other that luxury even though we haven't spent enough time together to make it official. Olivia and I have discussed having children but neither of us are committed to setting a timetable. It doesn't seem a pressing matter for now. We have plenty of time or at least that's how it feels.

There are stories here to be told as well as fodder from my own life and experiences. Crystal clear ideas emerge from the muddy waters of inspiration. Off to the west rain clouds make a surprise appearance on the horizon. Sudden summer thunderstorms are common in my neck of the woods. The musky smell of summer rain fills the air. Dog stirs for a moment then returns to his dream.

I see my wife's car cruising down Lambert Boulevard. The sight makes me smile. I always miss Olivia when she's not around. It doesn't matter whether she's in the same room with me as long as she's within my vicinity. When she's not on my radar, I miss her presence, her energy. I lift Dog from my lap and drape him around my neck like a mink collar. His eyes open briefly then close from the weight of his eyelids. I want to be there to greet Olivia with a big hug and a kiss, to meet her needs, and lend a patient ear for her to tell me all about her family dinner.